I0768793

# Explore the Rest of
# Earth M23

## Fear Itself
## Sinful Habit

# Fear Itself

Ink & Paint Publishing

Copyright © 2024 by Aura Nyxx and Ink & Paint Publishing
All rights reserved.

No part of this publication may be reproduced, distributed, or transmitted in any form or by any means, including photocopying, recording, or other electronic or mechanical methods, without the prior written permission of the publisher, except as permitted by U.S. copyright law, including the use of AI training. For permission requests, contact inkandpaintpublishing@gmail.com.

The story, all names, characters, and incidents portrayed in this production are fictitious. No identification with actual persons (living or deceased), places, buildings, and products is intended or should be inferred.

Book Cover by Aura Nyxx
Edits by A. Nikole
Second Edition 2025

ISBN 9798218456474

*Dedicated To all those who struggle with anxiety, panic attacks, phobias, or trauma, keep pushing. You got this.*

*"You are braver than you believe, stronger than you seem, and smarter than you think."*
*- Christopher Robin*

*"Courage is not the absence of fear, but rather the assessment that something else is more important than fear."*
*-Franklin D. Roosevelt*

*This book contains subjects that may be difficult for some people to read. Domestic abuse, anxiety disorders, murder, sexual assault, bodily mutilation, stalking, kidnapping, as well as several common phobias are mentioned. Please take care of your mental health while reading!*

# One

I leaned forward in my chair, trying to get closer to the fan oscillating on the desk, but it was no use; the air blowing from it was just as hot as the rest of the room. I groaned and threw myself back in frustration. The digital thermometer that was sloppily adhered to the lobby wall flashed between the time and the temperature, "85° - 2 a.m.". The phone had been ringing non stop all night with guests complaining about their rooms being too warm or the air conditioners not blowing cold enough.

"I know. I'm sorry," I repeated for the umpteenth time on the most recent call, "they're not designed to keep up with this heat wave. We have free ice in the lobby if—"
*Click.*

*I don't get paid enough to deal with customers and this ghetto ass A/C system.* The phone rang yet again, and I sighed.

"Front desk," I answered with a forced smile.

"Hey, the A/C just stopped working completely. Like, it was barely working before but at least it was keeping it under 90 in here," a female voice responded.

"I'm so sorry about that, I'm not sure if I'll be able to get a hold of our maintenance guy at this hour but let me see what I can do. What room are you in?"

"232."

I thought back, and remembered checking a young woman into that room around 11 p.m. who was escorted by a man dressed in an over-priced suit. She was one of my regulars. The girls and I had an unspoken agreement about their use of the rooms for their work. They didn't cause trouble for me, and I wouldn't mention the nature of their services to my boss, who would definitely not approve of us allowing the hotel to be used in such a manner.

I personally couldn't give a shit. If I had the body and confidence to do what they did, making that kind of money? Hell, I'd ask for a job application in a heartbeat. Part of me was slightly jealous of the attention those women got. Not that meaningless sex was my idea of a perfect night out, but it had been months since I got laid and even these shady, rich assholes were beginning to look attractive.

The guy she was with left hours ago. I'd watched his walk of shame out the lobby doors, and shouted "hope you enjoyed your stay!" extra loud for my own personal amusement. If looks could kill. Whatever. I was going to do what I needed to make this job even remotely enjoyable. The job market sucked and I was lucky to have one, even a shitty one like this. Living alone in the city wasn't cheap, but I refused to leave. I refused to let *that asshole* chase me out of my home. He took everything else from me, I won't give him that.


"Okay, worst case, I can move you into another room."

"Thanks." *Click.*


I reached to punch in the numbers to call our maintenance guy, then hesitated. *He's not going to answer at this hour, and I'm not going to be the one to wake him up.* I made an executive decision and scanned the hotel's rooms on the computer. There was an unoccupied one a floor up. I activated the key, slid my chair back, and hopped off. My co-workers were always teasing me because I had to raise the chair up so fucking high to be able to see over the check in counter that my feet didn't touch the floor.

I wiped sweat from my brow with the back of my hand as the slow and stuffy elevator cranked loudly on it's way up. The brass colored doors warped my reflection, and I moved to cause a thin indentation at my waist; one I knew I would never be able to achieve without this funhouse mirror effect. If reality reflected what I saw in these doors, I wondered how many of my past mistakes could have been avoided.

I looked away from it as the elevator stalled between floors. *For fuck's sake.* Everything about this place was ghetto as fuck. I resisted the urge to give it a swift kick and it eventually remembered its sole purpose in life, bringing me to the correct floor.

The doors opened to an ugly, dimly lit, albeit quiet hallway, and I made my way towards room 232 with the new key. My footsteps barely made a sound on the thin, golden patterned carpet. I stopped outside the door and raised my hand to knock, but paused when I heard a thump and muffled crying from inside.

I knocked. "Uh, hello? It's Adelaide from the lobby. I got you a new room."

A suspicious silence replied.

"Is... your air conditioning still out?"

A muffled scream set my hair standing on end.

Something wasn't right.

"Are you okay?" I fought the urge to let myself in. There was always the chance she had a client in there who liked it rough, and the last thing I wanted was to walk into the middle of an "appointment". But I didn't see anyone come in after the last guy. In fact, no one had come into the hotel after her at all.

No. Last time I didn't trust my gut I regretted it.

"I'm coming in." I used the universal key to unlock the door.

I met eyes with a man crouching in the window, mid-step onto the fire escape. He had a mop of messy, dirty blonde hair and his eyes… I would never forget those eyes as long as I lived. They were dark and soulless, dilated like a predators', and when they fell on me he smiled. An unhinged, sinister smile that turned my blood to ice. I gasped, and in an instant he was out the window and out of sight. I ran into the room after him, thinking he was robbing the guest. But as I came out of the small hallway past the door, the bed to my right drew my full attention, and I staggered backward at the sight.

The young woman, or what was left of her, was sprawled naked across the mattress. Her arms and legs tied apart by ropes that were attached to the four corners of the bed, her torso covered in blood, and her breasts were gone. Just… gone. Sliced clean off. She had tape around her mouth and eyes, and through her neck, a giant hole that I could see straight through to the other side.

I was told that my screams woke everyone on the floor, and an older couple had to pull me out of the room. I was told that the same couple helped me back down to the lobby, where we called 911. I was told the police arrived within minutes, and evacuated the entire hotel. I was told my boss showed up and was screaming at me and the cops, blaming us for losing him money. I was told I agreed to accompany an officer downtown, was loaded into the back of a police car, and hauled away, sirens blaring.

I was told all this, but I didn't remember any of it.

What I did remember was sitting next to an officer's desk, a cup of something steaming in my hands, a blanket around my shoulders, wondering how the hell I got there. I mindlessly stared at the officer in front of me, her antennae twitched as she spoke. I saw her mouth moving, but the only sound I heard was a distant ringing in my ears.

"Hun, I know you're going through a lot right now, but we really need you to answer some questions," she urged me gently. "Can we start with your name? Can you tell me your name?"

The fog began to lift. "Adelaide... Adelaide Quinn."

"Good, good," the officer coaxed. "Okay, and you work at the Sunrise Hotel?"

I nodded slowly.

"Now, what can you tell me about last night?"

My mind was both a blur and blank somehow.

"Take your time." Her antennae curled delicately.

"I think... there was a man..."

The officer typed something out on the computer. "Do you remember what he looked like?"

I couldn't. The images in my mind stopped after the elevator doors opened. I knew there was a figure there, but my brain blacked him out. I could only draw out the eyes...

"Evil," I whispered.

"Yeah, I don't doubt that, but I need more detail. Anything you can give will help us hunt him down," she sighed patiently.

A stern looking officer came up and stood with his hands on his belt. "Singer, Captain wants to see you."

Officer Singer stood. "I'll be right back, hun. Just try to think of any details you can, okay?"

I nodded and both officers walked away.

I stared into the cup in my hands in disbelief. What the fuck was even happening right now? It was a boring night at work. The guests were complaining, I got a call, an A/C unit broke, I went up to give the guest her new key and... The body.

I suddenly felt very sick, and quickly looked around for any sort of receptacle, finding the plastic trash can just in time to cough up bile. I was thankful I had nothing in my stomach, not having had my break before the... *murder*.

Holy shit. I was a witness to a murder.

I stood suddenly in a panic as my adrenaline kicked in, knocking my chair over with a loud thud. The blanket fell from my shoulders as I took in where I was for the first time. Police station... there was a murder... the man in the window...

Several other officers began to approach me cautiously. I was hyperventilating, my skin felt like it was on fire.

"Settle down now, miss, you're alright."

"Whoa there. Take it easy."

"That guy!" I screamed. "That guy killed her!"

As an officer tried to put his hand on my shoulder, I panicked. "Don't fucking touch me!"

I watched myself cause a scene as though I was outside my body; I tried to tell myself to stop, that if I didn't calm down someone was going to fucking taze me. But nothing was connecting.

"She's freaking out," a man's voice called out. "Restrain her."

I bolted. I ran out the office door and down the hall blindly.

"God help me, Nyte, if you get in the way of our investigation again..." A man raised his voice ahead of me.

"I wouldn't have to if you and your team would do your fucking jobs—" Another man with a soft but deep voice responded argumentatively as I ran right into him. "Whoa, what the fu—"

"Grab her!" An officer shouted from behind me.

I looked up into a pair of bright yellow eyes, not registering the face looking down at me.

"Hey, chill out." The man I ran into held his hand out to stop the   horde of police chasing me. "Can't you see she's having a panic attack?"

"Stay out of this Nyte," a different officer warned.

"Alright, whatever, but you'll get more from her if you give her a minute to breathe," the man raised his hands in defeat.

The sound of someone coming to my defense was so unusual it drew my focus back to reality. The man I ran into was tall, wearing dark jeans, moto boots, and a black leather jacket over a heather grey zip-up hoodie. His dark hair was shorter on the sides than the top, causing it to flop messily over his face as he looked back down towards me. Once again I noticed his eyes were brilliantly bright. Even in our day and age, where genetic mutations were no longer considered "abnormal", and people had a multitude of traits such as wings, tails, and superhuman abilities, yellow eyes were uncommon.

Officer Singer emerged from a side hall, "I'll take it from here boys." She motioned for me to follow her, and led me into a smaller room.

"I'm sorry," I whispered. "I don't know what just happened."

"It's alright, I know what you saw was horrible, but if you saw the man who did it, we need your help to catch him. Now tell me everything you remember."

I shook as I spoke. "He jumped out the window."

"When was this?" Officer Singer wrote on a notepad.

"After I opened the door..."

"I know that hun, I mean what time?"

"Uh." I racked my memories, and remembered the clock flashing 2 a.m. right before the girl called. "It was sometime after two, the guest called down... The A/C was broken... so I went upstairs to give her a new key to a different room... when I heard..."

She waited for me to continue. "Yes?"

"Screaming. She screamed twice... I opened the door after the second one... It didn't feel right."

"Did she check in with this man?"

"No. There was a guy with her, but he was different, and left an hour later, around midnight."

"And you're sure that man left?"

"Yeah, I saw him."

"Did she tell you if she was expecting any other guests?"

"No."

"So it's possible she was expecting this man?"

"I mean, I guess, but no one came in through the lobby after she checked in."

"I see. And the door was locked when you opened it?"

I stopped for a moment and realized. "It was locked with the key lock, but the metal latch was open."

"Alright, so what happened after you opened the door?"

I closed my eyes, and forced the image back. "He was already halfway onto the fire escape."

"Can you describe him?"

"Uh... I don't... remember..." His dark eyes were all I could see. "His eyes were black."

"Could you tell how tall he was?"

I shook my head.

She sighed, "hun, you looked right at him, you're telling me you don't remember more than his eyes?"

"I'm trying but... it's blank." My head was beginning to hurt.

"Alright, well, if you do remember more," she pulled out her card, "please call me okay? What we have from tonight isn't much to go on."

After hours and hours of questions and paperwork, the police finally released me, and I stepped out of the station into a hot, bustling city street. I checked my phone, and not surprisingly, no missed calls or texts. Scott did a hell of a job alienating me from people, and since the break up I rarely heard from anyone. Our "friends" of course took his side. As for family, my parents kicked me out after I voiced my beliefs about mutant rights when I was a teenager. Once in a while I would hear from my sister, but we lived on opposite ends of the country, and she led a busy life as a successful attorney.

The clock on my phone read "10 a.m.". If last night had been normal I would have been off work four hours ago, and would now be comfortably snuggled up in bed with my cat and the A/C blasting. The police station was in the middle of downtown, and it was going to take at least an hour to get back to my apartment with this stupid public transportation system. So much for sleeping. Not that I expected to be called into work tonight; the police said the hotel was still an active crime scene.

My head, which was used to a constant supply of caffeine through the night, pounded from the lack of it. So I walked down the block to a coffee shop that had decently good reviews and stepped into the refreshingly cold interior.

This was clearly a mutant friendly place, as the barista was a four armed man who was doing the job of two people. The tables were occupied both by obvious mutants, and those who looked human. I still couldn't wrap my head around how humans could be so prejudiced. You could have the most unusual looking mutant standing next to the most normal looking human and not be able to tell who was a good person. In fact, my personal track record shows that the most horrible people hide it exceptionally well.

I ordered my coffee and stood by the pick up area, zoning out on a younger couple who were obviously on a date. The guy pulled her chair out for her, tucked her in, and had already ordered her coffee. *Just wait girl. His demons will come out eventually.*

My name was called, and I turned before I looked, running into someone who had just stepped away from the counter, spilling their coffee all over us both.

"Shit!" He exclaimed.

"Oh my god, I'm so sorry!" I brushed whipped cream off my shirt and looked up at the man, meeting a familiar pair of piercing yellow eyes. I hadn't realized how tall he was when I ran into him earlier, my head barely reached his chest, nor did I notice how attractive he was. His un-styled, dark hair fell over his eyes as he looked down at me. He had a sharp jawline covered with a thick stubble of a beard, and full lips.

"For fucks sake," he sighed.

"You... You were in the police station this morning," I stated, forgetting my embarrassment and coffee soaked outfit for a moment.

"Yeah. And now I'm here, covered in latte..." He dabbed his jacket with a handful of napkins.

"Totally my fault." I felt terrible, and tore more napkins from the holder as I began cleaning his jacket instead of myself, causing him to pause and watch me curiously. "You can take mine," I offered as the barista slid my order onto the counter.

"I doubt you drink anything I'd like," he responded dryly.

Wow, what a dick. "Well fine then," I huffed and grabbed my coffee. "Maybe you deserved it," I added under my breath.

"Seriously? You lose me a $7 coffee and then give *me* attitude?"

"I apologized and tried to be nice about it. You're the one who's being an asshole."

"Fucking typical," he huffed a laugh. "She spends the morning in police custody, slams into me twice, then tells me *I'm* the problem. Why don't you watch where you're going?"

My cheeks began to redden. "Fuck you, asshole." I threw the dirty napkins at him, then stormed out the door. I was way too tired to deal with anyone's attitude right now, no matter how hot they were.


It was almost noon when I trudged through the door of my fifth floor apartment. Exhausted, covered in coffee, hungry, and a ball of nerves, I threw my purse on the kitchen counter, adding to the clutter that I kept telling myself I was going to pick up "tomorrow." A small calico cat pranced out of the hall from the bedroom, meowing desperately.

"Okay, Dinah, okay, I'm sorry, I know, breakfast is late. Nice to see you too."

Dinah rubbed frantically against my legs, purring.

I fed her, dragged myself into the living room, and threw myself across the sofa. I stared at the wall absentmindedly scanning the titles of the books on the shelves, too tired to change, too tired to eat. My eyelids began to droop, but to my dismay, the moment my body began to relax my mind flashed back to visions of the mutilated body on the bed, and the blood… All the blood...

"Nope. We're not doing that." I scolded my brain and sat up quickly, clicking on the TV. An on field reporter was in the midst of talking about the newest hover gadget that was hitting the market this year. I began zoning out, letting the distant voice of the reporter lull me to sleep, when suddenly the screen flashed a graphic stating a special report was just coming in.

"Tragedy struck last night when the police discovered the mutilated body of a young woman at the Sunrise Hotel..." An anchor covered in scales announced. I was wide awake at the sound of my workplace and turned the volume up.

"...Police suspect this to be the work of a serial killer who has been haunting the west coast for the past several months. Because of the brutality of his murders, and the trophies he likes to take from the victims, he has earned the equally dark nickname 'The Coastal Carver'. Though for once, this killing might have led to a crucial clue about his identity…" My breath caught in my throat. *Serial killer?!* "…A hotel worker spotted the man as he was escaping out the window, and is currently working with police to give a full description…" *I am?!?*

Holy shit. This fucker escaped and the news just announced that I was about to give a full description of the guy. I'm pretty sure I was clear with Officer Singer that I didn't remember anything. What the actual fuck? What if he was watching the news? He'd come after me. Aren't they supposed to put me in the Witness Protection Program or something? My heart began racing again, the same sensation I felt at the station came over me… *That asshole said I was having a panic attack.*

I sprang up from my seat and looked around frantically at all possible methods of entry into my apartment. My giant windows that overlooked the city were once a main selling factor for me, but now? *Perfect access for a serial killer.* I quickly drew the curtains shut, double and triple checked the front door, and even went as far as wedging a dining chair under the knob. I was literally running in circles; What the fuck was the protocol for this? My phone rang and I screamed, then sighed at my stupidity. Rory's face was on the caller ID.

"Tell me there is more than one Sunrise Hotel in your city?" She sounded so much like mom when she took that tone.

"Hi, long time no talk, how are you? Good to know you're not *dead*," I sighed.

"Sorry, I just saw the news. That is the name of that hotel you work at, right? Please say it's a chain and you were nowhere near that incident."

"I would, but it would be a lie."

"Addy, what the hell?"

"You're acting like I *chose* to get involved."

"I know you didn't, but why is it always you?"

We were both quiet for a minute. She was referring to the fact that drama always seemed to follow me, not that I ever went looking for it or anything.

"Do you wanna talk about it?"

"Not right now, I'm tired. I just got home."

"I really don't like the idea of you being there alone, do you want to come stay with me for a while?"

"No… Thanks. I don't think I could afford a flight over there anyway."

"Do you have a security system? Does your complex have a security guard?"

I laughed. "What kind of money do you think I make as a receptionist at a hotel?"

"In that case, I'm going to text you every day, and if you don't respond Addy I swear to god—"

"I know, I know."

"Do you want me to tell Mom and Dad?"

"Absolutely not. They'd probably root for The Costal Carver."

She snorted. "Oh my god, don't say that."

I smiled. "Thanks Rory. I'm gonna try to get some sleep."

"Alright, call me if you need anything."

I laid back down on the couch and changed the channel to some good ole mind-numbing cartoons. Looking into getting a security system was probably a good idea, especially after last night. I yawned. Dinah jumped up onto my chest and curled up, purring loudly. I fought it with every fiber of my being, but my eyes finally closed, and I fell into a restless sleep.

Somewhere downtown, a man with bright yellow eyes and a coffee stained hoodie sat at his desk, scrolling through the latest article about The Carver. He scoffed to himself after reading about the unlucky hotel worker who caught him in the act.

19

"Stupid. They put them on blast."

His hope that the police would be keeping an eye on them went as fast as it came. "They don't know what the fuck they're doing. They're going to lose me the only lead we've gotten." He reclined in his chair, resting his arms behind his head. If he could only get a chance to talk to the witness himself. All he needed was a name.

# Two

I woke in a sweat soaked panic. The images of bloody hotel sheets and soulless eyes staring at me from behind the curtains faded into my subconscious. It was dark, too dark. I fumbled for my phone, accidentally throwing Dinah off my chest. She gave me a grumpy 'mrow' as she landed on the floor, and I flicked open the Home app and tapped on the lights.

I was hyperventilating, again. I sat up, and tried to focus on my breathing. *Deep breath in, and out... Slow it down.*

I couldn't stop it.

Panic rose in my chest, causing it to tighten. I began sweating, and felt my heartbeat in my ears. "Not again..." I said out loud and dragged myself to the bathroom.

I turned on the sink and let the water run over my hands. The cold water seemed to slow the pulse pounding in my wrists. I leaned against the sink on my forearms, letting the water help me do what I couldn't do alone.

After a few minutes, my body temperature dropped and my breathing calmed slightly. I turned the water off, and pressed my cold hands against my cheeks. The relief was immediate.

The tightness in my chest released, and I exhaled. After drying my hands and face, I stumbled into the living room.

Dinah cautiously approached, staring at me like I intentionally chucked her across the room. "Sorry, these panic attacks are getting old." I bent down and picked her up.

I don't remember the last time I got a full night's sleep. I had been living in a constant state of anxiety since I got back from the police station three days ago. The hotel had been closed since the incident, which meant no work, and that was totally fine with me. Even the thought of stepping foot outside my door was enough to drag me into another debilitating episode.

Though I was in a significantly calmer headspace, the prickly feeling on the back of my neck hadn't gone away. It never went away. The feeling of being watched hounded me day and night.

I checked the front door again. The chair was still wedged under the knob, as had become habit whenever I came back in from getting the mail or taking out the trash for myself and Mrs. Tibbet. The windows in the bedroom were locked, and the curtains in the living room still shut tight. But as I stared at them, something screamed at me to throw them open.

"This is how the dumb bimbos in horror movies die…" I scolded myself as I approached them with an outstretched hand and drew them back.

Darkness and nothing. Empty balcony, mostly empty street. Just the tree in the complex courtyard that rose up to the level of my floor and the few parked cars that became regular fixtures on my block. A crow cawed and flew off the branch of the tree, annoyed at the disturbance of the light from my window.

I laughed out loud nervously and closed the curtains again, realizing I was still shaking. *Gotta be low blood sugar.* I hadn't had much of an appetite, and had resorted to grazing on whatever was easily accessible in the kitchen. My stomach hadn't had a substantial meal in days. I made my way to the fridge and opened it to find a whole lot of nothing. "Dammit." I tried the cupboards. Peanut butter, but no bread. Pasta noodles, but no sauce. Cereal, but no milk.

"Fuck," I grumbled. The last thing I wanted to do was to venture out in the dark. I checked my delivery service apps. "Fuck me, $10 for a delivery fee???" I couldn't justify that when there was a 24/7 corner store right down the street. Could I wait until morning? My stomach growled in response. I just needed the essentials, just a quick trip, then back to my solitude. I changed out of my pajamas, threw on a tank top and shorts, and double checked the expiration date on my travel mace for good measure. "You've made this trip thousands of times. You can do this," I psyched myself up before I opened the door and headed down.

A streetlight buzzed as I passed under it reminding me why I prefer to work overnights. The city was so quiet at this hour. I could enjoy the lights and colors without having to push through crowds of people, or get yelled at by someone in a hurry. The older I got, the more I found I really didn't care for city life anymore, though as a young woman in her twenties who grew up in cookie cutter suburbia and was hopelessly in love, the city offered adventure and romance.

She was stupid. She got her heart shattered and stranded herself in the middle of this morally corrupt concrete jungle. Back then I thought we would be able to make a difference for mutant rights. That we could fight the law forcing mutants to register with the government. I was wrong, we lost, and with the law came thousands of losses of jobs. Humans were so hateful towards mutants, it became exceedingly difficult for them to find work. Many became desperate, fell to a life of crime to survive, turning into the monsters society had already made them out to be.

I rounded the corner into the shop, and breathed a small sigh of relief at being surrounded by the bright light. "I should grab some calming tea while I'm here," I muttered as I rubbed my sore neck, releasing the tension I held the entire walk.

I chatted with the cashier a bit, a young kid in his freshman year of college, purchased my groceries, and felt much calmer about the walk back. But as soon as I exited the store, there were three men loitering on the corner that set off my alarm bells. I turned my back to them as I began the walk home, when one of them shouted after me:

"Heyyy baby. Whatcha doin' out at this hour?"

I didn't respond, and of course this aggravated him.

"C'mon. You could at least say 'hi'. Don't be rude," his voice sounded closer.

"Stay away from me," I spun around, holding my mace out in front of me as my heart began to race.

"We just want to look out for you, right boys?" He chuckled to the other two men. "It's not safe out here for a pretty little thing like you…" They continued to approach.

"I'll spray you, I swear." I tried to keep my voice steady.

"Can't get all three of us." He smiled menacingly, and they all ran at me.

I didn't have time to think, I dropped my groceries and fled. I ran past my street, down the block and quickly turned a blind corner hoping to lose them, only to discover I chose a dead end alley. They rounded the corner after me barricading me in.

"What do you want?" I panted, backing away slowly.

"Well at first I just wanted you to say 'hi', but then you threatened us," the man in the middle spoke. "Now we want you to make it up to us…"

"I don't carry cash on me," I began to shake. "You can take my wallet, but I'll just cancel the cards."

"Well then, we'll have to take our payment from you in other ways." He nodded to the other men who rushed me.

I sprayed the mace, only managing to get one of them. The other tackled me hard, knocking my head on the concrete.

The one I sprayed wiped his face, seemingly unaffected by the chemicals, as the man who tackled me stood and dragged me by my feet towards the wall, then pulled me by my hair until I was standing.

Their leader took his place, wrapped his hand around my throat and pinned me against the brick. I swung my hand up and raked my nails across his face as hard as I could, leaving a series of red welts over his eyes and nose. He cried out, but didn't release me.

"Bitch!" His free hand connected forcefully with my cheek, leaving my eyes watering, then he began undoing his belt.

I screamed and thrashed my legs, managing to kick him in the shin. He grunted, but simply adjusted his stance and pressed his entire weight on me, increasing the pressure around my throat.

There was no physical possibility of me overpowering him. He stood heads above me, and must have weighed at least two-hundred and fifty pounds. A tear fell from the corner of my eye. "Please... Don't..." I choked out, knowing my plea would be ignored.

"I'd keep your pants on if I were you. Much easier to run away," a low voice spoke out from the darkness above me.

"The fuck?" My assailant turned his head to look in its direction.

"Let her go," it commanded.

"Or what?" One of the other men pulled out a gun and pointed it above my head, his eyes seemed to be searching for the source.

"Or you'll end up in a psych ward, or worse," the voice answered.

"Fuck you," the man holding me spat into the darkness. "Take care of that asshole." He commanded his men behind him and continued undoing the buttons on his pants, clearly unashamed to have an audience.

The clang of boots landing on metal echoed through the alley as whoever the voice belonged to jumped down another level of a fire escape. "Funny, that's twice this week I've had that offer. At least the first one was my type."

The second of his men pulled out a gun as well, it seemed like they both had found their target.

"Heh. You've got to get yourself braver goons. This is gonna be too easy." The voice mocked right before a figure leapt from the last level over my head and landed somewhere in front of us.

One of the men fired at the shadow as it fell and missed. My assailant turned to face the threat as it rose from the ground.

Thin, spindly legs sprouted from the darkness. The man who fired first screamed and dropped his weapon as he turned to run, but a long leg shot out in front of him, grabbing him around the waist.

The other man's gun clattered to the floor as he bolted down towards the dead end, plastering himself against a chain link fence, while the man holding me dropped his hand, and I fell to the floor.

An enormous black widow stepped out of the shadows with the first man in its grasp. It brought him to its clicking pincers and pierced his body with its huge fangs. The scream he released before he fell silent and limp would haunt me for years. The spider dropped his body, turned its attention to my tormentor, and leapt at him.

He screamed and ran forward, trying to get underneath it, but the spider turned agilely and swiped at his legs with one of its own, sending him crashing to the ground.

It pinned him with one giant leg, as another pulled his pants down, turned him over, and stuck a third leg all the way up his ass forcefully.

A sound had barely escaped his lips before blood pooled around him from multiple orifices, causing his screams to become gags as he writhed on the ground.

The sucking, squishing sound made me sick to my stomach, but I was frozen in place in absolute shock, unable to look away.

Finally the spider clacked towards the last man, who was still scrambling, trying to get up the chain link fence. It turned and shot a mass of sticky web against his body, plastering him in place.

Then it turned its attention to me.

I screamed, found the feeling in my legs, and *ran*. I ran out of the alley, down the street, and away from my apartment and my neighborhood.

I wasn't paying attention to where I was going, and I found myself on an unfamiliar street. I stopped, looked behind me, and not seeing signs of a giant spider anywhere, collapsed against a building and let the tears fall. "What the actual fuck?!" I cried out. "Why is this happening to me?" I looked around at the strange buildings and reached into my pocket for my phone. It was gone. "Right, perfect."

Out of the corner of my eye I saw a figure down the street. I quickly scrambled to my feet and faced him, still shaking. "You might as well kill me after the week I've had," I yelled with tears in my eyes. "If I give you permission at least I can say it was my choice…"

The man stopped and lowered his hood. "I'm not going to hurt you," he calmly responded, and I recognized his voice from the alley.

"You… You killed those guys…" I stammered and took a step back, but he didn't move.

"Only two of them."

I expected him to come at me, turn back into a giant bug, demand something for his services. But he just stood there, as if waiting for an invitation. "What do you want?" My voice shook.

He tilted his head as if to think, then said simply, "to make sure you're alright."

"I'm fine. You can go now," I lied.

"May I walk you home? It's dangerous—"

I scoffed. "You think I'm stupid? I just watched you turn a man into a human hand puppet and you want me to show you where I live?"

"You were stupid enough to run down a dead end…" He mumbled under his breath.

"Excuse me?" I crossed my arms over my chest. "That was just bad luck, it had nothing to do with my intelligence."

"Yeah, 'cause you *totally* don't have a history of not paying attention to where you're going."

That tone… "Wait, coffee guy?"

"Not the nickname I would have chosen, but sure."

A slight relief washed over me at the realization. Did I really know him? No, but something about even a slightly familiar face was reassuring.

"Are you going to take off again if I come closer?" He questioned with an air of mockery.

I considered it. If he wanted to hurt me, he would have already tried. "No. But if you touch me I'll kick you in the balls."

The whites of his teeth glinted in the dark, "noted."

He slowly came towards me, stopping just out of arm's reach. Once again I took note of his appearance, this man liked black. Black wash jeans, a dark blue v-neck, and a black half-zipped hoodie under his leather jacket. Even strangely over-dressed for this insane heat wave, he'd totally be my type if he wasn't such a dick.

"Warren." He held his hand out to me in introduction.

"Adelaide." I took it in mine, his hands were freezing. It had to be at least 85° out...

"Nice to finally meet you without you assaulting me," he smirked.

"Says the bug man who just killed three people."

"Two," he corrected. "Not a bug, arachnid. And you're welcome."

"Whatever. Do you normally hang out on fire escapes in alleys, waiting for women to get abducted?"

"Not always. Sometimes I just follow around the ones who I know are bound to get into trouble," his eyes glinted.

"Hilarious," I rolled my eyes. I really did want to go home, but I didn't want to admit I had no idea how to get there.

"So... Are you just going to spend the night here or...?"

"No," I responded defiantly. "I just don't want you to follow me."

He stepped back against the building and placed his hands in his jacket pockets. "I'll stay right here."

"Good." I felt his eyes on me as I began walking towards the end of the block. I hesitated, not seeing anything familiar. I ran from the other way, so at least I know I should go back in that direction. I turned and walked past him, keeping my sight straight ahead. I came to the corner, then paused again.

*Which way do I go?*

"You lost?" There was a smile in his voice.

"I just need to get my bearings…" I didn't turn towards him, not wanting him to see the concern on my face.

"There's an app called 'Maps'. It's great for that."

"I lost my phone, asshole."

I could practically feel his eyes roll as he sighed, and walked past me to the left.

"Where… Where are you going?" I took a few steps after him.

He stopped and turned slightly back towards me. "Why?"

"I just want to know…"

The corner of his lips curved, revealing a dimple in his left cheek. "I'm headed back towards the alley."

I followed, keeping half a block behind him. He knew I was, but pretended not to notice me. That is, until I lost him around a corner.

"Warren?" I called out in panic as I stood alone under a streetlight at an intersection. Not hearing a response, I crossed the street and called again.

"Wrong way." He came around behind me.

I jumped. "*Shit.* Where did you go?"

He chuckled, "I thought you didn't need help?"

"Okay fine. I'm a little lost. But if you lead me down a dark alley and turn back into a giant spider…"

"I can't. You're not afraid of spiders." He motioned for me to walk past him, taking the outside of the sidewalk.

Huh, how gentlemanly. "So, your mutation is to turn into a spider, but only if someone is afraid of them? That's oddly specific."

"I can turn into the greatest fear of the people near me."

"Oh," that's terrifying. "So one of those guys was afraid of spiders?"

"Mhm."

"What if someone was afraid of balloons?"

"I'm limited to animate objects."

"So… Clowns?"

"Yes… Although I never really understood that phobia, clowns are harmless."

"No one is naturally that happy. It's creepy."

He released a small breathy laugh, and my defenses lowered a bit. I suddenly felt much more confident about walking in the dark, barren streets next to this intimidating dickhead.

"How long have you known?"

"Mmm" he thought, pursing his lips. "I think I was 12 when it first manifested."

That was young. Most abilities don't manifest until they're triggered by a traumatic event. I fought the urge to ask him about it.

"Where did you lose your phone?" He changed the subject.

"I don't know. I had it when I left the store, it must have been when the guys attacked me."

"The alley is around this corner here, we can go in and look for it."

"Uhh." My steps stalled. I had no interest in seeing the carnage left over from the attack.

He turned, "there's nothing to be afraid of, they can't hurt you anymore."

"I'm not afraid." I was.

"I can also sense fear. And you're radiating it."

"Okay well, sorry if I'm not cool with being around a bunch of dead bodies. One is enough for a lifetime." I added under my breath.

He pulled his phone from his pocket and swiped at the screen. "What's your number?"

"Hell of a time to ask a girl for her digits."

He glanced at me from under his brow. "So I can call your phone and find it?"

"Oh." Heat rose in my face as I recited it to him.

He handed me his phone, "dial it again if I don't pick up." Then  disappeared into the dark.

*Stupid. Of course he wasn't trying to hit on me.* I smacked my forehead. Did I want him to? Jeez, what was wrong with me? I put the phone up to my ear to listen to the dial tone.

"Got it." He answered from the other end, and hung up, emerging a few seconds later. "Really, the song from 'Princess Bride'?" We traded phones.

"What? It's a good movie." Who the fuck was he to judge my ringtone?

He rolled his eyes, "figures."

"You're the one who recognized it."

He looked like he was going to retort, but changed his mind. Neither of us moved, or steered the conversation in the inevitable direction it was headed. He stood with his hands in his pockets, looking to his side at nothing in particular, showing off his chiseled jaw. While I stared past him into the alley, pretending not to notice it. If he hadn't come across me when he did, my body might be the one left in there tonight.

"Thank you, by the way. For my phone, and for saving me."

He turned back to me, "you're welcome."

"You said you could sense fear too, is that how you found me?"

"Yeah. When I felt you, I thought maybe The Carver had finally caught up with you."

"If it was him, I'm not sure you would have had time to— Wait," my brow furrowed. "How do you know about my being on his radar?"

His eyes widened slightly, "uh…"

I backed away from him. "Who the fuck are you?"

"Shit," he sighed. "Alright, alright. Don't freak out, I'm a P.I."

"Bullshit!" I moved further.

"Seriously, here," he pulled a bifold out of his back pocket and held it out to me. "My license."

I stretched as far as I could without moving my feet, and snatched it from him. He was, in fact, a licensed private investigator, the name "Warren Nyte" was typed next to his photo along with all his personal information. "Why the fuck are you investigating me?"

"I'm not investigating *you*, I'm investigating The Carver case." His voice remained low and calm even though I was all but shouting. "You just happen to be the only witness."

"I already told the police everything I remembered! What else could you want from me?"

"Just… To keep you alive, alright?"

"Why!?"

"Do you *not* want to remain alive?" He tilted his head. "Did the cops promise you any protection after telling the media you gave them a full description?"

"Well no… But… I didn't! I can't remember anything!"

He shook his head. "Regardless, the world, including The Carver, thinks you did."

"So, what, you've been watching me all day?"

"And for the last two."

I gaped at him. "Un-fucking-believeable. Stay away from me you fucking stalker!" I hurried away from him, rounded the corner, and to continue my shock, my groceries were still sitting where I had dropped them. I snatched them up and rushed home.

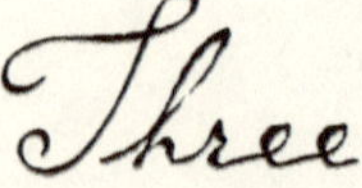

# Three

"You know, it might not be so bad to have someone keeping an eye on you right now. *If* he's legit." Rory contemplated on the other end of the phone after I recalled the events of the previous evening to her. "What did you say his name was?"

"Warren. Warren Nyte." I peered out my curtain, half expecting to see him lurking on my balcony.

She typed something in the background. "You said he's a mutant?"

"Yeah, why?"

"He's not registered. I mean he's in the system as a P.I., but it's not stated that he has abilities."

"You know how I feel about that law." I let the curtain fall back into place.

"You and me both," she paused, "huh."

"What?"

"He's cute."

"Yeah, but he's a dick, and a creep," I admitted.

"Not that I'm condoning it or anything, but it's not totally unusual behavior for a P.I.. It's *possible* he actually was just keeping an eye on you. It's also possible he's hoping to learn something from you, if you said he was already working on the case."

"But I told him I didn't know anything. Plus why would he go out of his way to watch me? I didn't think investigators acted as bodyguards?"

"They don't… Usually… You must hold some value to him regarding this case."

"I have no idea what that could be."

"Well, whatever it is, just remember you don't owe him anything. If he wants to volunteer his time and skills to keep you safe, I say let him."

I tried to put him out of my mind and go about my days as normally as possible. The hotel had opened back up, but today and tomorrow were my regularly scheduled days off, which meant this afternoon was tea with Mrs. Tibbet across the hall. Strangely enough, she had become as close a friend as I could have hoped for. She was mostly deaf, and pretty damn blind, but she was the only friend that stuck by me after my breakup. Not that I think she was even aware of it.

I knocked loudly on her door. "It's me Mrs. T!"

"Come in dearie!" She announced, "it's unlocked!"

Her four cats greeted me as I entered, and I moved past them to find her in the kitchen. "Mrs. T., I told you not to leave your door unlocked. It's not safe," I scolded her as she hugged me.

"But I knew you were coming dear, here, take the tray for me." She handed me a pewter tea tray with a full teapot, cups, and saucers, which I then took to the living room. A fat orange tabby named Gunther gave me the nastiest side eye as I sat down next to him on the sofa, disturbing his nap. She shuffled out after me with a plate of fresh baked lemon squares. "So tell me about your week." She sat down as I poured us both a cup.

I always had to be delicate with what I told her, not that she wasn't dying for all the drama, but I didn't like to worry her. So I told her how I ended up having the week off, neglecting to explain why, what books I read, and what shows I watched. Keeping everything as PG as possible.

"Oh Addy dear, you live like an old soul. You should get out there and have an adventure while you're still young!" She patted my knee, "meet a nice young man, have some *fun*. Live a little!"

"Trust me, I've lived enough."

"Fiddlesticks. When was the last time you went on a date since you broke up with that colorful fellow?"

I spit a bit of tea back out in my cup. *Well shit, she does remember.* "Uhm. It's been a minute."

"See? Exactly. What are you afraid of?"

"Getting murdered... For starters," I mumbled.

"What's that dear?"

"Oh, nothing. I'm just not ready yet. How has your physical therapy been going?" I changed the subject.

"I'll tell you, that doctor is a pain in my rear. He's always lecturing me about taking those horse pills."

I laughed, "well, are you?"

She looked away mischievously. "No. I ran out."

"Mrs. T..." I sighed.

"Now, don't you start too."

"They're good for you, you know that. You need them after that hip surgery. If you don't take your vitamins, they're going to have to replace the other one too. What would I do without you for another week of you being in the hospital?"

"It's so difficult for me to get to the pharmacy! And that cashier is so rude!"

"Ohmygod..." I mumbled. "If I go and get them for you, will you promise to start taking them?"

"Only if you promise not to keep skipping out on all the fun life has to offer."

I laughed again. Crazy old lady. "Alright, fine. I'll make sure I include more adventure if you take your vitamins." I set down my cup and checked the time. "I better head out then if I'm going to make it before they close."

"Oh, it can wait another day."

"How many days have you missed already?"

She purposely didn't respond.

"Yeah, that's what I thought," I chuckled, "I'll be back in a little bit."


The trade of having to deal with crowds during the day was that it wasn't as frightening to be walking around the city alone, even knowing I was being watched. The freakiest thing about it was the feeling. He never once actually *did* anything inappropriate or creepy, that I knew of, it was just knowing he was somewhere.

I decided to test him a bit by going down a few deserted aisles in the drugstore to see if I couldn't separate him from the crowd. I found a nice corner that would be blind to anyone not coming directly down it, and waited. Sure enough, those golden eyes appeared minutes later.

"I thought I told you to stay away from me." I pretended to look at something on the shelf.

"Am I not?" He responded from way down the aisle.

"Why are you so obsessed with me?"

"'Obsessed' is a strong word. I'd say 'concerned'."

"Okay, why are you so *concerned* with me then?"

"Because I can't trust you to keep yourself out of harm's way, and there's a very high probability that a serial killer is after you," he sighed dramatically.

"Have I not been completely safe these last two days?"

"Yes. Until you ventured out in public again, then went straight for the only corner of the store that was hidden from view. Literally anyone could have turned that corner and you would have been fucked."

I opened my mouth, then snapped it shut. It didn't even occur to me. I was so focused on him… "Don't you think if The Carver was going to come after me, he would have done it by now?"

"Not if he knew I was watching you. He's not stupid."

Fuck, another good point.

"Can you just hurry and get whatever you need for your grandma so we can go?"

"Stop being such a creep." I huffed and stormed towards the vitamin aisle, then turned to see if he followed. He was nowhere in sight. I grabbed what I needed, checked out, and left.

I tried to avoid the homeless man standing outside the entrance, begging for change. Not only did I not carry change on me, but the half empty bottle of alcohol sticking out of his jacket pocket was only made more obvious by the smell seeping off him. Though my active avoidance didn't seem to deter him.

"Spare some change for the bus?"

"Sorry, don't carry any on me." I responded passively.

"Bitch," he spat.

I turned to him, "excuse me?"

"Fucking cunt." He threw his collection can at me, scattering his few coins all over the sidewalk.

The voice in my gut told me to just walk away, but my anger pushed it aside. "You've got some fucking nerve, you piece of shit!" I stormed back towards him.

He pulled the half full bottle out of his pocket, aiming to throw it at my head, when his gaze drifted up to someone behind me. I quickly turned to find Warren with his arms folded, glaring down at the man with such intensity that even I shrunk in his stare.

The homeless man froze, considering his options, then grumbled something incoherent and shuffled away.

"That drunk has a stronger sense of self-preservation than you," Warren snorted.

He wasn't wrong. This had always been an issue with me, and as my adrenaline dissipated I began to realize the situation I almost put myself in. I turned on my heel and continued the walk home without a word to him.

"Really?" He raised his eyebrow and followed, not attempting to keep his distance anymore.

"I've lived my entire life without your help," I snapped.

"Attract many sociopaths along the way?"

"A few," I retorted.

"You're incredible," he laughed sarcastically.

I spun and he almost ran into me. "Why do you care so much about keeping me alive, huh? What do you need from me?"

His jaw clenched. "Why are you so determined not to let me?"

"Because I don't know you! You've fucking stalked me for what, a week now? Why didn't you just come to my door and knock, ask me questions like a normal fucking investigator?"

"Have the 'normal fucking investigators' solved the case yet?"

I glared at him. No, they hadn't, but I wasn't about to agree.

"Would you have opened the door for me? Answered my questions willingly?"

Again, probably not. A strange man knocking on my door would have sent me running to my room and barricading myself in, especially right now.

"Exactly." He didn't wait for a verbal acknowledgment from me. "I'm fucking good at my job.

The cops know it, and they don't want me making them look bad by solving this case before them. They aren't clamoring to help anyone but themselves, in case you haven't noticed. Why do you think they lied to the media? How would it look if they couldn't even get a description of the murderer from the only witness?"

I looked down. Several valid points were made. The reality was he already saved my life once, and protected me a second time. I searched my feelings to find that even through my consistent state of anxiety, not once had I felt uncomfortable around him. Sure, he scared the shit out of me that night in the alley, but if I was honest with myself, him walking me home was also the first time I felt truly safe since my ordeal.

"Fine," I sighed.

"Fine what?"

"You can keep stalking me." I half smiled as I turned back home.

"It's not stalking, it's my job." I could hear a smile in his voice as he came to my side, once again putting himself between me and the street.


He stopped beside a black truck as we came up my block. "This is me," he claimed, putting his hands in his pockets.

I looked at the truck, and then down to my building. "You've been parked here the whole time?"

He nodded.

"How… How were you watching me from way over here?"

"There's a lady in your building who's afraid of crows." He replied as if it was the most obvious thing in the world, and looked up the tree that reached my window.

"Wow. No shame." I shook my head and began to walk away. "Do me a favor?"

41

"Mmm?"

"Don't be so creepy about it anymore."

His dimple betrayed his smile. "I'll do my best."

That night as I peered out my curtains, a new black truck was parked on the street in front of my complex.

I woke up with my heart thudding and a sense of dread fading into my subconscious. It was now dark, the TV was on, and Dinah was perched on her tree. My sleeping pattern was all shades of fucked. When I tried to go to bed at my normal time, the fear of waking up with nightmares and anxiety were enough to send me into another panic attack. So I had taken to forgoing a bedtime routine, and just letting myself fall asleep whenever and wherever I was, which meant 90% of the time that was on the couch in the living room.

I sat up and checked outside again for the millionth time in the last 48 hours, Warren was still parked on the street, and a sliver of my anxiety subsided. Part of me hated that I had come to find comfort in the sight of his truck, it's fucking weird. He's an ass, and he's definitely hiding something, but dammit if I didn't feel safer knowing he's out there. My stomach growled.

I closed the curtain and checked the time. *Yeah, it was about dinner time for me.* I scratched Dinah under the chin as I passed by her. "What do I want for dinner? Cereal again?"

She purred and jumped off her tree, landing on the remote, accidentally changing the channel. A commercial for some pizza chain showcased their gooey, cheesy new recipe, and I salivated.

"Good choice," I chuckled at her. Hmm, I hadn't been to Tony's place for weeks, and with Warren watching me I was willing to brave the night.

As I washed my face and reapplied deodorant, I examined my reflection. *You could look cuter…* Why should I care what I looked like? It's just pizza. I dried off and crossed my room, subconsciously glancing into my closet at my favorite sundress that I hadn't had an excuse to wear for ages. *He's going to be watching you anyway, you might as well ask him to come with you.* I shrugged. I *had* shaved my legs that morning…

I stopped at his truck *just* to be courteous and let him know I'm going out. He was reclined back in the driver seat when I peered in the passenger window and tapped on it.

He sat up and rolled the window down for me. "You okay?"

"Yeah, uhm… I'm going to walk to the pizza place on the corner." Before I knew what I was saying the words slipped from my lips. "Wanna come with?"

He stared at me. "Are you actually inviting me to join you?"

Dammit. "I figured you'd follow me anyway. At least this way it's less awkward."

He shrugged, "sure," got out of the truck, threw on his jacket, and came around to the street. "I was beginning to think you'd never leave your apartment again."

"It was a serious consideration. But now, I have scary dog privileges," I smirked.

"Funny," he rolled his eyes and moved to the outside of the street.

I hid a smile at the protective gesture he habitually practiced with me and attempted to discreetly look him over. No hoodie today, but the same leather jacket, a dark purple v-neck, and dark grey jeans. His look was definitely a vibe, and damnit, I was feeling it.

"So are you bored of me yet?"

"Being bored is part of the gig."

"I mean, I could go down another dark alley for you, to keep things interesting?"

"I would prefer you didn't, knowing your luck."

"Aww, you're no fun."

"You think getting attacked is fun?"

"No… *But you coming to my rescue is kind of entertaining,*" I thought.

He smirked.

Shit, did I say that out loud? Stupid internal voice, her and my vagina were always sabotaging me. I blushed, and kept quiet the rest of the walk.


He held the door open for me when we arrived at Tony's, and my lips curved at the unexpected gesture.

"Adelaide! Bella Mia, I have not seen you for weeks." Tony, the restaurant owner, greeted me immediately, drawing my attention from Warren. "How have you been?"

"I've been better Tony, but nothing one of your pies can't fix," I smiled at him.

"Anything for you, Principessa, your favorite is still the same, yes?"

"Yeah." Tony never failed to make me smile. I had no idea what he was calling me half the time but he said it so gleefully I just accepted it.

"And your gentleman friend?" Tony looked up to Warren.

"Uh…" He scanned the menu board quickly, "I'll take the veggie."

"Very good! Sit, sit. I bring it out." Tony gestured to the empty tables, and I picked a booth by the window.

Warren sat across from me. "Is it always so empty in here?" He looked around.

"It didn't use to be. Tony's daughter came out as a mutant last year and they lost a lot of business because of it," I said sadly. "It's the best pizza in the city but people don't seem to care."

"You're not bothered by mutants?"

"Why should I be?"

He shrugged, "everyone's bothered by us."

"There are horrible, sadistic humans out there, and people are less concerned about them than a middle-aged Italian chef who is just trying to run a family restaurant." Righteousness swirled inside me. "People are fucking assholes."

Warren smiled, "yes. They are."

Tony brought out two modestly sized pizzas, and set them on the table in front of us. "Buon appetito!" He smiled and blew us a kiss.

I made a face at Warren's pizza after seeing the mushrooms on it. "Gross."

"What?" He asked as he took a bite.

"Mushrooms."

"Says the girl with pineapple on her pizza," he raised his eyebrow.

"Don't tell me you're one of the uncultured swines who hates pineapple?"

"I don't hate pineapple. There's a place for them, and several good uses. Pizza isn't one of them." He took another bite, and the melted cheese stretched between the slice and his mouth. His tongue reached for it, curling inwards against his lips.

*Stop staring.* I quickly looked back down at the table. "You're the one eating fungus."

He plucked a piece of mushroom off his slice, and made direct eye contact with me as he sucked it off his fingers. "And it's delicious," he emphasized.

Heat rose in my cheeks and I looked away, chewing in silence, until I realized he was still looking at me. "What?"

"Cute dress."

"Thanks," I responded shyly as I swallowed.

"Not your usual dress code."

"And what do you know about my dress code?"

"You prefer comfort and practical to cute and dressy," he shrugged, "and you avoid wearing a bra or shoes when you can."

I flushed pink. "You gained all that from creeping on me?"

"And not even for a full day," he winked.

I bit my lip and looked away from him, but my attention was pulled by a group of men who had just entered.

Tony attempted to greet them. "Good evening gentlemen, please sit wherever—"

"We're not here to eat old man." One of the men replied angrily, and I zeroed in on their conversation.

"We don't need you mutis taking up retail from actual people who need it," another man interjected. "Mr. Hillcrest gave you a generous offer for this dump, and we're here to *persuade* you to accept it."

"Please, men, my family has owned this pizzaria for generations..." Tony stammered. "I respectfully declined Mr. Hillcrest's gracious offer."

"And that was *your* mistake, wasn't it?" The first man replied.

Warren sat very still, listening intently.

The first man pulled a knife out from his belt, and I shot out of my seat. "Don't!" I yelled as I ran towards Tony, who had backed up against the wall.

Warren was faster than I was, and stood between me and the group of men, his hand flat on my chest to stop me moving forward. His back was to them, but he didn't turn when he addressed them. "Guys, I'm going to ask you to leave now," he demanded calmly. "You're upsetting the owner."

"Get a load of this guy…" A third man chuckled. "Mind your business or we'll mind it for you."

"Clearly you didn't understand the gravity of my request. So I'll say it another way. Get the fuck out of here," Warren threatened menacingly.

"Buddy, there's four of us, and one of you. You don't think this old geezer and that bitch of yours are going to help you?" The first man laughed, clearly under the impression they had the upper hand.

Warren's lips curved into a sinister smile. "Huh. Wouldn't have guessed that one…" He turned his head slightly towards them as his body began to swell.

His bones cracked and clothes ripped off as his skin began sprouting brown fur. He hunched over, going on all fours, and a tail shot out from his back end. He let out a horrible squeal as his face elongated.

In the blink of an eye I went from staring at a man, to a giant fucking rat.

The group of men gasped and backed away, all except the second one, who screamed and dropped the knife.

"Fucking mutant!" The fourth man yelled, and ran at the giant rat.

It rose on its hind legs, so tall that it had to hunch before it hit the ceiling tiles. Three of the men came at it with their weapons drawn, and began slashing and stabbing at it. I had never heard a rat scream before, and it's something I never want to hear again.

The rat jumped forward, biting hands and arms clean off with its sharp, razor-like teeth. Its giant glass eyes darted from man to man as they continued their attempts to attack.

It pinned one man against the counter with its giant body, while it slashed at another with its claws. The first man, who had initially dropped the knife, cowered on the floor. A puddle formed around his body that definitely wasn't blood.

The commotion stopped as quickly as it began. The giant rat twitched its whiskers frantically in expectation of another attack that never came. Its once brown fur was red and sticky with blood. The men's bodies  lay strewn about the restaurant floor.

The rat turned to me, blinked, and began to shrink. Fur dropped off its body in clumps as it quickly returned to human size, leaving Warren, on all fours, surrounded by a heap of bloody fur and severed limbs, panting heavily.

He stood, and turned his head over his shoulder to the first man who was still crouched on the floor, covered in his own piss. "Tell your boss this space is unavailable. Get." He growled, and the man scurried out the door.

"You... You mostro..." Tony stammered to Warren from behind the counter. "I do not need your kind of trouble here. Get... Get out!"

I looked from Warren's bloodied body to Tony, who was white as a sheet. My nerve returned to me for Warren's defense.

"Tony, they were going to—"

"Don't bring this *uomo maledetto* back here again, Signoria, and may God save you if this is the company you keep."

"But, Tony—"

"Come on," Warren sighed and gestured for me to follow, once again holding the door open for me. "Sorry about the mess," he apologized over his shoulder before letting the door swing shut behind him.

We didn't speak on the walk back to my apartment. What I just watched was horrifying, but Warren was only trying to protect Tony and Tony only focused on the resulting carnage. The way he looked at Warren, like he was a demon… I glanced over to him. He walked with his hands in his pockets, staring down at the sidewalk.

He didn't initiate the violence. "Those guys had it coming." I suddenly broke our silence.

Warren didn't respond.

"Tony didn't say it, so I will. Thank you."

"I don't think Tony was very thankful," he muttered.

"He was scared, what you did was terrifying, but, if you hadn't, Tony might not be here still."

Again, no response, so I didn't press it. We arrived at my complex, but as I turned to go inside, again my voice escaped before my mind had a chance to reel her in. "Wanna come in?" I asked, turning back to him.

"You're… inviting me in?"

"I mean, you've been watching me for days, and you're going to keep watching me. Might as well be comfortable while you're doing it. You've had a night of it."

49

He squinted his eyes at me, as if concentrating on something behind my gaze. "But you're afraid of me."

"Don't take it personally. I'd be afraid of inviting any strange, creepy, stalker into my place. But as long as you promise not to turn into a giant rodent and eat me, I'll take my chances."

His eyebrows raised in amusement. "Yeah. I promise."


"You can throw your jacket anywhere." I gestured to the sofa or dining room table once we were inside. "I don't even get how you're wearing that right now, it's a billion degrees outside."

"Let's just say I'm cold blooded." He shrugged as he began walking around the apartment. "It's smaller than it looks from the outside…"

"Well if you don't like it you can go back out to your lonely truck." I huffed.

"No… it's… nice."

"You sure know how to sweep a gal off her feet." I bent over the fridge. We needed alcohol after tonight.

He joined me in the kitchen, leaning over the island that separated it from the living room. "Sorry, I didn't mean to offend you. I'm not used to socializing, especially after someone sees me… change."

I paused at the apology. That definitely wasn't something I was used to hearing from any man. "You don't say?" I opened a beer and handed it to him, but then moved my hand away as he was about to take it. "Oh wait, that's right. I don't drink anything you like…"

His bright eyes glinted at the backhanded comment. "Very funny."

I smiled and handed him the bottle, then opened my own. Dinah meowed loudly and pranced into the room. I picked her up. "Dinah, Stalker. Stalker, Dinah."

"For the millionth time," he sighed looking up at the ceiling, his hair flopping back. "It's my job."

"Yes. It's your job to stalk people. You're a professional stalker." I poured Dinah's dinner into her bowl.

"Ugh. Whatever," he rolled his eyes and walked into the living room. "You're the one who invited me in…"

I watched him as he inspected my library, running his fingers over a few of the titles. Learning to trust my instincts again had been a constant struggle. When it came to men, they had been extremely unreliable. I knew I should feel perturbed by this man, knowing what he was capable of. Watching him kill people on two separate occasions should have been enough to send me running. But I was more concerned with the fact that I didn't feel driven to, than I was about the killings.

He moved towards the curtains, parted them slightly, and peered out. The silence between us began to make me nervous.

"Sooo, how long have you been working on The Carver case?"

"Months, since the third murder." He responded, still looking out the window.

"Who hired you for it?"

He let the curtain fall closed as he turned to me. "No one."

"So why then? I mean, if you're not getting paid to do all this work?"

"This one's… personal."

I waited for him to continue, but apparently he felt that was enough of an explanation. I sighed and moved into the living room, plopping on the sofa. "Fuck dude, it's like pulling teeth, trying to talk to you."

"Sorry, it's the nature of my profession," he smiled, but his eyes carried sadness. "I knew the third victim." He joined me, taking the edge of his seat. His elbows came to rest on his knees as he played with the label on the bottle in his hands.

"Oh." I looked down guiltily. "I'm sorry."

We sat quietly again.

He peeled the corner of the sticker up, and tore at it. "Her name was Jenna. She was like a sister to me," he finally spoke.

I turned my body towards him but held my tongue, letting him decide if he wanted to share.

"It was two days before they found her." A darkness fell over his face and he picked at the paper aggressively. "No one was looking for her. Not her pimp, not even the other girls she worked with. If the cops had done their fucking jobs to begin with, he would have been caught and she'd be alive right now."

Poor girl. How many others shared her story? My thoughts swirled around the woman I found, how she died alone and terrified. If I had only opened the door after that first scream… "Did she die in a hotel too?"

He nodded slowly. "Every girl, same line of work, same cause of death, same scenario."

"How many?"

"Your's makes twelve. Twelve girls, five cities, in eight months."

"Shit." I looked away, how could there be so many and this guy still hadn't been found? "Don't the police have any leads?"

He shook his head. "No. This guy doesn't leave fingerprints, the blood is always the girls, and no one has ever seen him. Except you." The shredded pieces of the label were now scattered over the coffee table. "You really don't remember anything?"

Guilt and fear consumed me as my eyes flashed back and forth. The empty eyes… The blood…. A figure crouching in the window… A surge of panic erupted into my chest and I closed my eyes. "No," I responded quietly, swallowing it before it took over.

He eyed me intently. "The memories are in there, you're terrified of them."

"Of course I'm fucking terrified! What sane person wouldn't be!" I glared at him.

"I didn't mean it as an insult," he softened his voice. "I just meant you *do* remember something. Even if your brain won't let you recall it… Huh." He studied me, making me feel like I grew horns.

"What?" I snapped.

"I almost got an image. I haven't been able to pick out your actual fear so far, it was almost as if you were afraid of the memory itself, but that time—"

"You know, I'm not sure I like this ability of yours. It feels a lot like mind reading." I brought my knees up to my chest, as if covering my body would make it more difficult for him.

His eyes glanced quickly down to my legs, and he looked away, a faint blush falling over his cheeks.

*Shit.* I forgot I was wearing a dress. I turned and sat facing forwards again, the heat rising to my face. He probably got an eyeful of my ass and panties. This was why I didn't wear girly shit.

He cleared his throat, fighting a smile. "It's not mind reading, it's more like another sense for me. I only get an image of the fear, but once I become it…" His eyes widened as an idea flashed across them. "If I *became* him. Adelaide." He turned and set his bottle down roughly. "If I could become him, I could use his abilities. I could ask Paulie…" He stood and began pacing. "That's so much better…"

"Better than what?" I gaped at him.

He stopped and looked back down at me. "Never-mind. Would you be willing to try and remember him?"

53

My mouth dropped open. "I… don't know I mean… I already tried…"

"But if it meant catching this guy, would you be willing to dig deeper?"

My instinct was to say yes. Of course I wanted to help catch this monster, but was I really ready to go digging into the greatest trauma of my life when I hadn't even finished unpacking the first one? I wasn't sure I had it in me.

He dropped to his knee in front of me and took my hand in his, startling me again with his icy touch. "Please Adelaide, help me catch this fucker."

My gaze shifted from our hands to his eyes, and they locked. Warmth spread down my stomach to my girl. Before I even had a chance to reel her in, she responded for me. "Okay."

His eyes lit up as he revealed an absolutely gorgeous smile. Every ounce of resistance left in me melted away. That fucking dimple.

# Four

Dark eyes, a crooked smile… I gasped and opened my eyes. My heart was racing.

"I'm sorry, I'm trying." I shook my head and put my hands over my face.

"I know," Warren righted his posture with a sigh, "but you got his mouth that time."

"This isn't working," I rubbed my temples. "We've been at it for hours and all I've managed is his freaky smile and his hair color, and I'm not even sure that was right."

"That's not nothing, but you're right, this is beyond my expertise." He bit his lip. "Have you heard of regressive hypnosis?"

"I've heard the term, but I'm not sure what it is."

"I'm guessing your mind is blocking out the memory of that entire encounter because it's trying to protect you. But we can get around that part of you, open a back door so to speak, and dig into the subconscious to pull those memories to the forefront."

"Uh, yeah, that sounds dangerous?"

He chuckled, "not if it's done correctly. Your mind is really good at burying trauma, if it wasn't, you couldn't function properly after witnessing something like that."

"I wish my mind would erase the memory of my ex…" I muttered. "Who knows how to do something like that?

"I have a buddy with telepathic abilities. He's a therapist."

"Ew," I took a drink. "Therapy and I don't really mix."

He smiled, "you've been to therapy before?"

"Yeah, in middle school. My parents thought I was 'troubled' because I got into fights a lot."

He sipped his beer and hummed a laugh, leaning back into the cushions. "Why am I not surprised?"

"Kids are mean. I didn't like it when they picked on others. So I got in the way."

"Your parents thought you were the problem?"

"Yeah, but probably more because of the kids I was standing up for, the mutants. My parents pulled me out of public school after the third fight, put me in an all human private school."

"And the therapist suggested that?"

"He was a quack. That and he tried to put me on all sorts of drugs to keep me sedated, wanted to send me to a human advocacy camp. I was eleven for fuck's sake. I didn't understand why everyone was so mean to those poor kids, and no one was standing up for them."

"That explains a lot." He stretched his arm over the back of the sofa, the length of it nearly reaching me. "Well, I can at least say that my guy is good. I've seen him work. Though I can't promise you don't need to be medicated, bringing stalkers into your apartment... " He smiled as he brought the bottle back to his lips.

"Oh my god, was that a *joke*?"

"Mmm," he hummed as he finished off his beer, and stood. "Want another?"

"Yeah, thanks," I smiled. Both at the offer and at the crack in his surliness I just caught a glimpse of.

He handed me a fresh bottle and sat back on the sofa. "So, what do you think?"

"I'm not sure I'm brave enough to try that," I looked down. "I want to help you, really, but… My mind locked these memories away for a reason. Maybe I'm not ready to deal with a second trauma."

"A second one?" He raised his eyebrow.

"Oh, uh." *Fuck, alcohol makes me loose lipped.* "I recently left a pretty bad relationship, you don't want to know the details." I quickly took another swig.

He studied me for a moment, as if he wanted to ask, but decided against it. "I know it's a big favor. But if it means anything, there is no question in my mind about your bravery."

I looked up at him. "How would you know?"

He leaned forward. "I could feel how afraid you were of those guys at Tony's tonight, yet you were willing to stand up to them anyway. When those guys cornered you in that alley, your terror rippled for blocks, but you still fought back. And even though you're afraid of me, you invited me in, and tried to recall the face of The Carver for me. You're a tough chick, braver than most other people I know."

"I didn't think before standing up for Tony, someone had to. Those guys were gonna take me, I knew it, but I wasn't gonna make it easy for them, and you…" I blushed, "well, that was just me being stupid."

He smiled. Dammit that smile. "You finally admit it then?"

"No." I looked away, turning redder. "I'll think about it, okay?"

"Fair enough." He pushed himself up off the cushions. "I should get going, I don't want to keep you up."

I tapped the screen on my phone '2 a.m.'. If I were at work, this would still just be the middle of my shift. I had hours before I would begin to get tired. I looked up at him, "where do you stay? When you're watching me?"

"In my truck." He stretched skyward and his shirt lifted slightly at his waist, exposing the edges of tattoos underneath.

My mind went to unholy places at the sight of his v-line. I tore my gaze away. "That can't possibly be comfortable? Where do you shower? Eat?"

"I've got snacks," he lowered his arms to my disappointment. "And showering, I just wait until I can shift into something small enough to use a birdbath or something..."

"That's so ghetto," I laughed.

He shrugged, "all in a day's work." His fingers combed through his hair, ruffling it slightly.

I imagined what it would feel like to run my fingers through it before forcing my mind back to reality. "Are you going to keep watching me?"

He looked down at me, and put his hands in his pockets. This time, he looked almost ashamed. "Yeah. You still need protection."

I hesitated at what I was about to offer. It went against every ounce of common sense. "Then... You might as well just stay here..."

"Here? Like, in your apartment? With you?" He was just as shocked as I was.

"Yeah... Fuck this is stupid, but you're going to watch me anyway, and I honestly feel safer with you here..."

He blinked at me. "Huh."

"What?"

"You're still afraid of me. But you want me to stay... That's... Weird."

"Stop reading my mind, you creep."

"I told you, I'm not reading—"

"Well stop sensing, or whatever. Most people keep their fears private for a reason."

"I can't help it. Can you control what you smell or hear?"

"I can plug my nose or ears if I don't want to."

He chuckled, "I don't have an opening to plug for this."

There's a dirty joke in there somewhere but I was too buzzed to find it. "Do you want to stay or not?"

"Sure, thanks," he relaxed his shoulders.

"I should warn you, I keep an odd sleep schedule, working the night shift and all. This is still early for me."

He shrugged, "I'm used to not falling asleep until my assignments do anyway."

"Wow, is that what you call me?" I laughed dryly, "how impersonal."

"I can't let it get personal. It would impede my work."

"Good to know." I finished my beer. "Well if you don't mind, your *assignment* is going to take a long overdue shower. Remote is right there, help yourself to the kitchen. Dinah, watch him," I commanded her as she was curled up in her tree. She blinked at me sleepily. *Yep. She totally has it covered.*

"Have fun." He relaxed back into the cushions and picked up the remote, making himself at home.

The hot water trickled down my body and I let out a deep sigh. I needed this. For the time being having a strange, dangerous, mutant man in my living room didn't bother me in the slightest. In fact, he could burst into the bathroom right now and slice me open Psycho style and I would be blissfully content with it. Okay not really, but there were worse ways to go. I recalled the sight and sound of a giant spider leg going up a man's ass and shook my head aggressively, immediately trying to forget it.

I took my time finishing my shower and cracked open the bathroom door. The sounds of some crime show came from the living room, and I quickly snuck down the hall into my room and shut the door. I threw on my pajama pants and a tank top, and returned to the living room.

He glanced at me as I emerged from the hallway, and smirked. "Nice pj's," he turned back to the TV.

I looked down at my Hogwarts crest-covered bottoms. "What? You're not a Potter-head?"

"As a matter of fact, I am."

I smiled and plopped down on the sofa, facing him. "So you *do* realize then you're basically a living bog—"

"*Yes.* Yes, I realize," he sighed. "In my defense I was born way before the books were released. So technically *they're* imaginary versions of *me.*"

I chuckled, "so what's your house?"

"Slytherin." He answered without turning his head.

"I could have guessed that." I laughed through my nose, and unwrapped my wet hair, letting it fall over my shoulders.

He glanced at me out of the corner of his eye, then refocused at the screen. "Bet I can guess yours."

"Yeah?" I began scrunching my curls in the towel.

"Gryffindor." He replied without missing a beat.

"Huh. Good guess."

"It's obvious."

"How so?"

"Aside from your impulsiveness and lack of self-preservation? Your emotional decision making, sense of justice, love for arguing—"

"Alright, alright. It's fucking creepy how much you know about me... Nerd." His lips curved and he turned toward me slightly, not saying a word. A tingling sensation ran over me. "Alright, your turn," I adjusted myself on the sofa to face the TV.

"My turn?"

"To shower?"

"You want me to shower... In *your* apartment?" Now he turned his head completely toward me.

"I don't *want* you to, I just figured I'd offer you something other than a birdbath for a change," I shrugged.

He blinked a few times in thought, then stood and moved towards the door.

"Where are you going?" I turned quickly.

"My duffel is in the truck." He smiled at my reaction, "don't worry, I'll be right back."

"I'm not worried," I huffed and turned back to the TV. But as soon as the door closed I hurried to the window to watch him walk to his truck, grab a bag out of the back, and return towards the building. *Now who's being a creep?* I returned to the sofa. Why should I care if he left? He could do what he wanted. Relief surged through me when he knocked softly and announced himself.

I stood and answered the door.

"Did you miss me?" He smirked.

"Hardly," I smiled and he stepped inside. "Towels are in the closet in the hall," I gestured.


Only once I heard the bathroom door close and the water turn on could I relax back into the sofa. My notification went off. One new text from Rory:

*"Morning. Checking if you're still alive."*

I always forgot she was three hours ahead. I chuckled to myself and typed back, *"for now."*

*"You doing okay?"* She responded immediately.

*"Yeah…"* I began typing, then hesitated, wondering if I should tell her about my chaotic night. I knew this whole situation was insane and she would berate me for allowing this hunk of a stranger to stay with me. But at the same time I knew she was the only one who would keep tabs on me in case this went south. I deleted my previous words and texted, *"I'm going to call you"*, instead.

"What's up?" She answered the phone.

"A lot happened today, and I need to talk fast so just let me finish before you judge me."

"Okaaay."

I quickly and quietly recapped the events of the last few hours, and she only interrupted with a few gasps or groans of disapproval until I was finished. "And he's in your shower right now?!" She finally responded.

"Yeah…"

"Addy, you crazy bitch. It's one thing for him to keep an eye on you from outside, it's another to invite him to stay with you!"

I knew this was coming. "I know… I know…"

"Goddamnit, I know he's the poster boy for 'Addy's heartthrobs' but think with your brain woman!"

"He's just here for protection," I insisted.

"Riiiight. I know you…"

"Listen, I'm over whatever my heart used to throb over," I thought back to Scott. "I learned my lesson. These guys are great to look at but I can't trust them further than I can throw them."

"Are you seriously considering this regression therapy? I'm not sure I like the idea of it."

"I said I would think about it. If it could help catch this guy—"

"You don't owe the world anything. You need to worry about you right now."

"As long as he's still out there, I'm always going to be looking over my shoulder."

"I just don't want you to get manipulated into his revenge schemes…"

"Don't worry. I'm never letting a man manipulate me ever again."

"Just please be careful. I have to head into the office now, lock your bedroom door when you go to sleep?"

"Duh."

"I'll check on you tomorrow."

I hung up just as the water turned off. A few moments later the door opened, allowing the steam to escape into the hall. He appeared in the doorway, dripping wet, dressed only in his jeans sitting very low on his hips, and a rolled towel around his neck. If my eyes could pop out of their heads like in the cartoons, they would have.

He had a thin frame, but perfectly toned, and *covered* in ink. It was difficult to distinguish one art piece's boundaries from another. His wet hair fell casually over to one side, dripping water down his pecs and stomach, betraying the existence of the curves of his abs. A small trail of body hair ran the length from his belly button down to where my imagination had to take over. I had to fight not to gawk, or drool for that matter.

He toweled his hair as he approached the sofa and sat down with a sigh, wafting a spicy, woodsy aroma in my direction. "Thanks. That felt really good."

I had trouble forming a single cohesive thought. *Get a grip woman.* My breath returned to me, and I noticed he was shivering. I thought of his icy hands. "Are you always so cold?"

"Yeah, thank my father for that part of my mutation."

"He was a mutant too?"

"Something like that."

"And your mom?"

Something dark flashed over his eyes, and he nodded.

I got the feeling he didn't enjoy talking about his family, so I changed the subject. "Tell me something about yourself."

"What?"

"You've been stalking me for a week now, you know more about me than I do of you. If you're going to stay, I should at least know you better."

"*You* asked me to stay, remember?"

"I did. And now I'm asking you to tell me about yourself."

He sighed. "Alright. What do you want to know?"

"Open mic. You pick."

He thought, then leaned forward onto his forearms, his hair flopped down over his eyes. He took a deep breath, "There *is* something you should know about me..." He began dramatically, "I'm... A mutant."

I rolled my eyes, laughing. "No shit, Sherlock."

He chuckled, "I have no idea what you want to know."

"What's your favorite color?"

"Uh, I guess black?"

"Figures. Okay. Favorite food?"

"The blood of my enemies," he growled, then smiled.

I attempted to hide the lust that surged through me with a sarcastic laugh. "You're hilarious."

"Blueberries," he chuckled.

"Really?"

"Why is that surprising?"

"It's just so… Normal," I chuckled.

"Is that it?"

"No," I thought. "What's the weirdest thing you've turned into?"

"Someone's mother-in-law," he responded without hesitation.

I snorted, "seriously?!"

He hummed and nodded. "Dude was terrified of her. I totally thought she was some horrible, dangerous, mutant woman but when I transformed she was just a normal, bitchy, old lady. It was so hard to keep a straight face while he screamed."

"What the hell kind of assignment was that for?" I burst out laughing.

"His wife thought he was cheating, I was trying to scare him into admitting that he was."

"Did he?"

"Yup."

"Serves him right then." I exhaled slowly as I calmed myself. But my mood darkened as I thought about all the things people were afraid of, about how debilitating some people's phobias were. It almost seemed an unfair advantage to be able to use that against someone. Those deep seeded fears were private. It was natural to keep them hidden for our own protection, and this man could pull them out of us without even a thought.

"What's wrong?" He studied my face.

"Have you ever used your abilities on innocent people?"

He looked down. "Not on purpose."

I stared at him, wordlessly pressing for more information.

"It took a long time for me to be able to control my abilities. For a while it was a reflex response. Someone thought of something they were afraid of and my body would just change. I grew up in a foster home, and there were a lot of kids…" He paused. "I didn't blame them for hating me."

"A foster home? What happened to your parents?"

His lips thinned.

I recognized that expression anywhere. Whatever happened in his past was exceedingly painful to recall. "Never-mind, you don't have to tell me if you don't want to."

He picked at a loose thread on the towel that now lay across his lap. "I never knew my father. And my mother died when I was 12. I've been on my own ever since, well, except Jen. She was the only kid who wasn't afraid of me."

I instinctively leaned forward and put my hand on his forearm. "I can't imagine what that must have been like for you." He flinched slightly at my touch, but didn't pull away. I could almost feel his skin thawing under the warmth of my hand. "Your ability is terrifying," I acknowledged, "but you know, *you* aren't so scary."

His eyes met mine, "no?"

"No. You're just a dick."

He hummed a laugh. "For a moment there I was afraid you were going to give me a compliment."

"Oh, well, good to know what *you're* afraid of."

"Why, plan to use it against me?" He smirked and his lips parted slightly.

My gaze traveled down to them. "Maybe, a girl's gotta have some leverage."

"There's a lot you could do to me with the right leverage…" His eyes flashed down to my lips, and back up.

Heat shot down between my legs. *They're great to look at, but you can't trust them.* My words rang in my head, and I moved away. "I should go to bed. I'm getting tired."

"It's been a long day," he smiled.

I pulled the blanket off the back of the couch and handed it to him. "Are you going to be okay out here?"

He nodded, "it's more comfortable than my bench seat, for sure."

I stood and turned back to him. "Goodnight."

"Goodnight, sweet dreams."

I blushed, then hurried to my room and locked the door.

# Nine

I lay on my back staring up into nothingness, and I couldn't move. My arms and legs were bound by ropes pulling them apart. I lifted my head slightly and looked down at my naked body. Panic struck as I pulled against the bindings which seemed to get tighter the more I struggled. I screamed, but nothing came out. Out of the darkness above me a face appeared, distorted, manic, with blank eyes, and a hideous smile. Clawed hands reached down and raked at my skin leaving bloody scratches. A single finger pressed down onto my chest, piercing my skin with its sharp nail. "Please, keep struggling… I like it when you struggle…" A raspy voice wheezed from above as the nail plunged through my heart…

I shot straight up in bed, panting, sweating, my heart racing. "No… No, not again," I murmured, fighting the feeling of sheer terror that threatened to take over. I threw off the covers, leapt out of bed, and fumbled for the doorknob, forgetting I had locked it.

The realization brought the reason why to my forefront. A strange man was in my apartment. I took a deep breath and opened the door quietly, creeping down the hall. I stopped in the doorway to the living room to find him sound asleep on the sofa with Dinah curled up on his bare chest.

My pounding heart steadied for a moment at the sight. He looked so non-threatening with his hair messily sprawled across his handsome face. His chest moved up and down gently as he slept. Dinah opened a single eye when I entered the room, but decided she was comfortable with her current accommodations, and quickly closed it again.

I quietly stepped into the kitchen and set the coffee maker. I continued battling the rising panic as I leaned backwards against the counter. Closing my eyes, I inhaled, counted to five, then exhaled, and again. When I finally opened my eyes Warren was sitting up on the sofa, staring at me.

"Sorry, did I wake you?" My voice shook in spite of my attempts to calm down.

"What's wrong?" He asked and stood, causing Dinah to jump down and the blanket to fall onto the floor.

"Nothing, I'm fine," I lied.

"You're not fine. I can feel—"

"Stop it." I turned around, sounding angrier than I actually felt. "Don't do that."

"I told you, I can't help it. Your fear is so strong it woke me." He walked into the kitchen and looked down at me, frowning. "You saw him…"

"It was just a nightmare," I shook my head.

"You're trembling."

"I'll be… Fine…" I gasped as I lost my battle with the oncoming attack and started hyperventilating.

"Whoa, whoa…" He caught me by the arms as I began to collapse onto the floor.

His cold hands relieved the burn on my skin, and I impulsively pressed my face against his bare chest.

"Oh…" He immediately raised his hands up to his sides and  stiffened.

I set my attention on the gentle rhythm of his heart thumping against my ear, willing my own to mimic its beating.

69

Slowly and hesitantly, he began stroking the back of my head. "You're okay. You're going to be okay…" He spoke softly. "He can't touch you. You're safe…"

My heart rate slowed and my breathing calmed. I shuddered an exhale, and was suddenly overcome with embarrassment. "Sorry," I pushed away from him.

"It's alright. Are you okay now?"

"Yeah. That was…" I cleared my throat. "I'm still getting used to them."

"Have they been happening a lot?"

"They've pretty much become a nightly thing since —"

"The murder?" He finished for me.

I nodded in response as I moved toward the cupboard and pulled out a couple of mugs, going about preparing the coffee as if nothing happened.

"Can you tell me about the dream that triggered it?"

I hesitated when I realized I couldn't recall it. "I don't remember."

"Let me do that." He reached over my head and took the creamer from my hands. "Go sit down."

"I'm fine," I replied defiantly, but I couldn't even look him in the eyes.

"Last time you said that you collapsed."

This gentler version of him was harder to argue with. I admitted defeat and settled myself down on the sofa. Dinah jumped on my lap as if to second his opinion that I should take it easy.

He brought two mugs and the entire bottle of creamer over to the coffee table. "I don't know how you like your coffee," he shrugged.

"Thanks." I smiled gratefully and poured what a normal person would consider a ridiculous amount of creamer into my black coffee. He watched me silently as I stirred it. "What?"

"You sure you even like coffee? Or should I just bring you a mug of creamer next time?" He smirked.

"Shut up," I hid a smile behind my mug as I sipped.

He pulled a shirt on, then took to preparing his own coffee.

"Did you sleep alright?" I attempted polite morning conversation.

"No," he said plainly. "You kept me up half the night with your nightmares."

"Oh, sorry. Was I talking in my sleep?"

"Your fear." He sipped.

"You can sense it even in my sleep?"

"Especially in your sleep. That's when people are most afraid, when their conscious mind isn't trying to block it."

I thought hard, but couldn't remember any dreams or nightmares from last night. "Do you know what my nightmares were about?"

"Vaguely. A few about me, most about The Carver, one about a guy with weird colored hair…"

I turned red at the mention of my ex.

"But the theme was all the same, it was about you getting hurt in one way or another," he continued. "It's a very primal human fear, pretty common."

Dinah moved from my lap to his, reclaiming her bed from the previous night. I smiled, "she likes you."

"She kept me warm all night." He scratched the top of her head gently and she purred happily.

My heart softened at the memory of her sleeping on his chest. The same chest that I was very recently pressed against as he held me, talking me down from a panic attack. That soft skin, his strong arms as he held me up… whatever

71

that body wash was smelled amazing... I began to feel extremely warm again.

I cleared my throat. "So, I'm scheduled to work tonight."

"Uh huh?" He brought his coffee to his lips.

"Are you going with me there too?"

His eyes smiled behind his mug and he placed it down gently. "Do you want me to?"

I meant to phrase that differently, but the insinuation wasn't entirely unintentional. "At the risk of sounding needy, yes. I'm not sure I feel entirely safe being there alone just yet."

"I was already planning on it." His eyes remained soft, and something fluttered in my stomach.

My phone rang on the coffee table and we both glanced down at it, reading the name of my boss on the caller ID. "Speak of the devil... Hey..." I stood and took the call into the bedroom.


His gaze dropped to her back end as she walked away, and he immediately scolded himself. Dinah looked up at him inquisitively. "*Alright*, she's gorgeous," he sighed, as if Dinah was the one pointing out all the little things he found endearing about her. "But trust me, you don't want me pursuing your mother in that way. I'm not a good guy." Dinah meowed defiantly, stretched, and jumped off his lap. "Fine. Be that way," he huffed, but began to feel guilty, and that worried him. He couldn't afford to let her get under his skin, his priority was catching The Carver, no matter the cost.


I came out of the room holding my phone at my side, dejectedly.

"What's wrong?" He asked.

I shook my head. "I… I just got fired."

"What?!"

I crossed the room and sat on the couch. "He said he didn't want the bad publicity of my face being the one everyone saw at check in. That they'd associate me with the murder…"

"That's the biggest load of bullshit I've ever heard. What a fucking dick."

It's not like I loved that job or anything, and the thought of going back to sitting in that overheated lobby, alone, for eight hours made me feel sick, but this was just the cherry on top of a shit sundae. "He said I have to go pick up my stuff before he leaves for the day or he's going to throw it away." I scrolled my phone for the bus schedules.

"I'll take you," Warren offered. "It's not a good idea for you to take the bus anymore."

I looked up at him, "are you sure?"

"Yeah. Go get ready."

No wonder he slept in his truck, it was like driving around in a living room. The seats were deep and comfortable, with plenty of legroom. I unashamedly began snooping through his center console as he drove, pulling out random snacks, tools, notepads, pens… condoms.

"Oh ho…" I smirked, flashing one up at him.

"Do you mind?" He glanced down, a flash of pink crossed his cheeks as he pushed my hands away from his compartment, and slammed it shut. "Nosey."

73

"*Curious,*" I corrected him. "What's back here?" I turned around and glanced in the back seat where he had thrown his duffle bag. There was a rolled up sleeping bag, a blanket, and a camera bag among miscellaneous wrappers and empty fast food containers.

"Seriously. So nosey." He shook his head as he flicked on his turn signal.

I reached forward and clicked on his radio, which was set to Bluetooth, then picked his phone up from the cup holder and tapped the screen. "What's your password?"

"None of your business." He snatched the phone from my hands and put it in his jacket pocket. "Fucking hell..."

"I just wanted to listen to music. Sheesh." I folded my arms and sat back roughly against the seat.

He shifted his eyes in my direction, rolled them, took the phone out of his pocket and scanned his thumb. "There. Spotify," he held the phone out to me, "and don't go clicking through my phone. I actually have sensitive information from other cases on there."

"Fine, fine," I smiled, tapped the app open, and scrolled through his playlists. Classic rock, hardcore, pop-punk, metal... "I'm gonna go out on a limb and guess you're a hip-hop fan?"

"Funny."

My eyes fell on a specific playlist and my smile widened. "No way..." I tapped it excitedly, and a song from the soundtrack of Wicked came on. "You're a theater buff?"

"You look surprised."

"Just didn't take you for the artsy type."

"I happen to be a pretty decent photographer, thank you very much."

"Somehow I don't think creepy pictures of cheating spouses will win any art shows."

"You better cut it out or I might crash from laughing so hard," he replied dryly.

"Dick."

"Pain in the ass."

I selected the show-tunes playlist and hummed to myself as the buildings sped past. There weren't many people out, I suspected most were still hunkering down in whatever air-conditioned buildings they could find. His phone vibrated from the cup holder.

He turned to me, "I know I'm going to regret asking but, can you see who that is?"

I picked up his phone, still unlocked, and swiped down from the top. "Uh, whoever 'Captain Dickhead' is wants to know if he has you to thank for the cleanup in the alley? This isn't the police Captain asking about the night you saved me is it?"

"Tell him 'I have no idea what you're talking about'."

"But it was us…"

"No, it was a giant spider," he smirked.

"Oh my god," I smiled, feeling guilty that I didn't feel more guilty. I typed it out and hit send. "Well at least I know I can get a new job as your secretary…" I put his phone back in the cup holder.

"You wouldn't last one day as my secretary."

"How much you wanna bet?"

"You don't have a job, you have no money to bet."

He was right, I was jobless. My face fell. How was I going to support myself? Wherever I went next, I would have to start over completely, probably fight to get anything above minimum wage… What if I couldn't find another job that payed enough to keep me independent?

"Sorry," his voice softened, "too soon. But don't worry about that, you'll find something. You deserve better than that shithole anyway."

"I hate when you do that…" I muttered looking out the window, not wanting to admit that his words did bring me a bit of comfort. My heartbeat sped up as he pulled into the unloading area in front of the hotel.

He turned to me, stretching his arm across the back of the seat. "Do you want me to go in with you?"

"No. I'll be okay. It shouldn't take more than a few minutes."

"Alright. But if you're not back here in ten, I'm coming in after you."

I smiled, and got out.


The lobby looked completely normal, though I wasn't sure what I expected. Maybe a small part of me thought there would be random blood splatters on the wall, or police tape everywhere. But there was no indication that anything horrific had occurred mere days before. My now ex-boss was sitting behind the check in counter as I approached.

"I'm here for my stuff." I greeted coldly, and he nodded to the back office.

I went in and began gathering the few belongings I kept there. A change of clothes, my lunch bag, water bottle, and some random desk decorations. He walked in, handed me a sealed envelope, and went back out to the front. I opened it to find my final paycheck, but as I examined the hours on the attached slip of paper I noticed the entire last shift was missing.

"Hey," I walked back out to the front, "I think you forgot to add the last day."

"You walked out on your shift. You don't get paid for that day."

"What? No I didn't. The cops made me come down to the station…"

"Exactly. You didn't finish your shift, and I didn't give you permission to leave."

"You've got to be joking, did you forget I witnessed a murder?!"

We both looked up as Warren entered through the front doors.

My boss greeted him with a fake smile. "Welcome Sir, I'll be with you in just a moment."

Warren ignored him and looked down at me. "Everything okay?"

"No, actually." I turned back to my boss. "You need to pay me for my last day. It's on record that I was clocked in."

"You left your shift early, got one of our guests killed, and caused the cops to shut us down for an entire week, making me lose thousands. No. Be happy I'm not suing you for misconduct. Now leave before I have you arrested for trespassing."

Angry tears pressed against the back of my eyes, and I opened my mouth to argue further, but Warren stepped in front of me.

"Hold on a minute, are you trying to tell this woman the incident the other night was her fault? *And* you're trying to cheat her out of her paycheck?"

My boss looked up at him. Warren was a good foot taller. "This is none of your concern young man."

"As a matter of fact, it is my concern." Warren straightened up and his pupils contracted. "Here's what's going to happen. You're going to go into that office, write her a personal check for what you owe her, plus one-hundred for pain and suffering. Then we will leave, and you will never hear or see either of us ever again."

My boss stuck out his round belly stubbornly. "Or what? If you touch me I'll have you arrested for assault."

"Adelaide," Warren's voice lowered. My skin tingled at the sound of my name on his lips, "will you please shut the curtains for me?"

"Don't you touch anything, girl," my boss threatened emptily.

I ignored him and drew the blinds. The lobby darkened significantly.

"I'm not going to touch a hair on your bald little head…" I recognized the tone Warren took all too well, and held my breath.

I watched in fascinated horror as his body bent and twisted. His bones cracked, and he groaned as he changed into the shape of a man- sort of. I gasped as a creature I didn't recognize stood awkwardly in Warren's place on one leg, while the other dragged limply behind him. Half this man's face was missing and bloody, as if it had taken a shotgun shell at point blank. He groaned in agony as he stretched his arms towards my boss who now cowered on the floor.

"Johnny?! No… No Johnny… I didn't mean it! They made me… I swear!" He crawled backward towards the office.

"Write cheeeckk…" The zombified man gurgled through a hole in his throat.

"Sure Johnny, whatever you want… Just, stay away from me!"

"Johnny" gurgled something incoherent, and my boss scrambled into the office. I swore the zombie winked at me, which would have been the funniest thing I ever saw if I wasn't in utter shock.

"Here… Here Johnny, take it…" My boss held out a violently shaking hand with a check in it.

The zombie looked in my direction, then looked back down at the check.

I cautiously reached forward, and took it out of my boss' trembling hand, and read it over.

The zombie watched me, as if waiting for my approval.

I nodded.

It reached its arms over its head and gurgled "braaaaaainnsss" as loud as it could.

My boss screamed, ran back into the office and slammed the door.

That was the final straw, I burst out laughing. The scene was too cliché not to find absolutely hilarious.

The zombie twitched, its skin began to peel and its bones cracked loudly back into place, until it began to look like Warren again. Hunched over, hands on his knees, and cracking up.

Oh my god, the sound set something alight in me.

"Let's get out of here," he gasped through a chuckle.

"That was the craziest fucking thing I've ever seen…" I was still laughing in the car as we drove away from the hotel.

"Did you see his face when he recognized me?" Warren laughed. The sound was so damn infectious.

"Oh my god… Am I a horrible person for thinking that was funny as all hell?" I caught my breath.

"No more than I am. Which sorry, doesn't mean much." He smiled at me, and my heart skipped a beat.

"Thank you. You didn't have to do that."

"That asshole got off easy."

I fell silent. No one had ever stood up for me like that, ever. It was strange to be on the receiving end.

He cleared his throat. "Hey so uh, I was wondering if you would be cool if we stopped by my office before I took you back home. I need to refresh my wardrobe."

My female sirens went off. *Don't let him take you to his place alone, he was waiting for a moment like this to take advantage of.* "Uhh."

"I get it if you're not comfortable," he quickly added. "I was going to just deal with it for a few more days because I didn't want to leave you, but since I can keep an eye on you and not have to go commando anymore…"

Fuck, he had to go and plant that image in my mind. Realistically, he had already been in my place overnight. If he wanted to do something to me he would have. "Yeah, sure."

The building in which Warren's office was, was one of the oldest in the city. Made from red brick, and it still had the original moldings around the doors and windows. It would have been a beautiful building if it were well maintained, but alas; Crumbling plaster, exposed wiring, and creaky wooden floors greeted us as we entered.

"Mmm, lovely." A cockroach scurried into a crack in the wall.

"Rent's cheap, what can I say?" He shrugged as he led the way down the hall, and stopped in front of a door with the words "Warren Nyte: Private Investigator" on the frosted glass.

"Tada…" He announced as he opened the door to a surprisingly large office. A very messy desk, covered in papers, files, photos, and a few empty coffee mugs stood against the wall opposite of us. A rather worn fabric sofa leaned on the wall to my left, and was kept company by a side table piled with a stack of books. The right wall was postered with papers upon papers, and just like the movies, lines of red marker, string, or both strung across certain ones, connecting them to other certain ones.

"This is… Exactly what I expected, actually…" I stepped inside and walked around the room.

"Is that a compliment or an insult?" He asked, leaning against the doorframe with his arms folded. "Wait, coming from you, I already know the answer."

I made a face at him.

"Make yourself at home." He walked past me and through another doorway, pushing a curtain open, revealing a small kitchenette. "Bathroom's down here if you need it," he called out as he disappeared around the corner.

I moved back towards the right wall, the red lines piquing my curiosity. There were printouts of articles about The Carver dating back months, photos of women, presumably the victims, and post-it notes with handwritten words and questions sprinkled throughout. I looked at each of the women, most of their photos were mugshots, some were candid pictures from a distance. Some of them looked so young, my heart broke. Their eyes were tired, defeated, the weight of a world of judgment and hate behind them. I scanned the notes and articles for their names, wanting to remember them as people, but there were a few who were simply "Jane Doe". My breath caught at the mention of a "Jenna Sinclair".

That particular article stated she was discovered in a hotel bed, her arms and legs bound, tape over her mouth and eyes, her breasts taken, and a hole in her neck. Exactly like the victim I found. It was strange knowing I saw her, knowing the image of her mutilated body was in my head, but I couldn't recall the scene. What I knew of it, I knew from what I was told, as if I wasn't even there.

Jenna's picture in the article looked nothing like the one he had hung up above it. She was caked in makeup, her sad eyes distant and suspicious. While the photo *he* chose of her looked like a purposefully taken selfie where her head leaned on the shoulder of someone who was cut out of it. She was a pretty little thing, her eyes were bright, her smile wide, a totally different woman than the one pictured in the media.

"That was the last time I saw her alive," Warren spoke softly as he approached from behind. "I took her to the beach, she loved the ocean."

"She's beautiful," I whispered.

"She really was. And she was so smart, she could have been anything, done anything she wanted... If the world didn't hate us so much." His finger trailed sadly down her photo.

"She was a mutant too?"

He nodded, "an empath. She understood me in a way no one else could." He blinked back tears that flooded his eyes, and turned his head away from me, clenching his fists.

I placed my hand on his back. Even through his leather I could feel his muscles tense. "I'm sorry."

He coughed to cover a sniffle. "If I wasn't there to identify her body, she would have just been another 'Jane Doe'."

I looked back up at the photos. Twelve women, murdered and mutilated. They each died alone, their bodies used one last time for a sick man's pleasure. My sympathy churned to anger. What was it with men and seeing women as objects? A means to their own ends? This guy won't stop. How many more women have to suffer before he fucks up and leaves a clue for the authorities to follow?

"How would you knowing his abilities help us find him?" I asked, still facing the wall.

"I have connections, someone who keeps an unofficial record. He knows a lot of mutants and there's a good chance he can give me a name." His voice was still quiet.

"Alright. I'll do it." I ran my fingers over Jenna's photo.

"Wait, what?" He turned. "Really?"

I nodded. "I'm not willing to let him hurt anyone else."

I gasped as he suddenly hugged me, picking me up slightly. My blood rushed at his scent of sage and cedar wood.

He put me down, smiling. "Thank you, Adelaide."

I blushed and stepped backwards, running into his desk, knocking his lamp over. The clattering shattered whatever thin pane of sensuality that encompassed us. I looked down at it, and noticed a blinking red light under a pile of papers. After shuffling them aside an office phone screen read '10 new messages'.

"Looks like you had some missed calls." I choked out, quickly changing the subject.

"Always." He sighed with a smile, and leaned over me, pressing my body further onto his desk.

I held my breath, and he pressed a button. Voices spilled out of the recorder:

*"Mr. Nyte, my name is Stephanie. I heard you're good at catching good for nothing cheating husbands. Boy, have I got a job for you."* Stephanie recited her phone number and hung up.

*"You good for nothing piece of shit! My wife left me because of you! You're dead! You hear me!"*

"Charming." I looked up at Warren who just rolled his eyes.

*"Heeyyy cutie. It's me. I've been missing you these last few nights—"*

Warren's eyes got wide. He quickly picked up the receiver and hung it back up.

"Who was that?" I was surprised to hear a slight twinge of jealousy in my voice.

"No one," he cleared his throat.

"No one who calls you 'cutie'?"

He didn't respond, but his stoic expression was betrayed by a brush of pink across his cheeks.

I jumped a mile out of my shoes when the office door flew open violently and slammed against the wall. A huge man in a white tank top took up the entire door frame.

"NYTE!" He boomed.

Warren turned and stepped between the intruder and myself. "Yes?"

"You son of a bitch." The man stormed into the office, stopping inches in front of Warren. They stood at equal heights but the angry man was twice as wide. "Where do you get off…"

Warren widened his stance and folded his arms across his chest. "Wherever I'm given consent to," he smirked.

"My wife hired you to find our baby girl, and you have the balls to take her money and not even bring her back to us?!"

"I did exactly as your wife asked. I found your '*baby girl*'. She's safe and happy. I stated that in my report."

"Where is she?" The man's face reddining by the second.

"That was not part of the contract," Warren stated simply. "I was hired to find her, and I did."

"You tell me where she is or I'll…" The man took a step toward Warren, who's eyes flashed with anger.

"You'll what? You won't do *anything*. Because you know, that I know *why* your 'baby girl' ran off in the first place. Your baby girl who is now a legal adult and can finally choose to live out of your reach. Your baby girl who you raped and molested repeatedly from childhood. If your wife really has no clue, then you can be the one to explain to her why she won't be coming home. And no amount of money will convince me to force her back to the hell you call home. I fulfilled my contract Mr. Johnson, and I suggest you let it end at that."

All the color drained from Mr. Johnson's face, "you… You can't prove anything…" He stammered.

"Sure you wanna test that theory?" Warren raised his eyebrow.

"This… isn't over." Mr. Johnson stepped back toward the door. "You'll regret sticking your nose in my fucking business."

"Sure I will."

Mr. Johnson opened his mouth as if to retort, but then thought better of it, huffed, and slammed the door behind him as he left.

"Holy shit." I gasped.

Warren's shoulders relaxed at the sound of my voice and he sighed. "Sorry you had to see that." He turned back to his desk and began to gather some papers, putting them into a backpack he had brought out.

"Is that... A common occurrence for you?" I turned to him.

"Pretty much an average workday," he shrugged.

A surge of defensiveness swarmed me. "That's not right, people have no right to treat you that way."

He stopped what he was doing and looked at me as if I just told him I was the second coming of Jesus. He blinked a few times, studied my face, then smiled. "I can handle much worse than 'Wifebeater Joe', but thank you."

I smiled, trying to lighten the mood. "I honestly thought you were going to turn into some crazy creature again."

"Not everyone's fears are physical things." He returned to his packing.

"Did you know all that from his fear?"

"No. That was simple detective work. It just so happened to also be his greatest fear for his wife to find out about it." He straightened up and zipped his bag closed. "Alright, let's get out of here before another angry client storms in."

"Aren't you going to call your girlfriend back?"

His eyes glinted, "no." He moved towards the door, and opened it for me.

My brain began down the rabbit hole as I passed him. He had said she was 'nobody', so either she doesn't know that or he's lying. But... She called him on his work phone, not his cell, *that I know of*. He was awfully quick to shut the message off, he clearly didn't want me to hear too much, and that condom in his truck? I suddenly realized I was staring down at the floor, and looked up.

Why did I care? Why should I care about any of it? So what if he has a girlfriend? So what if he doesn't and just has side chicks? It didn't affect me either way. I agreed to meet with his psychic friend to help catch a murderer. At most, this was a professional relationship. That was it.

"You coming?" He held the building door open, watching me.

The heat from the midday sun began to fade as it set outside the city. I should have been walking to work, getting ready for another boring eight hours of no air conditioning. But instead, I was bringing a guy I barely knew back to my apartment, to plan… What exactly?

"What's next?"

"I assume you want to go home?" He walked me to the passenger door and opened it for me.

I fought a smile. "For my memories. Since we're doing this crazy hypno-thing."

He closed the door and went to the driver's side. "I'll call my buddy when we get back to your place, see when he's available."

"Have you seen him do it before?"

"I wasn't present for the actual session, but I met with the client after. It helped us reunite her with her mother."

"Did she seem… Okay afterward?"

He smiled, and without looking brought his hand down and patted mine softly. "Yes. She was fine. You'll be fine."

I froze. My skin still tingled even as he returned his hand to the steering wheel. *If it feels like this on your hand, imagine his fingers elsewhere…* NO. For fucks sake. No man's touch was worth the heartbreak. I crossed my legs and turned away from him, refusing to forget the years of self-loathing and isolation that came from guys like him.

It was dark when we got back, and I hadn't spoken much to him the entire ride. He dropped his bags by the sofa before letting me know he was going to step out on the balcony and call his therapist friend. The minute the glass door slid closed, I pulled out my phone and called Rory.

"So, did you sleep with him yet?" She wasted no time.

"No," I grunted and sat on the couch. "I told you I'm not interested in that."

"Who are you trying to convince?"

I pursed my lips, then sighed and lay flat. "I don't know anymore."

She laughed. "Look, he's cute, your type, and you've already asked him to stay with you. How many more steps do you have to go?"

"Well, first of all, no one is saying he's even interested in me like that. Second, I'm pretty sure he has a girlfriend. Third, I cannot handle another Scott situation, and fourth, I agreed to see his friend to do that regressive hypnosis so I'm pretty sure that would break some sort of rule—"

"Wait, what? You agreed to it?"

"Yeah. There's no way I couldn't have." I explained to her about Jenna, and the other women, nameless or not, who I felt responsible for bringing justice to.

Rory was silent for a moment. "I get it Addy, I really do. I know how you go all warrior queen on the helpless but, this is a major thing you'd be dredging up. I mean, have you even uncovered the full length mirror in your room yet?"

I know she didn't mean it to hurt me, but I felt a jab in my heart with the last comment, mostly because I hadn't. I still couldn't look at my own body without feeling disgusted by it. Though I got past my unhealthy relationship with food, and had begun to start wearing my favorite clothes again, I couldn't bear to see how I looked in them. She took my silence as confirmation.

"I don't want to lose you to another bout of depression Addy."

"I know. But hey, at least I'm seeing a therapist this time," I chuckled.

"I'm serious. Did he pressure you to do this at all?"

"No, actually, he only asked the one time then dropped it. He's been a total gentleman this whole time…" I tilted my head back on the sofa to look upside down towards the balcony door as the latch clicked. "I gotta go Rory, I'll text you later."

I hung up as he stepped inside and closed the door. "So, he's booked tomorrow, but he's free the next day at 2." He sat down next to my head as I looked up at him. "I told him I'd let him know if that worked after I asked you."

"Sure. It's not like I have a job to go to anymore or anything. Where is he?"

His eyes kept flicking between my face and down past me, then he turned away, smiling. "Sorry, I'm having a hard time concentrating with you laying like this."

I glanced down my body, and my boobs were all but spilling out of my top. I blushed and quickly sat up. "Sorry," I muttered.

"Please, don't be." He smiled as he shifted in his seat, crossed his leg in a figure four, and cleared his throat. "What was the question?"

"Uh... Where he's located?" I asked to the coffee table, unable to look up.

"About two hours south of here. So we'd have to leave by 11 a.m. with traffic."

"That's going to be miserable for my sleep schedule," I sighed. "But I guess I have to retrain myself sooner or later."

"We can always head down tomorrow, get a hotel over there for the night so you don't have to get up so early?"

"Yeah? You wouldn't mind?" I turned to him finally.

He smiled, "not in the slightest. I actually thought you would."

"Not having to get up early? Hell no."

He chuckled. "Alright, I'll let him know. I was kind of worried I'd upset you earlier."

"What? Why would you think that?"

"You've been uncharacteristically quiet since we left the office."

"Oh." The last thing I needed was to let on that I was fighting dirty thoughts about this man. "You're saying you missed my talking?" I smirked.

"I didn't say I was complaining about it." He turned away from me, hiding a smile. "Maybe I just wanted to know what I did to keep you quiet."

"Fuck you," I chuckled.

His lip curved as he looked down at his lap, "mmm."

My heart pounded, and I jumped up. "I better go pack," I gasped and quickly went to my room, as if I could outrun the tension. I cannot, I *will not* crush on this man. Focus on packing, focus on prepping for tomorrow.

I flung my closet door open and scanned for my overnight bag, which of course was on the top shelf just above my reach. Why I even bothered to put things up there, I had no idea. I jumped, hand stretched upward, snatching for the handle that hung just over the edge. "Yes!" I grabbed and pulled it, but of course, it was the only thing that *didn't* come down on me.

"Motherfucker!" I groaned, rubbing where the corner of a book hit me square in the forehead.

"What happened?" He rushed in, and immediately came to me.

"Nothing. I'm fine," I huffed stepping over the pile.

"Did all that fall on you? You've got a lump going there." He cupped my chin in his hand and moved my face up to his, pushing a stray curl away. He furrowed his brow as he examined me, his finger gently circled around my forming welt. "We need to ice that. It's going to bruise."

I gasped at the chill of his fingers. His grip was so light, so gentle, but I couldn't pull away. Goosebumps broke over my skin. "You could just use these icicles you call fingers," I whispered.

He laughed, "come on."

He sat me back on the sofa, went into the kitchen and came back with a bag of frozen veggies. He sat in front of me. "Turn," he commanded, gesturing me to face him.

I obeyed, and winced as he gently placed the bag against my skin. "I can hold it myself, you know." But I didn't move to take it from him.

"I know," he smiled, locking his gaze with mine, "but I can't keep my eye on you if I don't."

"You don't *always* have to watch me."

"Apparently I do," he chuckled. "This is the third time I've let you out of my sight and you've gotten yourself in trouble."

"I've gotten myself in and out of trouble plenty of times before I met you," I grumbled.

"Sure you have," he goaded, adjusting the bag slightly.

"I avoided getting arrested during the protests without you."

"Is that right…"

"I got myself and my friend out of a crowd fight at a concert."

He hummed a laugh, "which I'm sure you started."

Fucking asshole. "I didn't need yours, or anyone's help when my ex threw me against a wall!"

His face hardened. "What?"

I dropped my gaze and pushed his hand away, fire swelling in my cheeks and eyes.

"What did you just say?" He demanded.

"Nothing… Forget it."

"There's no fucking way I can forget that. Your ex… *Threw you?* Against a wall?"

I swallowed the lump forming in my throat. Shit. I didn't mean for that to slip out. Not even Rory knew that Scott laid hands on me. To her knowledge, it was all psychological abuse. The body shaming, name calling, and isolation were bad enough, but if she knew about the fights, and rape…

"Adelaide, look at me." He still stared intently at me.

I shook my head. I couldn't. If I looked at him, I wouldn't be able to hold back the tears.

"Fine. Don't look at me. Just listen. That is *not* alright. I don't know anything about your past relationships but no matter what, he was wrong to do that to you." He shook his head. "You're absolutely right. You don't *need* me, you survived him on your own. But now you *have* me, so please, for fucks sake, let me protect you. At least until this is all over, then I'll fuck off, okay?"

I smiled at his final offer. "Fine. Until we catch that monster. Then you can pick another girl to stalk."

"Deal," he smiled. "Now, what the hell were you trying to do in there?" He looked toward the bedroom.

"Get my bag down from the top shelf."

He rolled his eyes and laughed, then stood and held his hands out to me. "Let's get you packed, brave little girl."

I packed, we had a light dinner, and I called it an early night. Not only was I absolutely drained from my emotional rollercoaster of a day but I knew I was going to take forever to get going tomorrow. Though no matter what I tried, I couldn't sleep. I tossed and turned as nightmares of my ex, The Carver, and getting fired all fought for first place in the "fucking up my life" category. It was late when a soft knock came at my door, and without waiting to hear a response, Warren spoke quietly: "You don't have to be afraid of them anymore, I won't let *anyone* hurt you."

It was the first time I slept through the night in days.

After breakfast and annoying Dinah to death with hugs and kisses, we went across the hall to ask Mrs. T for the fairly common favor we asked of each other; To watch the fur babies while the other was out of town.

"Addy! Would you like to come in?" She greeted me enthusiastically.

"No, thanks Mrs. T. I'm on my way out of town and was hoping you could check in on Dinah for me? We should be back in a few days."

She looked behind me toward Warren with her giant glasses, examining him up and down. "Oh? Did you finally take my advice?" Then she added in a "whisper" loud enough for the whole floor to hear, "My, my, this one's a stud. When you go looking for 'fun' boy do you find it."

Warren coughed as he suppressed a laugh.

"Oh… No, no. We're just working together," I stammered, turning beet red.

"Hmm." She stared at me, then at him, then back at me and smiled as she attempted another whisper. "Maybe for now, but show a little skin dearie, you'll get him," she winked.

"Oh my god," I actually whispered, so she didn't hear, and continued talking as if she didn't just embarrass the hell out of me.

"Of course I'll check in on Dinah for you dear, I'd be happy to."

"Thank you, Mrs. T. I'll call you if anything changes."

"Enjoy your trip!" She stepped back into her apartment and closed the door.

Warren burst in laughter. "Good to know grandma approves of me."

"Shut up," I mumbled as I slammed the elevator button, face bright red.

"I mean, if you're just looking to have a little 'fun' you could have just said so," he sniggered. "You didn't have to put yourself in danger for my sake—"

The elevator door opened and we stepped in. "If I were looking for some *fun*, you are the *last* person I would want to have it with, asshole."

"If you say so." But the grin on his face indicated that he didn't believe me.

"HOW?!" I shrieked from the passenger seat.

He shrugged with both hands on the wheel. "It sounds disgusting."

"But you never even tried it! How do you know you don't like it?!"

"Have you ever tried dog shit? No? How do you know you don't like it?

"Oh my god. You haven't lived. What is wrong with you?" I dipped another french fry into my chocolate shake and stuck it in my mouth. "Mmmmm" I moaned exaggeratedly, drawing his eye, though he was trying to be sneaky about it.

He looked away when I caught him. "Gross." He shook his head, hiding a smile.

"Just try it. You'll be surprised," I begged.

"I'm good."

"Wooow the man who can sense everyone's fears is afraid of a little culinary exploration. So pathetic."

He sighed. "If I try one will it shut you up?"

"Yes."

"Fine." He consented, moving the arm closest to me across the back of the seat.

I beamed at him, and shook my fries looking for the crispiest, most perfect fry in the container. Then I dipped it in the shake, achieving the perfect chocolate to fry ratio and held it up for him to take. He leaned over towards me and opened his mouth, and I put it in, his lips pulling the rest. He chewed in silence, his expression blank.

"Well?" I asked impatiently.

His eyes glinted. "It's not as bad as it sounds."

"You love it and you know it." I smiled triumphantly as I dipped another one. "Want more?"

He chuckled, "sure."

I held another fry for him to take with his mouth, but he miscalculated the distance and ended up biting my finger slightly, pulling it with his lips as he took the fry into his mouth.

"Oh..." I gasped involuntarily, as a patch of wetness spread inside my panties.

"Sorry," he whispered and licked his lips.

I was so focused on hiding my own obvious arousal, that I didn't notice him move his hand to his lap, concealing the rising bulge in his jeans. Conveniently enough, the song on the stereo was about sex, and though the volume was turned down, it was deafening in the silence between us.

"So, are we there yet?"

"Really?" He raised his eyebrow. "You're going to be that girl?"

"If it annoys you, then yes."

He rolled his eyes, "pain in the ass." But they blazed with fire when he turned to me.

My text notification went off, and I glanced at my phone to see Rory's daily check in.

"Shit," I murmured.

"What's wrong?" He had a slight panic in his voice.

"My sister, I forgot to tell her the therapist was out of town. I'm about to get an earful."

"Because you went out of town, or because of who's taking you?"

I looked up at him guiltily.

"Ah," he noted.


*"So, don't be mad, but I forgot to tell you that the therapist was two hours south of here. I'll be back the day after next though."* I typed.

*"Uhh… how are you getting there? You don't have a car…"* She responded, and I could just imagine the tone in her voice.

I cringed as I typed, *"Warren."*

Immediately the phone rang, and I thought for a split second about not picking up. "Heeyyy…" I answered sheepishly.

"Addy are you fucking serious? You go from telling me you can't decide if you want to fuck him or not, to GOING OUT OF TOWN WITH HIM?" I had to hold the phone away from my ear.

Warren's eyebrows shot up. I hid my face in my free hand.

"What, is the hotel room going to end up mistakenly only having one bed too?" She continued. "Is he there with you right now?"

I looked at Warren, who shook his head aggressively. "Yeaaah?"

"Put me on speaker."

I held the phone out in front of us. Warren mouthed "nooo" to me, and I responded with a silent "sorry" before clicking the speaker button. "Alright… We can both hear you…." I shut an eye, waiting for the explosion.

"Warren, is it?" She sounded like she was in court, addressing the jury.

"Yeah?" He answered cautiously.

"Listen closely to every word I'm about to say to you. I don't care what you two have agreed to as far as your sexual escapades, she's a grown ass woman and can handle herself. BUT. If you hurt my sister, in any way. If she even comes back with as much as a splinter, I will fly down there, find you, cut off your dick, cook it on the grill, slap it in a bun, lather it with mustard and feed it to you. *Do you understand me?"*

97

I covered my mouth with my hand to keep myself from busting up out loud.

"Yep. Yep. Hurt sister, gourmet dick dog for one. Got it," he responded quickly, "loud and clear."

"Good. Addy, make out with him, suck his dick, fuck him… Whatever, have fun. Just don't let this be a repeat of last time."

"Ohmygod. GOODBYE RORY." I hung up, mortified, and hid my face in both my hands.

After a painfully obvious silence, he asked; "So, I'm curious. Where did you finally land on wanting to fuck me then?" I could hear that smug grin in his voice.

Seven

We arrived at the hotel as the sun set. This one, significantly nicer than my previous place of employment. It had a valet, (though Warren refused to let anyone touch his truck), a pool, hot tub, gym… All the typical amenities one would expect from a hotel, but none that I was used to providing.

"Checking in for Nyte." Warren told the lady at the front desk.

"Yes Mr. Nyte, we have you booked for two queens for one night?"

I released an exhale at the confirmation of the number of beds.

"Yes."

"Would you like to charge the credit card on file?"

"Yes."

She handed us each a room key and thanked us for our patronage.

"How much do I owe you for the room?" I asked him in the elevator.

"Don't worry about it. It's a tax write off for me."

"Oh." I wasn't entirely sure I was comfortable with that. "Are you sure?"

"Yeah," he looked down at me and smiled. "You're helping me out by doing this, it's the least I can do."

The elevator doors opened and I froze at the all too familiar sight of a long empty hallway with doors lining the walls.

Warren stepped out, and looked back when I didn't follow. "What's wrong?"

"Nothing." I took a breath and stepped out.

He tilted his head slightly as he looked down at me. "Would it help if I went ahead and checked it out?"

"It's fine." I shouldered my bag and walked past him to our door, again freezing as I slid the key card in the reader.

He spoke softly from behind me. "You know I can feel it…"

I stared at the door handle, terrified to open it. Terrified to be greeted by another gruesome scene.

"Here, let me do it." He gently moved me aside, unlocked the door, and opened it. "Wait." He squeezed my shoulder, and walked into the room.

Even though logically I knew the chances of seeing another dead body across the bed were highly unlikely, I couldn't convince my instinct to run otherwise. "It's an empty hotel room, stupid. It's fine. Just go in." I whispered to myself, but my legs didn't move. I was on edge, ready to sprint away from here, my ears sharp against even the smallest sounds. I jumped slightly when he reappeared.

"All clear. I checked everywhere." He smiled softly down at me, "come on." He held his hand out, and I took it, allowing him to lead me in. He closed the door behind us, locked it, latched it, and chained it, then tested the door by pulling on it. "No one's getting in. You're safe."

I finally forced myself to look up and around the room. It was a spotless, tidy, empty hotel room with two beds. Just as it should be. I gave a little sigh of relief, and as I relaxed I realized I was still holding his hand.

"Sorry," I quickly dropped it.

He brushed his fingertips over mine, "don't be."

My heart gave a small flutter. *What was so wrong with crushing on this guy again?* He moved away and began unpacking his backpack, spreading his laptop and papers all over the desk, and I sobered instantly. This was a work trip for him. He may be a shameless flirt but I was only here as an asset to his case. If I let my feelings get involved I would end up getting hurt.

"Is that all on The Carver?" I moved towards the desk.

"Hmm? Oh no, I have a couple of cases I've fallen behind on, thanks to *someone*," he smiled down at me. "I have to keep up with my paid work too, you know."

"Did you want any help?"

"It's alright, it's not as fun as it sounds."

I put my hands on my hips. "We have an entire evening to kill, and what else am I gonna do? Just lay on the bed and watch you all night?"

"I mean, I've heard I'm not completely unappealing to look at…" He smirked.

"By whom? Mrs. Tibbet? She's blind and deaf. I wouldn't use her as a reliable source," I pushed him.

He laughed, *God, his laugh did something for me,* and pretended to fall into the chair. "We're gonna have to work on your aggression problems…"

"Maybe your therapist can fix me while I'm under," I smiled.

His eyes flashed up at me. "I've got a better idea of how we can get all that out."

My girl quivered, and I gave him another shove in the chest, causing the chair to tip back. "Get back to work," I laughed softly.

He grinned mischievously, but sat up in the chair. "Still want to help?"

"Sure." Anything to keep my mind occupied.

He leaned across the desk and grabbed a notebook. "This is what I've got on The Carver so far," he handed it to me. "My notes on the latest victim are on the last few pages, but the cops didn't give me much. Would you be willing to fill in any blanks you can remember?"

I flipped through the pages of hand-written notes. "I'll try." It was strange that he preferred to hand write things still, most of his notes and work were on scrap papers and notebooks. "You don't want to type all this out?"

"I write and think faster than I type," he shrugged. "It helps my ideas flow better when my hand is moving."

I lay on my stomach on the bed and opened the notebook. His writing was surprisingly neat and compact, easy to read, which was fortunate because I found myself devouring every word. The Carver's victims ranged in age from 18-35, he didn't seem to have a preference except for their line of work. They were all sex workers, all died in hotel rooms, each one with their breasts cut off after they were found bound and raped. Though the police were unable to determine if the rapes happened before or after the mutilations, they were able to tell that their deaths always came last. It made me angrier. As if it were even possible for these murders to be more horrific, he made sure these women suffered before taking their life.

I finally got to the latest victim, and as Warren said, the police didn't offer him much information. I flipped to a blank page and began jotting down what I could remember. He had her legal name, but I knew she preferred "Punky", as I heard a few other women greet her in the lobby in passing. I also added that she was a regular, knew the area very well, checked in with a man that night and wrote a description of him. I broke down the night step by step, but once again, anything after I exited the elevator was fuzzy, as if trying to recall an old movie I had only seen once as a child. I squeezed my eyes shut, concentrating, and got a flash of her bloody face plastered with duct tape.

I gasped and sat up, my heart raced.

He came and sat on the bed. "You're okay, breathe…"

I nodded and focused on slowing my inhales. "Sorry," I breathed out.

He tilted his head as he looked at me. "You know, you don't need to apologize for feeling vulnerable."

I turned and met his gaze. "What?"

"You do that. Whenever you feel afraid or upset by something, you always apologize."

I didn't even realize it. "I guess, I don't want to be an inconvenience to you. I don't want to upset you."

"You're not," he placed his hand on my back. "Your anxiety is completely understandable, and it's just a part of who you are. I accept that. Besides, if anyone is used to feeling fear from others all the time, it's me."

His acceptance of my burden somehow made it easier to bear. I relaxed under his touch and picked up the notebook. "I wrote down all I could remember." He took it from me and scanned the page. "It gets fuzzy when I go upstairs. Sor—"

He raised his eyebrow at me.

I laughed through my nose, "I guess I do, do that."

He smiled and looked back at my notes. "Wow this is a lot…"

"I'm not sure it's all useful information but—"

"Thank you," he smiled. "This is more than enough. Now," he closed the notebook. "What do *you* want to do?"

"Don't you have work to catch up on?"

"The rest can wait."

I stood and went to the window, thinking. It was still early for me, and after sitting in a car for two hours I wanted to move around. Our room happened to face down into the currently vacant pool area. "Let's go down to the hot tub," I turned and smiled at him.

"Uh, I didn't pack trunks."

"And I didn't bring a swimsuit. But that's not going to stop me."

He raised his eyebrows and smiled. "What? Are we going skinny dipping?"

"You wish." I rolled my eyes, and motioned down to my current outfit of a tank top and jean shorts. "I'll just take my shorts and bra off."

"You're going in your underwear?"

"Why not? You can too."

"How am I supposed to resist that?" He smirked.

A warm breeze blew through the clear, moonless night. I was exceedingly grateful at the deserted pool, as I wouldn't have had the confidence to undress in front of other people. Though I decided that as long as I remained submerged so he couldn't see my body, I'd be fine, and god did I need to relax. I turned the jets on, tested the water, and dumped my towel on a beach chair nearby. I had just begun to unbutton my shorts when I noticed him watching me intently.

"Turn around… Perv."

He smiled and averted his eyes.

I shimmied out of my jeans, unhooked my bra, skillfully pulled it out from under my top, and quickly sunk into the water. "Fuck, that's nice…" I groaned as I slid down.

He stood above me holding his towel, still fully dressed.

"Aren't you coming in?"

"I'm content to just watch," he smiled.

"Whatever. Creep." I closed my eyes and tried to relax.

He sighed and unzipped his hoodie.

I peeked an eye open at the sound of him tossing it aside, and hypocritically watched as he stripped down. He pulled his shirt over his back and tossed it carelessly on top of the pile of our clothes, the rippling water reflected off his chest. My attention caught on a series of circular, puckered scars along his inner elbow, which from further away disguised themselves as a part of the tattoos that circled his arms. *Did the injuries he sustained in other forms carry over to this one?*

He kicked off his boots and socks, unbuckled his belt, and pulled it off with one hand. My heart raced and his fingers worked on his button and zipper, and he slipped out of his pants. I inhaled a quiet gasp. This man was a work of art, his entire body covered in ink. Different designs of horrifying creatures, skulls, spiderwebs, and thorns were intertwined flawlessly, even up past the seams of his boxer briefs, leaving me to imagine how far they went.

He lowered himself into the water across from me. "Shit. That's hot," he hissed.

I opened my eyes fully as he stood only waist deep. "I mean, it's called a 'hot' tub…"

"Smart ass," he growled at me as he stood in the same place. "It's probably at least ten times hotter to me than it is to you."

A surge of guilt washed over me. I forgot about his body temperature. "Right, hang on." I hurried out of the water and to the temperature gauge, turning it down. "There, that should be better." I broke out in goosebumps as a light breeze hit me, and moved back towards the spa. He was staring at me, and I panicked.

In my concern for him, I completely forgot I was in just panties and a soaking wet tank top. Shit, whatever chances I had of him being attracted to me just flew out the window. There was no hiding my belly, huge ass, stretch marks…. I folded my arms over my chest, feeling the nipples of my not so perky breasts clearly pressing against the fabric of my top. I felt completely ashamed, embarrassed, and angry at myself for exposing it all to him. I fought tears as I slid back into the water, attempting to hide from him, and preparing for the verbal assault that I was used to receiving.

"Thanks." He continued to stare as he slid further down into the water.

"If you want to stare at a freak, buy tickets to the mutant circus." I rested my head against the ledge nonchalantly. I refused to let him know how I felt. If I didn't give him ammo, he couldn't use it.

He tilted his head, "what?"

"Like I didn't just see you look me up and down? Go on… Say whatever backhanded, sarcastic, rude comment you're dying to express. Get it out of your system."

"You think I have something uncouth to say about your body?"

"Don't you?"

"Why the hell would I?"

"Don't fuck with me! I know I'm fucking fat okay? Trust me, I'm working on it. But just because I'm unattractive doesn't mean I don't have feelings—"

He sat straight up. "Adelaide, who told you those things?"

"It doesn't matter who."

"It most certainly does, because they are a fucking liar."

He took the wind out of my sails. "But… You were staring…"

"Uh. *Yeah*. I was checking you out," he said angrily, "and even if I wasn't, what kind of asshole says those things to another person?"

He was... What?

"Fuck! What kind of fucking idiot was that boyfriend of yours? Anyone who sees *that*," he gestured up and down in the water with a splash, "and doesn't immediately get a hard-on and tongue-tied, deserves to have both parts cut off since they're not *fucking* using them." He threw himself back into the water, "for fucks sake."

I wasn't sure how to take the overly aggressive compliments, so I just stared down into the water, focusing on the foaming bubbles.

"Adelaide," his voice was much softer. "What did this guy do to you?"

Once again, I felt the pressure of tears threatening to fall. "It's not important," I replied meekly.

"It is to me."

"It's kind of a lot to go over…" my voice cracked.

He pushed off the side and settled next to me. His eyes mirrored the spa lights below as the patterns of the water surface reflected in them. "Tell me?"

I cleared my throat. "You really don't need my baggage."

"But I want it," he ran his fingers gently up and down my arm. "Please?"

My breath shuddered as I inhaled. "I was 17 when we first met, and he *told* me he was 23, but I found out much later he was actually 27."

He looked down and tensed, "go on."

"It was fun, at first. We met at a mutant rights rally that he organized. He was funny, and handsome, and being by his side made me feel powerful. I fell for him, hard… When I turned 18 I lost my virginity to him." I swallowed the tears. "He told me he was willing to wait for me, told me

I was worth it… He would convince me to drink with him, he'd pretend to drink as much as me then tell me to sleep it off in the bed…" A tear fell down my cheek and I closed my eyes.

He brushed it away with this thumb.

"I told him one day I didn't want to drink so much anymore and the fights started. He convinced me that I wasn't skinny enough for anyone else to find attractive. That if I didn't stay with him, I would end up alone. That became the reason I stayed for six years. But I finally had enough when I caught him cheating on me for the fifth time. I confronted him in public, he had the girl with him. He got mad, picked me up, and threw me…"

Warren roughly grabbed my chin between his fingers. The coldness of his touch stung against the heat from the spa. "He was a coward, Adelaide." He looked deep into my eyes. "So afraid to lose you, that he taught you to believe the most ridiculous lies. He saw the strength in you and knew if he didn't beat it down, you would see him for what he really was. He knew how gorgeous you are, and that you can literally knock anyone off their feet with one look. He wasn't good enough for you, and he knew it. Trust me when I say that fear turns people into monsters. But I need you to hear me right now; I was staring because you're a fucking knockout, and you're impossible for any guy not to drool over."

My heart threatened to leap out of my throat, and I trembled from the combination of nerves and his icy touch. No one had ever spoken to me like that. No one had ever made me feel afraid and wanted at the same time. Did I dare believe him? Was he actually attracted to me too?

His eyes flicked between my gaze and my lips, and he inched closer.

The burning desire I had been denying for days was impossible to ignore any longer. My head tilted towards his as my lips parted in anticipation.

Suddenly, he looked down, as if a thought crossed his mind, and let me go. "We should get dried off and get back upstairs. It's getting late." He smiled as he retreated, but there was a hint of regret in his voice.

*Stupid. Fucking stupid.* I lay in bed with my face in the pillow. I said I wasn't going to, I told myself it was a bad idea, but I let it happen anyway... I have a fucking crush on Warren. The man had my face in his hand, my lips inches from his, and he chose not to kiss me. He turned me down, but I still couldn't stop thinking about him. I should be worried about my session tomorrow. I should be focused on how terrified I actually was to face this horrifying trauma, but instead I was racking my brain about why he didn't close that gap... Why he left me there, wanting. Was it because of that girl in the voicemail? Did I try to get him to cheat? Was I a home-wrecker?

He shuffled in the other bed and mumbled, "I can feel you," sleepily.

"Sorry," I whispered and forced my eyes closed, willing myself to sleep. What if after pulling these memories from me I'd never be able to sleep again? I already had panic attacks and nightmares every night from what I *didn't* remember... What the fuck did I agree to? Rory was right, I couldn't handle this. I'm going to lose my goddamn mind. It's too broken to be subjected to that...

109

"Adelaide…" He grumbled.

He snapped me from another spiral. "I know, I'm sorry."

"Don't be sorry, just go to sleep."

I sighed, "I'm trying."

I flipped myself onto my back, and stared up at the pitch black ceiling. A vague memory of a dream ran through my mind, something about claws? I shuddered and turned onto my side. *Focus on the reason I agreed to it.* This was for all those women. For every one of them who thought no one would remember them, or care that they were gone. What if it was Rory? I would do anything to catch her killer. Oh god. The image of Rory's bloody, taped up face formed in my mind. My heart raced, my breathing shallowed… No… Not again…

He grunted.

"I'm afraid to sleep."

He was silent for a while, then he sighed. "Come here."

"What?"

"I'm not going to get any sleep at this rate. Come over here," he demanded.

I slid out from under the covers and stood at his bedside. I could barely make out his figure in the dark as he threw the blankets off and scooted over. *Was he wanting me to get in bed with him?* I hesitated. He turned to face me and grumpily thumped the mattress in confirmation to my silent question.

"I'm not going to fondle you in your sleep, now will you please get in here? I'm cold," he growled.

I thought to argue with him, but the company honestly sounded comforting. I lay down, careful not to get too close, and he pulled the covers over my shoulder.

Even in the dark his bright eyes seemed to glow as he blinked sleepily. "I'm right here, and won't let anything happen to you," he muttered. "You're safe. If anything happens I'll wake up. Now please, for the love of all things in heaven and hell, *go to sleep.*" His eyes closed as he settled into his pillow.

I didn't want to disturb him again, I really tried to stay quiet. "Warren?"

He sighed, "Adelaide?"

"If I have a nightmare… Will you wake me up?"

"Yes."

"Promise?"

He opened his eyes and stared into mine. "I promise."

I concentrated on his soft inhales and exhales from the other side of the bed as they slowly lulled me to sleep.

I was in the lobby at work, typing something on the computer when I heard the bell of the front door go off as someone entered. "Good evening," I greeted, expecting them to turn the corner. But no one came. I waited, but still nothing. Curiously, I pulled away from the desk and hopped off the chair. Turning the corner to the front door, I expected to see someone outside, but again, no one there. "Huh." I said out loud and turned back toward the desk when I saw a man standing in the middle of the lobby with his back to me.

"Oh sorry, Sir, I didn't see you come in." I took a step towards him, and suddenly my feet sank into the floor. I looked down as I frantically tugged at my legs trying to free them. A shadow passed over me, and I looked up. A hideous face with bulging eyes stared down at me. He opened his mouth in a grotesque smile that spanned the width of his entire head. Drool dripped from between his crooked teeth…

"Adelaide." Someone spoke my name from outside of my consciousness. I felt my body move back and forth, and again heard my name. "Adelaide, wake up."

I closed my eyes, and when I opened them, Warren was leaning over me in the dark, rocking me gently.

"It's just a nightmare."

I was breathing heavily, but the rising panic I expected never came.

He waited a moment, and once my breathing calmed, he asked, "you alright?"

I nodded, forgetting he couldn't see me. "Yeah." My voice was small.

He sighed and rolled back into the mattress.

"I'm sorry…"

"Don't be."

"If I could stop them I would…"

"I know. Just try and go back to sleep."

I woke to the feeling of warm breath on my neck. I became conscious of an arm around my waist, and soft, cool skin pressed against my back. I lay as still as I could, unsure if he was awake or not, but when he didn't stir I let myself relax against him, feeling slightly guilty at how good he felt. He pulled me tighter and murmured something in his sleep. I held my breath, hoping to hear what he was saying.

He spoke again, barely over a whisper, "no, don't be afraid…"

This man had one of the most terrifying abilities I had ever heard of, and in his most vulnerable state he begged for someone not to fear him. How ironic… And heart wrenching.

His breath became increasingly shallow and his muscles tensed against my back as he began to wake. I quickly shut my eyes, pretending to still be asleep, wanting to allow the man the dignity to be the one to remove himself from our accidental spooning.

He moved his arm slightly, and I fully expected him to pull away immediately when he realized its position, but instead he let it linger. His fingers traced over my skin as he buried his face in my hair. His chest swole against my back as he inhaled and held me for a moment, before gently sliding away from me.

I adjusted slightly to watch him as he drew the curtains open and looked out. He stretched upward, flexing his back and arms, unaware he was giving me a show. The diluted morning sun trickled through the sheer curtains, saturating the curves of his muscles in warm light. There was no way to fake sleep as I gawked shamelessly at him, and he must have felt my eyes because he turned to me.

"Morning," he smiled, with his hair messily tousled, grey sweats riding low on his hips, looking too fucking sexy for his own damn good.

God I'm fucked.

"Morning," I blushed, "did I finally let you sleep?"

"You did, as a matter of fact. Thank you," he chuckled.

"I should be thanking *you*." I sat up and stretched. "How did you know how to calm me down? I didn't even know."

"I was honestly willing to try *anything* to get you to sleep. I figured, at least if you knew I was right there…" He shrugged, "It was the easiest solution I could think of."

"And the hardest?"

"Guess we'll never find out." He gave me a suggestive grin and threw on a hoodie. *Poo.* "I was going to head down to grab some of that free breakfast. Did you want anything?"

*You.* I decided to censor myself. "Coffee? And I dunno... A muffin or something would be nice."

He sat on the chair and pulled on his boots. "Lock everything behind me. Don't open the door for anyone except me."

"Yes, Daddy…" I sighed sarcastically.

Something flashed behind his eyes as he looked up at me from under his lashes.

Oh my god, did I just discover a kink? I really couldn't help myself. "Do I get a reward if I behave?" I cooed.

"Mmm," he stood slowly, ignoring my comment.

I followed him to the door, feeling rather pleased with myself.

He looked both ways down the hall before stepping out, then turned his head over his shoulder to me. "Be a good girl," he growled with a smile, and closed the door, melting away any sense of dignity I had left.

# Eight

My anxiety surged as we sat in the way-to-fucking-quiet
waiting room. I leaned forward in my chair, rested my
elbows on my knees and my chin on my folded hands, not
paying attention to my bouncing leg until Warren reached
over and placed his hand calmly on my knee. He leaned
over and whispered in my ear, "it's going to be fine."

"I'm not sure I can handle this," I whispered back.

"Yes, you can. You're much stronger than you think
you are."

"Ms. Quinn?" The receptionist called out from the
doorway. "Dr. Austin is ready for you," she smiled warmly.

Warren followed me through the door and she
closed it behind us. I scanned the room. There were a lot of
leathers and woods mixed into its design, making it feel less
like a therapist's office and more like a rustic wood cabin,
which I supposed was the point. A loveseat, armchair, and
chaise sat in triangular formation in the middle of the room,
and the walls were lined with bookshelves full of leather
bound manuscripts. Against the window on the far right wall
stood a desk where I was surprised to see an almost normal
looking man in his 30's with blonde hair, in a casual button
up shirt and jeans. Except for the fact that he had no eyes.
Not just that he was blind, his eyes were missing entirely, as
if his face was designed without a place for them.

115

He moved his face in our direction when we entered, and smiled. "Warren, it's great to see you man," he stood and they hugged.

"Thanks for fitting us in." Warren took a step back to stand beside me, "this is Adelaide."

"Hi, Dr. Austin," I reached my hand out to shake his.

"Just Austin, please. We're calling this a therapy session for *this one's* anger management on the books, but we don't need to be so formal about it," Austin chuckled as he motioned to Warren.

"Really? Is that how we're billing this?" Warren sighed.

"It's the most believable thing I could think of," Austin laughed. "Please, sit wherever looks most comfortable." He gestured to the three options in the middle of the room.

I sat on the loveseat and Warren sat next to me. Austin took the armchair.

"Okay so, we're doing a regressive hypnosis session?" Austin looked between Warren and me. "Are we focusing on anything in particular from that night?"

My attention switched between Warren and Austin, feeling less like a person and more like a lab rat.

"I need her to remember as much detail from that night as possible," Warren explained. "Ideally about the killer, but anything could give me a lead at this point."

"What you saw was brutal," Austin spoke to me directly, "your brain is doing its job by blocking out some pretty traumatic stuff. We don't usually jump to this point in therapy until you've dealt with the basics."

"Like what?" I asked.

"Have you been experiencing sleeplessness, heightened anxiety, panic attacks, or flashbacks at all?" Austin asked.

"Uh, yeah… Like, all of that."

"Okay. If we do this, I *highly* recommend you practice actual therapy with me or literally anyone else. I'm not going to sugarcoat it, you'll probably need it."

Great. I was feeling less sure of this all of a sudden. I looked at Warren.

"You can do this," he encouraged and put his hand on my knee. "I'll be right here."

"Alright, how does it work?" I agreed before I changed my mind.

"You don't have to do anything but sit there. I'll use my abilities to look into your memories, and I'll be with you every step of the way." Austin assured me. "You'll be able to talk to, and hear me the whole time. You're going to feel a bit of a tingle, maybe a little pinch here and there, but nothing too physically painful. I just ask that you don't try to fight me. You're going to see things that you may not want to, but that's the point of this type of therapy. If it gets too much, just let me know, and I'll pull us out."

I nodded.

"Whenever you're ready, just close your eyes and take a deep breath."

I did just that. Warren turned to watch me closely.

It was the weirdest feeling… Like a little bug moved around inside my brain. Though I was surprised that it didn't feel entirely wrong, like an itch, but not in a way that made me feel like I needed to scratch. Then suddenly I was sitting behind the desk in the lobby of the hotel, hot and uncomfortable.

*"Adelaide, can you hear me?"* Austin's voice echoed all around.

*"Uh… Yeah?"* I looked around, but I was alone in the room.

*"I can see what you see, but as if I'm watching a movie through your eyes. You are in control of what we're looking at,"* he explained. *"Do you actively remember this?"*

> *"Yes."* I looked at the clock on the wall that flashed between "1:30 a.m. - 87°"
>
> *"This was a bit before she called down."* I fanned myself with my hand, actually feeling myself sweat.

*"You can interact with your memory. Touch things, feel things. I want us to try to pay attention to anything out of the ordinary."*

> I nodded.

*"Good. Is there anyone in the lobby with you?"*

> *"No."* I looked around to confirm. *"No one came in after she did."*

*"Look around. Even at things you think aren't important."*

> I obeyed. The desk was fairly empty, the computer screen was on screensaver mode, the curtains were flapping as the fan rotated toward them, headlights shown through the window as they passed...

*"What was that?"*

> My memory jumped back a few seconds, the scene rewinding in front of me made me feel slightly dizzy. *"Fuck..."*

*"Focus on the window."*

> I watched as the curtains slowly began billowing with the wind from the fan, and for a split second I saw the headlights of a large truck of some sort pass by the hotel, slow down, then shut off.
>
> *"Huh. That's weird. There aren't usually any cars at this hour. I don't remember even noticing it that night."*

*"If it's unusual, note it."*

*"Okay."* I continued to focus on the window, but aside from the curtains moving, I didn't notice much else. The incredibly boring night wore on, feeling like I was living it in real time. I answered the complaining phone calls, got yelled at, tried to pass the time playing games on my phone... Then I got the call from room 232.

"Front desk." I answered with a forced smile.

"Hey, the A/C just stopped working completely. Like, it was barely working before but at least it was keeping it under 90 in here," A female voice responded.

"I'm so sorry about that, I'm not sure if I'll be able to get a hold of our maintenance guy at this hour but let me see what I can do. What room are you in?"

"232."

"Okay, worst case, I can move you into another room."

"Thanks."

*"Was that the victim?"*

*"Yeah."*

*"She didn't sound distraught or panicked at all. Let's move forward."*

Again, the scene around me zoomed past at lightning speed, but this time I closed my eyes in anticipation for it.

When I opened them I had just gotten out of the elevator. I froze, and so did the scene.

*"This is where the disconnect is,"* Austin confirmed. *"You might feel a slight pinch..."*

*"Ow."* I rubbed the side of my head. It felt like something bit the middle of my brain.

*"Sorry, see if you can move now."*

I moved forward hesitantly, more from fear than inability.

*"Good. Okay, take it slow. A lot of this is going to feel unfamiliar."*

I walked extra slowly, taking my time to look around as I approached door 232. Thumping and muffled crying sounded from inside.

I knocked. "Uh, hello? It's Adelaide from the lobby. I got you a new room."

A suspicious silence replied..

"Is... your air conditioning still out?"

A muffled scream set my hair standing on end.

Something wasn't right.

"Are you okay? I'm coming in."

An immense sense of trepidation came over me, along with an instinct to run. *"I don't want to..."*

*"I know, it's not going to be easy. Your subconscious is going to fight us, but I'm right here with you."*

The door swung open, and there he was, crouching in the window. I immediately clamped my eyes shut.

*"Adelaide, it's just a memory. Open your eyes."*

I took a deep breath, and looked.

His grin widened as he watched me examine him.

My body trembled as he eyed me up and down, there was almost a hunger in his empty gaze.

A glob of drool fell from his lips onto his leg as he balanced carefully on the windowsill. His thin fingers that gripped the wall were covered in blood.

I felt like I was pulled off the top of a ladder. My body didn't move but I was falling… Falling… Then a sinking weight pounded in my head as the sensation stopped.
*"Austin?"* I called out, my voice trembling.

The Carver twitched his exceptionally long finger as he spoke in a sharp, whiny voice. "She breaks the rules… She is different…"

*"Dr. Austin? Make it stop… Please… I want to leave,"* I begged, but there was no response, no voice in my head. I was alone with my memories.

*"No…"* The tears poured down my face as The Carver jumped out the window. A key ring jangled loudly from his belt loop.

I turned to see the naked body of the woman, sprawled across the bed. Where her breasts once were, two bloody gaping holes. I could see tissue, tendons, organs, and bone all the way through her.

*"Warren!"* I screamed, begging for him on instinct alone.

On her face and the tape covering it were splatters of blood from the opening in her neck still spewing fresh fountains of it.

*"Warren… I need you…"* I whimpered as I curled up on the floor. My whole body shook uncontrollably. I couldn't breathe… My lungs felt like someone had clamped them shut. My heart was going to explode. I thought I was dying… At least if I died it would stop… Someone please make it stop…

*"Adelaide…"* Warren's voice whispered around me.

The crushing terror was burying me alive. My hands covered my head as darkness enveloped me.

*"Adelaide! Fight it!"* Warren called out again, this time much clearer.

I opened my eyes and tried to move. *"Where are you?"* I stopped focusing on the fear and honed in on his voice.

*"I'm here. Come back to me."*

The scene began fading as I was pulled by the back of my neck. I floated upward as it drifted further and further away…

I blinked, and found myself kneeling on the floor in Warren's arms. He held my face up to him, searching it frantically as if I wasn't there a moment ago.

"Adelaide?" He gasped as he recognized the light coming back into my eyes.

At his touch I was undone and I crumbled into him. His arms wrapped tightly around my body as his chin came to rest on the top of my head.

"You did it." Austin spoke from somewhere to my right. "You brought her back."

Whatever walls my mind had installed to keep me functional through any of this had been thoroughly demolished. The tears that I kept carefully contained for so long streamed down my face as my entire body convulsed with the effort of release. I clutched his hoodie in my fists as I soaked his chest with my sobs.

"I know… I know…" He whispered, "I've got you." His attention turned to Austin and his gaze hardened. "Did you really need to go that deep?"

Austin twisted his hands in his lap and shook his head. "She had pushed it pretty far down… I hope it was worth it, man. Take whatever time you need." Then stood and left the room.

I didn't hear a word Austin said, and I couldn't see where I was. The only thing my senses would take in was Warren's scent. I inhaled him deeply and let the soft cotton envelop my swollen face. His firm yet gentle grasp pressed against the back of my head.

"Brave girl," he muttered.

Every noise made me jump. Every man I saw had The Carver's distorted face. Every woman had his victims bloody stains. I was an absolute basket-case, and I just *knew* everyone was staring as we left the office. But the moment I was able to stand I wanted to get the hell out of there. I hugged my body and stared at the ground as we walked out, so afraid I would start bawling again if I opened my mouth, that we were back in the comforting isolation of Warren's truck before I uttered a word.

He sat in the driver's seat with his hands on the steering wheel, staring down at it as we sat in the parking lot. "I'm sorry."

"What?" My voice cracked from the unuse.

"I regret asking you to do that."

I didn't even have the capacity for regret at that moment. My eyesight blurred as it unfocused on my lap. "He… Said something to me." I whispered.

"Austin?"

"The Carver," I clarified. "I didn't remember it before. He looked at me, and said… 'She breaks the rules, she is different'." His voice rang in my head and the tears welled up again.

"You sure he said that to you? He wasn't talking to the victim?"

I nodded slowly, "she was already—"

His face tensed, "we don't have to talk about it now. Let's get out of here." The engine roared to life and he swung his arm over my backrest as he pulled out of the parking space.

We sat in silence as we passed storefronts, office buildings, and people waiting at bus stops going about their monotonous day. As we turned a corner I caught a glimpse down a side street where the less admirable businesses were lined up. Strip clubs, smoke shops, a bail bonds place… The Carver could literally be waiting in any of those places right now for his next victim.

The blinker clicked steadily in the silence, and Warren turned when the traffic light gave him permission. I didn't even notice where we were going, nor did I care. Nothing felt real anymore. I didn't feel curiosity, pain, or even fear. I was completely empty inside. Devoid of a sense of self-preservation or any will to defend myself. Wherever he took me, I was at his mercy. I was unaware of his hand on my lap, rubbing his thumb across my bare leg as I stared out the window. Though I jolted slightly when we stopped. He got out of the truck, came around to my side, and opened it.

"Come on." He held his hand out, and I let him help me down.

He held it his as he led me through the parking lot and up a cement path. When I felt the ground soften, I stopped and looked down.

Grass.

My gaze moved upward, to find we were in a huge park. Bright, green grass, trees, a pond with a fountain, somewhere in the distance kids played on a playground. I looked up at him. "Where are we?"

"Just a local park. I thought you could use some open sky. "

He took me to a partially shaded area atop a small hill looking down at the pond. Ducks and geese swam back and forth, while a family on the far end threw grain in the grass for them. I only realized he was still holding my hand when he dropped it to unfurl a blanket.

"Is this okay?" He looked around, "I can find another spot, I just figured you'd feel safer being able to see everything."

The warmth of the sun spread across my skin and I did feel a bit better. "Yeah," I attempted a smile, and sat.

A gust blew up the hill and I closed my eyes as it hit my face, opening myself back up to sensations. The tickle of the grass as I ran my hands over it, the sounds of the ducks quacking angrily as they fought over the free meal. I opened my eyes and looked up. The sky was as bright a blue as I had ever seen. I took off my shoes and socks and slid my feet onto the grass, pressing firmly against the solid ground. I felt myself reconnect with my body, and I took a deep breath.

Warren sat down next to me slowly, watching me as if I was about to spontaneously combust. "Are… You okay?"

I nodded, "I think so."

He shifted uncomfortably. "I really am sorry," he repeated.

"It's not your fault," I looked down. "I don't even know what happened. I just feel… Like shit."

"Austin said you sunk too deep, that you had buried those memories so far down, he lost you. But he also said you went into the darkness willingly."

I looked up, "I did?"

He nodded, "that you were terrified, but he felt like you were determined to see it, but he couldn't tell why."

I furrowed my brow and looked back down. "I don't remember anything but the memory."

"You don't remember getting lost?"

I shook my head, "I remember the fear…"

"You don't remember calling for me?"

"No," I remembered a feeling of crushing darkness, but then him calling me out of it, "but… I remember your voice… Pulling me out of the depths. If it weren't for you, I'd still be trapped in there," I looked up at him.

"You wouldn't have even been in it if it wasn't for me." He picked at a blade of grass.

"I agreed to it," I insisted, finding the smallest ounce of defiance. "I agree to a lot of things that end up fucking me up. Seems to be my special ability—"

"It doesn't help when someone pushes you to do it." He threw the shredded grass aside.

I shifted my feet, stirring up the scent of cut grass. "You didn't push. I did this for those women, for Jenna. It was the right thing to do."

The sun beat down on his side of the blanket and he slid off his jacket and hoodie. Once again I noted the small raised scars on the insides of his arms, seeing them clearly for the first time. They looked like puncture marks, but he had disguised them as textures among his tattoos.

"What are those from?" I asked, not having the energy for subtlety.

He looked up at me, "hmm?"

"Those scars." I tapped my own arms as an example.

He glanced down at his bare arms and quickly pulled his jacket back on. "An old fight," he responded dismissively.

Hint taken. "Sorry. I didn't mean to pry."

"It's fine." His voice softened, "I just don't like to think about it."

"I know the feeling," I looked away.

He bore an expression of pure guilt. "My mother and I have— *Had*... A difficult relationship." He suddenly admitted, lowering his voice.

I looked back up at him silently.

He plucked another long blade of grass. "My mother's mutation was that she could stay young, forever. But she had to consume blood to do so... Blood from children."

My breath caught. "That's horrible."

He nodded and continued. "The longer she lived, the more she needed, and the world was changing. She couldn't have children of her own, and with the advances in police work and security it made it difficult for her to keep kidnapping kids to drain them. So she made a deal with a demon, my father... And had me." He took a deep breath as he shredded the grass in his fingers. "She consistently reminded me the reason I existed was to serve her purpose. That I had no other reason for living. These..." He motioned to his arms, "are teeth marks from where she fed."

The color drained from my face. "Warren... That's... I can't even believe how..." I couldn't find a word for the level of disgust and heartbreak I felt. "Where is she now? Please tell me that's why you got put into foster care..."

"Sort of. Around when I turned 12, my blood stopped working for her. She was so angry at me, like it was my fault that I grew up. She said if I couldn't serve my purpose for living then I didn't deserve to be alive," he hesitated. "She came into my room one night with a dagger… And my body changed for the first time. I can't even tell you into what, but whatever it was, whatever her greatest fear was, scared her so badly she had a fatal heart attack. She died right there in front of me. She was my first murder."

I gaped at him. Whatever our parents did, whatever prejudices they attempted to instill in us, they never once tried to hurt us. Our mother was a close minded, religious lunatic, but she was nothing compared to his.

I looked around to ensure no one was listening and whispered. "It wasn't murder. It was an accident, self-defense, you were just a child…"

"That's what the jury ruled too," he shrugged, "but it doesn't change the fact that I took a life at 12 years old."

"Hardly an innocent one… She was a monster."

He huffed, "guess the apple doesn't fall too far from the tree."

"Fuck that." I adjusted onto my side to face him and cupped his jaw in my hand, forcing him to look at me. "You're not even in the same orchard." I brushed my thumb over his skin.

He looked into my eyes, "She's not the only one Adelaide. I've killed others, you've seen me do it."

"You were protecting me." Our faces drew closer.

His warm exhale brushed against my lips as his eyes fell to them. He released a pained sigh and stood to storm down the hill, his hand ran aggressively through his hair. "I hurt people without consideration, whether I intend to or not. I bring out the worst in people, their anger, their hatred, even when I try to do good, it's done in a horrible way." He came back up towards me, pacing back and forth like an agitated, caged panther. "I was literally created from evil. It's in my blood. This ability is a god-damn curse that I deserve."

I stood. "What are you talking about? It's not a curse. I wouldn't be here right now if it wasn't for you and your ability…"

"I'll take you home," he muttered, not listening. "I'll call a contact of mine to keep watch over you. But I'll leave you alone."

"What about The Carver? Figuring out his mutation?"

"You don't need to be involved with this, with me. You need to stay as far away as possible." He stopped pacing and put his hands on his hips.

"But… I want to be involved with you…" I whispered, surprised at my own admission.

"Don't you get it?! Dammit, Adelaide. I'm a fucking piece of shit. *I was using you.*" He threw his hands up and put them on his head as he paced again. "FUCK! Do you know *why* I was watching you in the first place? Because I was hoping, goddammit, I was *hoping* The Carver would come back for you. I was using you as fucking bait!"

My eyes pooled. "What?"

"Even after you invited me to say with you, this whole fucking idea of remembering him, I manipulated you into agreeing to it. Fucking hell!" He kicked at a rock and sent it sailing downhill.

"My ability allows me to feel *all* forms of fear. Anxiety, nervousness, *anything* that makes your heart rate increase. I *knew* you found me attractive. I flirted, sweet-talked, even took you back to my place to get you to do this.

I coerced you to unlock the most traumatic experience any human could go through, and almost lost you to it… All for revenge! I didn't give a shit about the other women or saving anyone else. I wasn't even all that concerned with protecting you. I only cared about gutting that bastard for what he did to Jenna."

Silent tears streamed down my face as I listened to him confirm how big of an idiot I had been.

"And you know what makes all of this *that* much worse?!" He scoffed a laugh and threw his hands up again as he faced me. "That I'm fucking *into you*. FUCK! Adelaide. I'm so *fucking* into you it's not even funny. Everything about you drives me wild. The smell of your hair, your gorgeous fucking eyes… And that attitude…" His jaw clenched and he sucked through his teeth. "Fuck if you don't make me want to do something about it," he shook his head. "From the moment you lost it on that homeless dude outside of the store, I knew you were going to be trouble for me. You strong, selfless, courageous little brat… You're so protective of everyone except yourself."

He dropped his shoulders and grabbed at his hair, pulling it back. "Adelaide… What I felt in Austin's office… What *you* felt… It was horrible. I didn't think it would affect me as much as it did. I feel other people's fears all the time, I force them to confront them *all the time* and it *never* bothers me. But with you, I hated it. It… *Hurt*. I… *Fuck*!" He turned away from me.

"You… What?" I sniffed.

"I actually give a shit about you. I don't *want* to hurt you. It wasn't supposed to go down this way. I don't *get* attached to my assignments. But dammit you got under my skin, and I can't even begin to express how much I regret ever intruding into your life. I'm a bad guy, a fucking asshole, and I'm sorry."

I stared at him, shaking and broken as a tornado of shame and rage spiraled inside me. But not at him, at myself. I was fucking pissed at myself for letting it happen again. This wasn't his fault, it was mine. I pushed blindly through a sea of red flags chasing the warm glow of romance at the end. Of course he was fucking using me, I would have used me too if I were in his shoes. What a perfect opportunity I was to catch this murderer, a perfect opportunity for revenge. I was the only one who knew what he looked like, and I allowed a stranger to dredge up the most horrific experience of my life, for what? For it to go to waste?

Fuck that.

I wiped my tears and moved down the hill until I was at eye level with Warren, and crossed my arms.

"How or what we feel for each other doesn't matter, there is still a serial killer on the loose and  now we have the means to do something about it. If we don't, and he kills again… Which you know he will, it would be our fault. I'm still willing to catch this guy, and you still need my help. However, you're going to be working for *me* now. I'm hiring you to catch this fucker, and you're going to do it free of charge. You owe me that much."

His amber eyes softened as he caught mine. "You're really wanting to keep working with me, even after today?"

"Shocking isn't it? But now *I'm* in charge. You got that?"

He tilted his chin upward and his dimple slowly formed. "Yes ma'am."

My girl clenched. Dammit. Was I really still attracted to this asshole after everything? What the fuck was wrong with me?

# Nine

The electricity that lingered between us was palpable as we drove in silence. I fidgeted in my seat, changing positions every five minutes to his great amusement. I pretended not to notice him smiling to himself as I crossed my left leg over my right while I stared out the window, trying very hard to focus on anything but his words.

He admitted he was into me, and he could tell I was too. It wasn't fair that despite my desperate attempts to hide it, this goddamn mutant could sense when he sent my pulse into overdrive. I found myself watching as he leaned his arm on the car door and played with his hair. Whoever decided to create this man so attractively could go right off and fuck themselves.

He chuckled as he stared straight ahead. "Alright. I'm calling a truce."

"What?"

"I'm evening the playing field. If you can't hide your desire from me, I won't hide mine from you."

"I don't know what you're talking about," I huffed.

He smirked and switched hands on the wheel, moving his right off his lap to reveal a swelling bulge between his legs.

I blushed and looked away. "I'm literally just sitting here," I muttered.

"Do you want to know what it feels like for me? Sensing fear?" He asked, seemingly out of the blue.

"Sure." I happily took the distraction.

"So, imagine you're on a roller coaster in the front car. You take off and you see the first hill coming up. The cars lurch as the chain grabs you to pull you up."

He slid his hand closer to my leg. Lightning shot between his fingertips and my skin. I attempted a sly glance down at it, he was literally centimeters from me…

"You begin the climb, the cranking sound echoes around you." His fingers found my knee, and I tensed as a tingle shot up my leg.

"The anticipation, the excitement builds as you inch closer… And closer…" He maintained a calm tone as he spoke, even as he began sliding his finger up my leg.

"You're almost there, you can see the top of the hill, you start to get that tickle in your stomach…"

His finger reached the hem of my shorts, and I released a quiet gasp as it began to trace down my inner thigh…

"You look over the edge, down the steep slope, and the cars catch for a second, right before they drop."

He moved his hand away, back to the seat, to my absolute dismay. I released a breath. My panties were soaked.

"That's what it feels like for me when I sense someone's heart rate speed up. When their breath catches and they decide if they're going to succumb to fight or flight. The second right before actual fear hits, the adrenaline surge… It can be totally intoxicating, and if I'm not careful, I could even get addicted to it. But when I sense that from someone… And it doesn't result in fear… Fuck, it's like the world's biggest tease."

"Why… Why are you telling me this?" I barely got the words out.

"You don't have to do anything to get me worked up, those thoughts of yours are enough," he almost growled.

"You're so full of yourself. Did it ever occur to you that what you're sensing from me is anger? Or actual fear?"

"I can tell the difference," he smirked.

That stupid, adorable dimple of his. My fists clenched. "Is this how you get all your girlfriends? By stalking and seducing them?"

"Are you admitting my seduction worked then?"

"Hell no," I turned red. Fuck his ability to turn everything I say upside down. "I meant that girl on the voicemail."

He quickly glanced at me, "what girl?"

"The one from your office?"

Now it was his turn to blush. "I told you, she's no one."

"Does she know that?"

"Yes."

I sat quietly, trying to force myself not to care at the lack of explanation, and failing.

He sighed dramatically. "Fine. We met at a bar. I only met up with her when I needed to blow off some steam. I haven't even spoken to her in weeks. The extent of my female companionship has been casual, meaningless sex. I'm not exactly great 'boyfriend' material."

I couldn't help a sense of relief at his current unattachment. "You haven't *ever* been in a committed relationship?"

His jaw tensed, and he took a deep breath. "There was one girl about ten years ago. Well, I was committed to *her* at least… Though I'm not sure you'd consider it a healthy relationship. Needless to say, it ended badly."

I empathized with him. Someone had fucked him over too, it's no wonder he chose to use me instead of actually gaining my trust. "What a pair we make…" I half mumbled.

He laughed, "we're a pair now?"

"Don't get all excited. That's not what I meant…"

"Mmm…" He smiled.

My phone went off in my pocket. *Saved by the bell.* It was Rory.

*"How did it go?"*

*"It's a lot to text."*

Her face came up on the caller ID. Goddamnit. If there's one trait we shared it was our nosiness. I mean, curiosity.

"Okay. Shoot," she sighed.

I told her about the therapy appointment but decided to leave out anything after.

"Jesus. Are you okay?

"Yeah. Better now. We got a lot of stuff out in the open."

"Like how you really need to get laid?"

Warren chuckled.

"No!"

"Girl. I can hear you blush," she laughed, "I was just kidding but, *did* you finally sleep with him?"

"Why are you so concerned about my sex life?!"

"First of all, I'm concerned about your heart, not your sex life. Second, we're both nosey bitches, you know that."

"No kidding," Warren muttered with a smile.

I shot him a look. "No one slept with anyone. No one's heart is at risk. Your concern is noted. Goodbye." I hung up, not entirely sure I didn't just lie to her.

There seemed to be an inordinate amount of cop cars buzzing around as we pulled off the freeway. They weren't at their usual speed trap locations, or posted around the seedy areas, almost as if they were looking for something, or someone. Neither Warren or I mentioned anything, but I could tell we were both thinking the same thing. As we turned onto my street my heart dropped.

Several police cars were parked up and down the street, and the entrance to my complex was taped off. There were barricades set up in a perimeter around the outside, and reporters, neighbors, and god knows who else were clamoring to get a peek as to what was going on.

"That's not a good sign," Warren commented as he pulled off and found a parking spot down the street.

We approached my building and were immediately stopped by the police. "Can't let you in, it's an active crime scene," a young officer put his hand up to stop me.

"I live here," I answered, expecting that to excuse us.

"Sorry lady, building's been evacuated," The officer didn't budge.

Warren stepped up and flashed his ID. "I'm investigating this case. Let us in."

The officer hesitated, looked between us both, but then stepped aside.

I let Warren lead the way, as we were consistently being stopped by other officers on the way up to my unit, and when we got off the elevator to my floor, I realized why.

My front door hung off its hinges at an angle inside my apartment. Warren got to the officer guarding the door first and pulled him aside to speak with him as I stepped past them into my home. It was in absolute shambles.

My kitchen cupboards were open, and pots and pans littered the floor and counters. Books were thrown across the living room floor, my TV lay face down, half on the coffee table, half on the floor, with its screen smashed to hell. The dining room chairs were flipped upside down, sideways, backwards, every which way but the way they were supposed to be.

I gasped and covered my mouth as I turned to the hallway. The photos mounted on the walls were askew or pulled off completely. The bathroom door was open and trash, toiletries, and liquids spilled out into the hall. My bedroom door however, stood conspicuously closed. My hand shook as I reached for the knob and turned it.

A wail escaped me when I met Mrs. Tibbet's lifeless eyes, as they stared up at me from the floor. Her body contorted into a shape I couldn't imagine she would have been able to achieve on her own. Warren rushed in behind me and pulled me around into him, hiding my face in his chest.

"Mrs. Tibbet..." I cried into him. "Why?"

He hugged me as he pulled me out of the room, closing the door behind us. But he didn't have an answer for me.

We were halfway down the hall when I panicked. "Dinah!" I broke away from him and ran into the living room calling for her.

"Adelaide," he calmly walked up to me and grabbed my hand. "They already have her. Animal control picked her up twenty minutes ago."

"Animal control?..." I looked up at him, not really understanding what he was saying.

"Let's go get her," he was so calm.

Nothing made sense, why was my cat with Animal Control? Why was Mrs. T dead in my bedroom? Why was my apartment torn apart? I stood and stared up at him, not moving. Not wanting to leave without answers. "Mrs. T…" was all my mouth could spit out.

"Dinah's waiting for you, come on." He used her as an excuse to get me to follow him out, and it worked.

He had me wait in the truck while he went into the shelter to pick her up. One of the volunteers was kind enough to come out to have me fill out all the necessary paperwork, and fairly painlessly Dinah was returned to me, terrified, but otherwise safe. Warren took us back to his place, where he had me sit on the couch while he moved some things around he didn't want Dinah to get into. I watched in silence, the entire evening blurring together as the sun set and the street lights came on outside his window.

"To take the edge off." He sat next to me and handed me a warm mug.

"My apartment…" I stared ahead into nothing.

"You're going to stay here tonight." He stated as he rubbed my back.

"What happened?" I finally got the words out.

"Someone broke in. The cops think they were looking for something when Mrs. Tibbet accidentally intruded on them as she came to check on Dinah."

"She…. Died… Because she was looking after Dinah?"

"No. She died because an evil fuck decided he wanted to break into your apartment and then hurt a harmless old lady." He knelt down in front of me.

I moved my eyes to look into his. "If it wasn't for me asking her to, she'd be alive right now."

"You can't think like that—"

"Do they know who it was?" I interrupted. I didn't want to hear the lie he tried to feed me.

"Not for sure…" I could see in his eyes he didn't want to say what he was really thinking.

"But *you* do."

"The cause of death *was* similar to how The Carver kills his victims, but her body was intact which doesn't fit his M.O."

"He was looking for me, and found her." My eyes swam and I looked at the floor.

He raised himself to be level with my face and moved my chin up with his hand. "This was *not* your fault. Do you hear me?"

I couldn't look at him, or respond.

"Dammit, Adelaide, look at me." His voice deepened, and I obeyed. "This is all on *him*. Not you."

I moved my face out of his hand and looked towards the corner of the room, where Dinah began to creep out of her carrier. "I don't have any of her stuff," I changed the subject. "She needs her litter box, cat tree, food…"

"I'm going back to grab whatever you need, as soon as they clear everything for evidence." He stood. "It should only be a couple of hours."

My mind scanned facts and ideas faster than I could keep up. "How long was she there?"

"They guessed the break in happened some time this morning. Why?"

"Mrs. Tibbet's cats… They need to be taken care of."

"Adelaide, I can't bring them here. I can't have five cats running around—"

"I meant we have to go take care of them for her now, at her place."

"Oh. Yeah, of course we can do that."

Mrs. T was gone, and it was my fault. I had taken it upon myself to watch out for her, bring her mail, take her garbage out. I was worried about her hip, about her taking her medications, not about getting her killed. What kind of psychopath murders an old lady? He could have just as easily tied her up and she would have been out of his way. She was too blind to have gotten a clear look at him, hell, if he was smart he would have just laid in wait for me to come back. What was this guy's end game here? Why go through the trouble of trashing my place, leaving her body…

"What's going to happen to her?" I looked up at Warren.

"The police will take her body. I already identified her at the crime scene. If she has any family, they'll contact them."

I shook my head. "I was the closest thing she had. What about a funeral?"

"Don't worry about that right now. Drink," he softly ran his hand over my hair.

I looked down at the mug I still clasped in both hands. "What is this?" I sniffed the sweet brown liquid.

"A hot toddy."

I let out a dry chuckle, "nothing cures trauma like getting drunk."

"I only put enough in there to calm you down," he gave me a little smile.

I sighed, "I might need a double after tonight…"

"Finish that one first, you drunk," he chuckled. "If you want another, I'll make you another."

I smiled up at him, thankful that he was still willing to poke fun at me, and took a sip. There was definitely more than a touch of whiskey in this… But the satisfying burn reignited my body parts that decided to seize up on it's way down. Dinah bravely decided to explore the office and began getting into his wastebasket. Warren quickly intervened in her snooping and scooped her up. She fussed in his arms as he brought her to me, placing her down on the sofa.

"Just like her mother," he sighed and rolled his eyes.

I scratched her chin. "We can find a hotel room for the night, I don't want to put you out."

He shook his head aggressively and sat on the other side of her. "You're staying right here." His eyes caught mine and he warned, "don't even argue."

I smiled, "thanks." The alcohol was kicking in, because I almost got a rise from his scolding.

He was deep in thought however, petting Dinah mindlessly.

"What are you thinking?"

He sighed grumpily. "I don't like that I can't figure out how the hell he found you, or how he got in. I assume he only finally took his shot because he knew I had gone, but no one knew your name or address. I had to fight really hard to get the Captain to give me that info. Unless he threatened your old boss?"

I chuckled, "I don't think he knew where I lived. I would be surprised if he even remembered my last name."

"Didn't he keep employee records?"

"I was in charge of all that. I promise you, he has no idea where any of that stuff is. All he cared about was seeing that the money was deposited in the evenings," I scoffed. "That hotel is going to fall apart without me there."

Warren was silent for a while, then, "it must be something to do with his abilities. What the hell could he be able to do that lets him track people, and kill without leaving fingerprints?"

"We have the tools to figure that out now." I put down my mug and stood, looking down at him. "All I have to do is think of him, and you can turn into him, right?"

"I'm not sure that's a good idea."

"What? Wasn't that literally the whole point of our trip?"

"It was. But after seeing what it did to you…" He looked into my eyes, "Adelaide, I almost lost you."

"But you brought me back. I've already relived it, it can't be worse the third time around."

He shook his head, "I can't."

"You can."

"You don't get it," he stood and began his signature pacing. "It's not just going to be reliving the memory. I have to turn into him, with you *in* the room. I can't stand to feel how terrified you were. I can't put you through that again…"

"What was it all for then?!" I raised my voice as my fists clenched at my sides. "I put myself through all that, almost got trapped inside my own mind, Mrs. Tibbet *died*, for *what?!*" My hands went to my hips. "This is what you asked for. This was what you wanted to use me for, *right?*"

He took two strides and was in front of me, grabbed my shoulders in his hands, and shook me slightly. "I can't stand the thought of being the cause of your trauma," his eyes begged. "I can't… I don't want you to be afraid… Of…. *Me.*"

It suddenly dawned on me, *he was afraid*. Afraid of me turning against him, like his mother, like the other children. Afraid that I, like so many others, would think of him as the monster he has been taught he was. I reached my hand up to his face, warming the chill in his cheek. "I'm not afraid of you," I spoke firmly. "You're not a monster, Warren."

He leaned into my touch and closed his eyes. "I am. Even when I'm in this form, I'm a monster. Look at what I did to you. I'm selfish, vengeful, bitter… I hurt you once already. I won't do it again."

"Maybe you did. But you did it because of the love you have for your sister, and honestly… I can't say I wouldn't have done the same for Rory, so… I don't blame you. What's more, you feel guilty about it. Monsters don't feel guilt, or love." He shuddered against my hand. "Warren, I feel many conflicting things for you, but fear isn't one of them."

He opened his eyes. "I don't *ever* want to make you feel the way he does…"

"Just because his form makes me feel a certain way, doesn't mean I feel that way about you. We need to do this."

With the most extreme resistance in his eyes, he looked down, then back up at me. After a long exhale, he stated, "you're not going to watch."

"What do you mean?"

"I want your back turned and your eyes closed. All you have to do is imagine him and I'll become him. But you don't need to watch it happen. I don't want you to see him."

I nodded and lowered my hand, preparing to step away, but he grabbed it and squeezed. I turned back and he brought it to his lips, and kissed it softly. "I'm sorry," he whispered, then turned me around.

I closed my eyes. "I'm ready."
"Whatever you hear, Adelaide, *don't turn around.*"

# Ten

I let myself sink into my memories, for once not giving in to the urge to banish them from my mind. My heart began to race at the sinister smile that materialized in my mind's eye. The hungry, empty eyes, the bloody fingers…

The sickening cracking of bones, tearing of tissue, and Warren's groans of discomfort came from behind me. What began as his familiar sounds changed to whining, sickly, animalistic noises, until they finally subsided into raspy panting. Dinah hissed and growled a warning from somewhere in front of me, and I recognized the scamper of her feet as she ran out of the room and faded into the distance.

I was afraid to speak, afraid to ask anything. He shuffled around behind me, his breath wheezing in his throat.

*"Holy shit.* I can *smell* you…" A horrible shrill voice caused me to tense. I listened closely as he moved around the room, sniffing loudly. "You smell… So… *Good…*"

A shiver ran up my spine and my heart rate sped. I squeezed my eyes shut, pointlessly hoping that the harder I held them, the less I'd feel.

"So *that's* how you do it you fucker…" A disgusting slurping sound accompanied the realization.

I began to tremble. "It's just Warren. It's just Warren," I repeated to myself in a whisper.

More shuffling, wheezing… Then a pause, followed by a sound I could only relate to a wounded animal that caused my body to jolt. Groaning, snapping, popping, then a familiar exhausted gasp for air. Footsteps approached, stopping directly behind me. I held my breath. A hand pressed gently on my shoulder, and I flinched.

"It's me."

Warren's comforting, deep, soft voice gave me such relief that I released a whimper and opened my eyes, blinking as they readjusted to the dim lighting in the office.

"Are you okay?" He asked disquietedly.

I inhaled, and held it, half-sure that I would turn and see the face of that monster staring back at me. "Mhm."

"It's okay, you don't have to look at me." He responded dejectedly and moved his hand away.

Guilt poured into my anxiety cocktail, giving it the kick I needed to finally turn. I spun around before I changed my mind, to see… Warren. Just Warren, looking incredibly timid for a change. I exhaled.

His eyes met mine and then quickly moved away in shame.

I put my hand over his heart. It pounded almost as aggressively as mine. He slowly and gently moved his hand over mine and pressed down. "I'm sorry," he repeated his earlier apology.

"You have nothing to be sorry for. I asked you to do it."

His relief was present in the smile that brushed his lips, and he pushed a stray curl from my face, but he still wouldn't look me in the eyes.

He was so vulnerable, so fragile at that moment, I couldn't help myself. Before I knew what I was doing, my hands slid down his jacket, grasping the folds, and I pulled him into me.

His hand reflexively fell around my waist as our bodies touched, and his eyes finally fell onto mine. His other hand moved up the back of my neck, winding its fingers through my hair. He leaned down, pulling my head towards him until we were inches apart, but again he hesitated.

"I can feel how afraid you are," he whispered. His breath warm against my lips.

"Some fears are worth facing," I whispered back.

With an exonerated smile, he pressed himself onto me.

His lips were cool and soft, and they sent a shockwave of shivers down my spine. He was gentle, as if he were afraid he would break me, but I would have none of it.

My tongue parted his lips in search for his, and at their touch he released a quiet moan. His cold fingers tugged at my hair as he gripped the base of my head, balancing the heat that rose in me at the sound.

He reciprocated my invitation of fervor with enthusiasm, pulling me closer as he emphasized his kisses by gently biting my lower lip. I gasped, and he smiled against me before slowly pulling his lips away.

"That was… unexpected," he hummed down at me.

"See, you can't tell everything just from sensing me," I smirked.

"Mmm. I gladly admit I was wrong."

His fingers still tangled in my hair as we stared into each other. I could still taste the electric charge as the invisible strand connecting us threatened to pull us back together. I smiled and licked my lips, severing it.

"So. What did you learn?"

"That you like when I bite…" He purred, leaning forward for more.

"No," I giggled, slapping his chest playfully, "about *him*."

"Oh," he chuckled, then looked down, his mood darkening. "He's sick. He's a sick bastard…" He shook his head.

"You didn't need to turn into him for us to know that."

He softly moved his thumb over my cheek before lowering his hand and stepping away. "I know how he found you." He inhaled deeply, "his sense of smell is ridiculously good, and there's something about your scent, at least to him, that's… I don't know how else to describe it but intoxicating."

"My scent? Like my body wash?"

"No. *You* give off a specific scent. I could smell everyone who had been in my office in the last few days. Me, you, Dinah, Mr. Johnson… But you stood out like a neon sign."

"That's unsettling."

"Yeah no kidding. There's more to his mutation too. I know what the murder weapon is, and how he's probably breaking in."

My eyes widened, "yeah?"

"His fingernails. They grow out like claws. Sharp, straight… Like a cone file… And he can grow and shrink them at will. One nail could easily bore a hole through someone's neck."

I gasped, "you mean he's just… Stabbing them with his… *Nails*?!" The image of his bloody fingers grasping the windowsill flashed in my mind.

"I'd bet my next case on it, and I'm sure it's just as easy to slice through tissue with them to take his… trophies," he grimaced.

My stomach soured. He had just been killing women with his bare hands… And he was following my scent. What the fuck.

"He's an animal, Adelaide. It was like I lost all sense of what it felt to be human when I was him. Our primal desires, hunger, lust, anger, instant gratification… That's what drives him. All other emotions are muted. I had to focus *really* hard on the reason why I became him in the first place, the logic behind it. I can't imagine thinking like that 24/7, I'd lose my mind…"

I sank into the couch as my anxiety began seeping through the flimsy barriers I had in place. Any and all feelings of happiness faded away.  "He's going to follow wherever I go…"

"If there's one thing I know about serial killers, it's that they have a compulsive need to follow their kill patterns. You don't fit his. He might be distracted by you but I don't think you're going to be his primary focus."

I knew he meant them to be comforting words, but they missed their mark. "So if not me, then some other innocent woman?"

He sat next to me, grabbed my face in his hands and turned it towards him. "I'm not going to let anything happen to you," he stated firmly. "I know this is fucked up to say, but fuck those other women. He can have them. Not you."

"Warren," I scolded, fighting a dark chuckle, "that's not okay."

"Yeah well…" He shrugged and released my face. "We're still going to catch him. Stop him. And now I have something to bring to my contact."

His phone went off, and we both jumped.

"Nyte," he answered shortly, listened to what the caller said, responded with, "yeah. Thanks," then hung up. "That was the police, they cleared your stuff to be picked up." He stood. "Wanna text me a list of what you need?"

"Can I go with you?"

"No. You don't need to see your place in that state. Plus it'll be harder to find you in this building. More rooms and floors to sort through. Just lock the door—"

"I know, and don't answer it for anyone except you."

"That's a good girl," he smiled. "I'll be back soon."

I suppose "soon" was a relative timeframe. After an hour of sitting on the couch, scrolling through my phone I began to get bored, and bored meant overthinking. The guilt of Mrs. Tibbet's murder, the new knowledge that I had a serial-killer-stalker, all sprinkled with the audacity I had to incite a romance with the man using me to catch said killer was too much. I began to hear things. The wind blowing outside was someone trying to get in the window. Dinah finally knocking over the wastebasket was the door being kicked down. If I didn't find something to entertain myself I was going to have an actual heart attack.

Snooping. Snooping was always distracting. I wandered into the tiny, yet surprisingly tidy, kitchen and began pulling open drawers and cupboards. It was such a man's kitchen… There was probably a grand total of three actual food items in the refrigerator. Although I gave him credit for the plethora of frozen foods, at least I wouldn't starve. His cupboards were equally sparse, but he owned more cooking utensils than I did, some which I didn't have a clue what they were used for.

After I fully inspected the kitchen, I moved into the bathroom and flicked on the light. A clawed tub and shower combo stood off to the far right with a circular, clear shower liner pulled around it. I was tickled to see matching bath mats on the floor in front of it, and the toilet which sat next to it. *Aww, he tries to accessorize.* To my left was a sink with a mirrored medicine cabinet above it, and the miracle of miracles, a set of matching towels hung on the rack to its right. He had already gained more points than any other guy I dated. *Are my standards so low?* I laughed at myself.

The front door rattled and I almost fell backwards into the tub. As I panicked, I looked around for the first thing I could use to defend myself, and quietly moved towards the main room. I froze in the doorway to the kitchen as the silhouette of a person on the other side of the door jiggled the knob back and forth. My shaky hands raised my weapon and held it at the ready. The door opened, and Warren tumbled in, awkwardly carrying Dinah's large cat tree.

"Could you come grab this?" He gestured to a bag behind him. "I've got my hands full—" He paused when he saw me and chuckled. "What are you going to do with that?"

I looked up at my weapon, which unfortunately happened to be the toilet brush. "Oh…" I faltered, turning red. "I thought you were him…"

"And you were going to what? Scrub him to death? Hope to scour the evil from him?" He laughed. "I mean it's a pretty good brush, sturdy."

"Shut up." I dropped the brush on the floor, my face burning. I quickly moved to grab the bag he had left in the hall as he heaved the tree in the rest of the way.

"I can rest easy now, knowing you can defend yourself." He sniggered as he stood the tree up in a corner.

I didn't respond.

"Aww, come on, don't tell me you're out of witty comebacks?"

I was, at least temporarily. The dissipating swell of anxiety and adrenaline left me completely drained and on the verge of tears again.

"I'm sorry," He spoke softly as he approached and took my hands in his. "I'll call time out on the teasing."

"Who knew, all it took to get you to stop being a dick was to find my closest friend murdered." I slowly raised my gaze to meet his.

His lips curved. "You get *one* night of me being nice, can't go and ruin my reputation now, can I?"

I couldn't help a smile. I gave his hands a grateful squeeze and let go to ruffle through the bag he brought. "Thanks for doing this by the way."

"You're welcome. I hope I got everything you asked for."

I pulled out my pajamas and toothbrush. "Do you mind if I change in the bathroom?"

"If I said I did, would you change out here?" His eyes glinted.

"Warren…"

He chuckled and gestured with his head to the back of the studio.

I locked the door behind me, flicked on the light, and immediately cringed at the the sight of myself in the mirror. I looked like death. My hair was in knots, skin pale, dark circles overtook my eyes… He kissed me looking like this? Eeesh. All this murder and panic was taking its toll. Not that I was much to look at before, but now I resembled something that Warren might turn into. I brushed my teeth keeping my sights strictly downward. Sleep. I needed sleep.

He was at his desk when I reemerged, and the couch had magically transformed into a bed.

"I was wondering where you slept," I motioned to it as I shoved my clothes into the bag.

"Honestly, I usually just pass out in the middle of working on something," he patted the desktop. "Or I'll just crash on the couch as it is." He reclined in his chair and stretched his arms above his head. The slightest patch of skin appeared above his belt line. I couldn't control my eyes as they shifted towards it. "It's all yours tonight," he spoke through a yawn.

"What?" I blushed. My blood raced to my chest.

"The bed? I set it up for you." He clasped his hands behind his head and crossed his ankle over his knee.

"Oh. Yeah, thanks." *Get your mind out of the gutter.*

He smiled, "what did you think I meant?"

"Nothing…" I hid a smile as I turned away from him.

"That heartbeat of yours is going to drive me crazy." He shook his head, not hiding his.

This heartbeat of mine was going to get me in trouble.

"Get some sleep." He righted in his chair. "I'm going to be up for a bit still, will it bother you if I leave this on?" He clicked the small lamp on his desktop, then stood. "I'll turn the rest of them off."

I shook my head and moved towards the bed. "I'm exhausted enough that it shouldn't matter." Then I added quietly, "I hope that's also enough to keep the nightmares away."

"If it's not, I'm right here," he spoke softly as he moved around the room turning off the lights.

I pulled back the top sheet and slid inside. "Goodnight." I looked up to him as he turned off the last lamp by the front door.

He crossed to me and paused at the bedside, contemplation written on his face. He bent over and placed a gentle kiss on my forehead, letting his lips linger for a moment. "Sweet dreams," he whispered, then returned to his desk.

I lay on my side as I watched him work. His brows furrowed as he read something on his laptop screen, then flipped through a stack of papers to his left. He pursed his lips as his eyes shifted to the right, then rolled when he found what he was looking for in his desk drawer. He bit his lip as he typed something out, and then stuck the end of the pen between them as he read back what he had written. He ran his fingers through his hair as he swiped across his phone screen single-handedly, then put the pen back in his mouth, using his tongue to push it around while it hung between his lips. There was something incredibly reassuring about his presence, and watching him work was almost hypnotizing. My eyelids fluttered under the weight of sleep, each blink a bit heavier than the last, until they finally fell, and darkness swept over them.

My text notification woke me. I pried my eyes open with extreme effort, and daylight flooded my vision. For a moment I forgot where I was, until my hand hit the armrest of the sofa. Right, Warren's studio.

The sweet smell of sugar and dough wafted through the air, accompanied by the sound of a sizzling of a pan. My stomach threw a tantrum over its neglect. I stretched and sat up. The bedsheets beside me were pulled down, as if someone were present in them recently. A twinge of disappointment flicked in my face at the realization that I missed out on waking up next to Warren. I remembered my phone, and grabbed it from the armrest.

*"Did you make it home?"* Rory asked.

How was I going to explain any of yesterday to her? *"Can I call you?"*

*"Oh boy."*

I took that as a yes.

"What happened?" She answered.

I explained as concisely as I could. From the scene we arrived at, to Warren offering me his place to stay. Amidst our conversation he appeared in the entryway to my right and smiled down at me. A swarm of butterflies erupted in my stomach. He turned and went back into the kitchen.

"Hello? You still there?" Rory barked.

"Yeah. Sorry."

"Addy, I'm really worried about you. None of this is something you should be going through alone."

"I'm not alone."

"A handsome stranger doesn't count. You need help. I'm coming down."

"You really don't have to. I'm fine."

"And that's what worries me. You shouldn't be fine."

Warren reappeared with a tray piled with coffee, pancakes, sausage, and scrambled eggs. I almost dropped the phone as he set it down on a small table next to the armrest. I was *starving.*

"Rory, I've gotta go."

"What? No, don't you hang up on me—"

"I'm fine. I swear. I'll text you later." I hung up. "What's all this?"

"You'd think you'd recognize breakfast when you saw it."

"I mean where did it come from? You didn't have any of these ingredients yesterday."

He sat at my feet. "Were you snooping in my kitchen? Figures. Fucking nosey," he smirked.

I couldn't help a guilty smile.

"As it so happens, there's a thing called a 'grocery store' where you can purchase various ingredients to—"

"Ohmygod. STOP," I gave him a gentle kick under the blanket and picked up the coffee mug from the tray.

He chuckled, "I snuck out this morning while you were still asleep. I don't have a reason to keep stocked since I'm never here."

"This is very sweet, thank you." I helped myself to the pancakes. "Mmm, blueberry… Wow. These are *really* good." *Holy shit, this man can cook.*

"My specialty."

"Aren't you going to eat?" I asked, swallowing another mouthful.

"I wanted to make sure you had enough. You haven't eaten since yesterday morning."

"Here," I held a forkful of syrup soaked pancake out to him. "We can share."

155

He smiled and leaned in. I watched his mouth with more focus than I needed to as it slid slowly off the end of the fork. His tongue ran along his bottom lip as syrup dripped off it. Fuck, bad idea.

"Hmm. I'll use less vanilla next time…" He pondered through his mouthful.

"They're perfect. Don't change a thing."

He looked up at me and chuckled, "you have blueberry on your face."

I haphazardly stuck my tongue out, licking around the edges of my lips trying to find it. "Where?"

"Here…" He wiped under my bottom lip with his thumb, then sucked the juice off it between his own lips. My eyes followed every subtle movement of his mouth.

"May I?" He whispered as he pressed his forehead against mine.

I nodded as warmth flushed my face, and he kissed me. The coldness of his skin would never cease to surprise me. His lips even colder in comparison to the breakfast we shared, but he tasted so much better. The sweetness of the syrup still lingered on his bottom lip. I sucked it between my teeth and bit down as I ran my tongue across it.

He grasped my neck in response, pushing me harder into him. Goosebumps broke across my skin at his icy touch. Our lips held firm as his fingers trailed down my bare arms and I reached for his waist, pulling him onto me by the elastic of his bottoms.

He obliged, leaned me back, and my legs opened in response to him as he situated himself over me. But he froze, panting heavily, and furrowed his brow.

"What?" I gasped breathlessly.

"We shouldn't. I shouldn't…" He gently moved off me with a weight in his eyes.

My thoughts fought between desire and logic. My body craved this man like nothing I had ever felt. Even though my heart was screaming at me not to get involved, I was drawn to him like a mosquito to a deadly bug zapper. I admonished myself. *Since when does a man have more restraint than me?*

"I'm sorry."

"Don't be." He turned and sat on the edge of the bed with his back to me. "I started it."

"Maybe this time..." I placed my hand on his back and his muscles tensed.

"I'm not exactly the kind of guy you bring home to the folks," he grunted. "My life is too unpredictable, I make too many enemies..."

"It's a good thing I don't talk to my parents then," I smiled.

He huffed a laugh and turned back to me. "You know what I mean."

"Maybe we just keep it casual then?" I shocked myself.

"Really? You don't strike me as the 'casual sex' type."

"Well, maybe that's been my problem." I brought my knees to my chest and wrapped my arms around them. "Maybe I need to give up on the whole 'feelings' thing and just have some fun."

"Are you sure that's what you want?"

I paused. *No.* I wasn't sure that's what I wanted. "I know what I *don't* want..."

He waited for me to continue.

"I don't want to get my heart broken again. I don't want to fall head over heels for someone who just wants to use me as a means to an end. But, I also don't want to keep pretending like there's not something here... It's exhausting."

His face was deep in thought. "I don't *want* to hurt you, but I can't promise I won't. I'm pretty fucked up... I *can* promise the whole 'using you as a means to an end' thing is a non factor though. I can't believe I ever tried to do that to you, and I'll never stop apologizing for it. We can keep our truce, you can't hide your feelings so I won't hide mine, but I won't push anything until you tell me you know what you want."

"I don't want you to feel like I'm leading you on or anything—"

"Don't worry about me," he smiled, "I just want you to be happy."

My heart skipped a beat.

He chuckled, "I'll pretend I didn't feel that."

# Eleven

I hate paperwork. I hate talking on the phone. And I HATE insurance companies. What the fuck did I even pay them for? I sat on the remade sofa, my legs criss crossed, scrolling through yet another form I had to fill out on my laptop. I thought the point of insurance was to make your life easier in case of emergencies, not to stress you the fuck out. They didn't want to pay for half of the damages to my apartment because "I didn't own the building and it fell onto the property management to fix this or that…" And of course the complex insisted that they weren't going to pay for shit.

"FUCK." I slammed my laptop closed.

"Who do I have to kill?" Warren looked up from his desk where he scoured over his own paperwork.

"No one. Because then I'd have to deal with the insurance claims again."

He chuckled, "we can make it look like an accident and just skip town?"

My shoulders relaxed as I turned to him. "I'll consider your offer," I smiled. "How are you getting on?" I stood and stretched.

"Still waiting to hear back." He checked his phone for the millionth time. "He's going to be difficult to get a hold of by design."

"I thought he was a friend?"

"'Friend' is not the word I'd use, acquaintance is even a stretch…"

"And you still think he'll help us?"

"I know how to trade with him." He replied cryptically as leaned back in his chair, allowing me to stand in front of him when I went around to see what he was working on.

I bent forward to read an incredibly thorough and well-written profile for The Carver he had come up with on his own. "You really should be a detective," I noted as I scanned his words.

"Hmm?" He clearly wasn't listening.

I turned back to find him staring at my ass, which I unintentionally positioned right in his face as I leaned over.

"Oh my god." I chuckled and spun around, leaning against the desk. "Focus."

"Yeah, that's impossible when you do *that*," He smirked.

"I didn't mean to," I rolled my eyes.

He eyed me up and down. "By all means, make more mistakes then…" He bit his lip.

My girl pulsated as I considered my next move, making it difficult to decide logically. I was stressed, turned on, and in desperate need of a way to release this tension.

Fuck it.

I pushed off the desk and moved towards him, positioning myself between his legs. My arms wrapped around his neck as I leaned down to him. "I want you, but, no feelings…" I murmured against his lips.

"Yes ma'am," he whispered against mine, and ran his hands up the back of my legs, stopping to fondle my ass.

He looked up at me and I took the opportunity to run my fingers through his hair. *So fucking soft, and he smelled heavenly.*

"I've been dying to feel *this* for days…" He smacked me *hard*. I gasped, and he chuckled. Keeping one hand firmly where it was, his other traced up my lower back and pulled me roughly onto him, forcing me to straddle his legs.

The feeling of his already hard manhood pressed against my girl made me so fucking wet. Desire raged through me. I leaned forward and bit down on his neck.

He growled a moan and thrust his hips, rubbing himself against me. His hand slid up my back and grabbed a handful of my hair, using it to pull me back.

I gasped at the force of it and smiled down at him.

He chuckled darkly. "You like it a little rough, don't you Babygirl?"

I bit my lip in response to the pet name, the way it rolled smoothly out of his deep voice set fire to me. His eyes flashed before he leaned me further back and pressed his lips back onto mine. His tongue ran against my bottom lip, before he pulled it between his teeth and clamped down, sucking it into his mouth.

I moaned against him, completely at his mercy as he kept me from falling backward. His arms tensed against my back and he pulled away with a grin. "I would do anything to have you make that noise for me again."

"Take me then," I whimpered.

His phone rang on the desk behind me.

He released a long sigh then rested his forehead against my chest with a grunt. He reached around me for his phone and answered it as he leaned back in the chair.

There was no fucking way I was done. I pressed against him, rubbing up and down his length through his fabric.

He glared at me. "Behave," he mouthed with the phone up to his ear as he responded to his conversation. "Yeah?"

Did he forget I was in charge here? I pressed my lips back on his neck, planing kisses up to his ear, then bit down on his earlobe.

He smacked my ass again in punishment, the sound reverberated off the walls. "Yeah. I just wanna talk to him," he forced out through gritted teeth.

He would have to do better than that. I softly trailed my tongue down his neck to his collarbone, forcing him to pull the phone from his face as he gasped "*fuck*" in a whisper. "Mhm," he responded to the person on the line, then quickly wrapped his hand around my throat, squeezing gently, and pushed me back.

My eyes widened, and he tilted his head with a triumphant grin. "Where is it?" He responded to his contact. "Yep. Got it. Thanks." He hung up and threw his phone aside. "*You* are in *so* much trouble."

"Yeah? What are you going to do about it?"

"Nothing. Because that's what will drive you crazy." He smiled and released me.

Wait. What? That's not what I wanted... "Warren..." I whined.

He chuckled, "I have work to do Babygirl, that's the call we were waiting for."

"Oh," I blushed again at the name. "Can he help?"

"That, I don't know. Getting his location was the easy part, now I have to go and talk to him." He ran his thumb across my lips as he cupped my face. "There's an event this weekend about six hours from here, out east. That's going to be my best bet."

"So you're leaving?" I stood and leaned against the desk.

"I hoped... I thought, maybe, you'd come with me? If you want..."

I did want. The thought of him leaving actually hurt (dammit), but... "What about Dinah? And Mrs. T's cats? And at some point I'll have to go back home and clean everything up…"

"I get it, it's okay," he was smiling, but only with his lips. He leaned forward and grabbed my hand. "I'll make sure you're safe. I'll get someone to watch over you."

I wasn't even thinking about that. My stupid brain was focused on not being with him. *Was it my brain?* "When do you have to go?"

"I should probably leave tomorrow morning."

I looked down.

"You can still stay here as long as you need to, if you feel safer…"

Here he was, thinking of my well being again while I was only concerned with being without him. "Thanks." I intended to sound more grateful than it came off.

"I'll only be gone a few days." He pulled me closer to him. "Then I'll go right back to stalking you," he grinned up at me.

I couldn't help but smile when he did. "You enjoy being a creep that much?"

"For you, absolutely."

It was my phone's turn to pop off. *Not a moment's peace.*

"What's his address?" Rory didn't even greet me.

"Why?"

"I'm on my way. I need to know where I'm headed."

I froze at the sounds of cars whirring, horns honking, and people chattering in the background. "Are… Are you at the airport?!"

"Come on. I need to know where to have the Lyft take me."

"Are you *here*?!"

"I mean I can Google his office if I need to…"

"Uh…" I looked down at Warren.

163

He sat up slightly.

"Never-mind. I already found it. You're useless. I'll be there in 20." She hung up.

I looked down at my phone as if it would hold answers. "My sister is on her way."

"Oh, that's good?"

"I haven't seen her in years."

"But you talk to her all the time?"

"I mean, increasingly with everything that has been going on but… She's kind of… a handful?"

"It'll be good for you to have some company, especially while I'm away," he rationalized.

"Yeah, I guess."

I was a nervous wreck waiting for Rory to arrive, though I really didn't know why. We got along just fine and it would really be helpful to have her here. I just hadn't seen any of my family for years, and the last time the two of us were together was the last Thanksgiving I spent with our parents… which did *not* end well. I kept playing our reunion in my head, what I would say, how I would introduce Warren…

Shit, how *will* I introduce Warren? 'Hey, this is my hired bodyguard slash P.I., that I kind of started to have feelings for that I don't want to acknowledge so we're just keeping it casual. Oh yeah, he can turn into your worst nightmare and has killed a few people, nothing to worry about…'

"Adelaide, will you please sit down?" He came out of the kitchen holding a dish towel. "You're driving me nuts."

"I can't, I'm freaking out."

"Clearly." He flung it over his shoulder and leaned against the door frame. "Want to tell me what are you freaking out about exactly? The only thing I'm getting is a vision of an angry woman… and turkey?"

"Interacting with my family has never been easy."

"But you get along with your sister?"

"Yeah, but the last time we were together…" I turned to him, "I kind of broke our family apart."

"Did you have a good reason?"

"I mean, it was kind of a long time coming. Remember how I mentioned my parents tried to send me to a human advocacy camp? Well my mother is a full blown anti-muti."

"Yeah," he smiled. "I figured as much."

"And… I kind of outed Rory as a mutant rights lawyer… without her consent."

"Is she still upset about it?"

"If she is, she hasn't let on. But we also only really started talking again when I witnessed a murder so she might be holding back out of pity."

He pushed off the doorframe, crossed the room towards me, and looked down into my eyes. "Don't assume to know other people's thoughts, unless you've been a mutant this whole time and didn't say anything, you can't actually read minds." He kissed me on the forehead. "Your sister is not your mother. She came all this way because she cares about you and was worried. She's going to be happy to see you safe, and you're going to be happy to have her here."

"But—"

"Look at me. It's going to be fine," he smiled. "If you're really worried about her being upset with you, just ask her."

As if on cue, someone knocked on the door. He answered it. "You must be Rory."

"Where is she?" She demanded.

He opened the door wider to allow her in, "right here."

She rushed at me and pulled me into a hug. Her curly hair was pulled back tightly into a bun, and she wore one of her many suits. Looking at us, you wouldn't know we were related if it wasn't for our hair. She was always in pristine condition, makeup done, hair neatly tied back, dressed to impress. While I was most happy in sweats and a tank top, my hair loose and wild, sans makeup. She always made me feel like Oscar the Grouch standing next to her.

"Hi…" I hugged her back.

"I'd say I'm sorry for surprising you, but I'm not," she sighed. "You would have never let me come otherwise."

"You're right," I smiled and pulled away. "This is Warren," I gestured at him.

He approached us with his hand outstretched. "Nice to finally meet you in person."

"I'd also say I'm sorry for threatening your manhood, but I'm not." She shook his hand firmly.

"As well you shouldn't be," he chuckled.

"Hmm. At least you don't give off rapey vibes." She moved further into the office.

"Uh, thanks?" He closed the door.

I smiled at her abruptness. She never wasted time with fake pleasantries.

"So, what's the situation with your place?" She asked, taking off her blazer and placing it neatly on the arm of the sofa. "Phew… it's warm in here…"

"Oh, yeah, Warren runs cold. Uh, I've been fighting with the insurance companies all day about getting the front door fixed at least so I can move back in. They and the complex have been arguing about whose responsibility it is—"

"That's going to end right now." She sat on the sofa. "Give me your insurance info, I'll handle this."

I forgot how bossy she was, but man does this woman get shit done. I always envied her drive. She was so strong, putting herself through college, moving across the country, fighting from an underdog position in almost every case she took. She seemed to thrive under pressure, like a fucking diamond.

In a few hours, with a glass of wine in hand and her heels kicked off, she not only had a repair person on their way to fix my front door, but she had the insurance cover an entire maid service to come and deep clean the apartment. By the time the sun set I could have moved back in, but I was enjoying being surrounded by the two of them, so I was in no hurry.

Rory and I were on the sofa, Warren on his office chair across from us, a few glasses in, and much more comfortable with each other.

"So, if I may ask, why don't you pursue a career as a detective? Why stay private?" Rory asked Warren as she curled her legs under her.

"Uh, other than not being registered?" Warren sipped his glass.

"I know it's a flawed law, but from what I've heard you could be very successful in the force. You definitely have the skills."

"I don't think any government organization would want me working for them," he chuckled.

"Why not? Because you're a mutant? I've represented several mutants who were rejected from good jobs they were more than qualified for, and I win every case. If you want—"

"Warren has kind of a checkered history with the government." I interrupted, "family stuff." Not to mention the non-family murders…

"Ah, yeah. I know how that goes. I guess, as long as you're happy."

"Mhm." Warren agreed, and gave me a grateful look.

"So tell me more about this contact of yours out east? You're going to see them tomorrow?"

"Yeah. He might have information that can help me… us," he smiled at me, "figure out The Carvers identity."

Rory looked between us, a knowing expression on her face. "Are you going with him?" She asked me.

"I can't. I have Dinah and Mrs. Tibbet's cats."

"But you want to?"

I took a larger swallow of wine than I meant to.

"Oh Addy…" she sighed dramatically, "you really can't resist these brooding types in leather jackets can you…"

I choked. Warren smirked.

"Alright. I'll watch them for you." She swirled her glass. "Someone is going to need to handle the rest of that insurance claim anyway, and lord knows you let them walk all over you…"

"What? Really? You came all this way—"

"To help you." She interrupted, "and this is what you need help with right now. Go. Go on your crazy road trip with your new… whatever this is…" She motioned towards Warren and took a drink nonchalantly.

"Thanks, Rory," I smiled.

"Just make sure you come back with answers, and in one piece?" She smiled back. "Now, if we're going to keep drinking I need to eat something. This wine is too damn good. What is it?"

She asked me, but I shrugged.

"A 2016 Malbec." Warren answered plainly, sipping from his glass. "I wanted to let it mature for another year or so but, eh."

"You know wine?" Rory turned with a huge smile on her face. "You might grow on me yet, lover boy."

"You can cook, and you know about wine?" I gaped.

"Man's gotta have a hobby," he leaned back in his chair. "If you guys are up for it, the Chinese place down the street is pretty good."

"Sounds good to me, Addy?" Rory looked to me.

I was still processing Warren's hidden talents. "Uh, yeah, sure."

"I'll go pick it up." Warren stood and finished his glass before heading out.

"Okay, spill it." Rory turned to me as soon as the door closed.

"Spill what?"

"Something happened since the last time we talked, you guys were basically eye fucking this whole time."

"We may have made out…" I swirled my glass "a couple of times…"

"Fucking called it." She smirked and finished off her glass.

"What about you?" I chuckled, "have you met anyone?"

"As a matter of fact, I have." She turned to face me. "I met her online."

"Have you met in person yet?"

"Yeeesss," she beamed. "She's gorgeous Addy… oh my god. And so smart. She's a high school physics teacher."

The longer we talked, the more we poured. Rory couldn't stop singing her new girlfriend's praises once I got her started, and though I refrained from telling her the details of the first two times I witnessed Warren's transformation, I happily dove in when it came to him defending my honor against my ex-boss at the hotel. We also didn't waste a single opportunity to complain about our parents, who as it turns out had attempted to contact her a few times in the last year.

Not once did she bring up Thanksgiving, or show any hints that she was still upset with me. I silently scolded myself for being so afraid that she held a grudge that I went months without having my sister in my life. I would never make that mistake again. By the time Warren returned with the food, Rory and I were more than a bit tipsy.

"It's about time!" Rory stood when he unlocked the door. "Starve a girl to death over here why don't you…" She took the bags and rushed into the kitchen with them.

"Thanks," I giggled as I stood to greet him.

"Enjoyed the rest of that wine I see?" He smiled as he looked from my empty glass to the almost empty bottle.

"Mhmm. Thank you very much." I reached up and pulled him down by his hoodie so I could kiss him. Which he reciprocated with a soft peck. I pouted, "that's all I get?"

"When you're drunk? Yes," he chuckled. "Let's get some food in you."

"I'd rather have something else in me…" I smiled up at him suggestively.

"Naughty girl," he chuckled, and tapped my butt towards the kitchen.


Six cartons of Chinese food, and two bottles of wine later, we were all deeply satisfied and extremely tired. Warren had pulled the bed out and  offered it to Rory who was falling asleep standing up. The moment her head hit the pillow, she was out.

"Hey," Warren whispered from the kitchen as I pulled the blanket over her shoulders, "round three?" He smiled and held up another bottle.

I giggled and nodded, creeping towards him as quietly as possible. "I don't want to wake her though, that jet lag has gotta be killing her," I whispered.

"I have a place. Grab a blanket?" He smiled and moved towards the window behind his desk.

I frowned questioningly, but did as he asked, and followed him as he slid out the window onto the fire escape. He took my hand to help me gain my footing as I stood and looked out at the twinkling city lights in the distance. The crescent moon aligned itself perfectly, fitting between two high rises. A warm breeze tickled my skin as I stood with my hands on the railing.

"What a view…" I gasped and turned to him, but it was dark and I could barely make out his silhouette.

"Oh, hold on." he pulled out his phone, tapped a few times, and immediately the metal balcony lit up with several strands of warm yellow lights. "Better?" He smiled.

"Wow, how many times has that trick gotten you laid?" I laughed softly, secretly thinking it would definitely work on me.

"None. I don't bring anyone out here." He set the bottle and glasses down on the floor and lay the blanket out next to it.

"But you have it all set up?"

"I come out here to get some fresh air, snap some landscapes, get my mind off things. It's kind of my 'quiet place'." He lay on the blanket with his back against the railing, poured a glass, and offered it up to me. I moved to accept it, but he pulled it down towards him and smiled.

"Nu huh. Come here," he curled his finger, beckoning me closer.

My cheeks flushed at the gesture. I knelt between his legs, and leaned forward, supporting my weight on my arms. "Is this what you wanted?" I asked against his lips.

"Mmm... if we hadn't been drinking..." He gave me a soft kiss, "turn around."

"Turn... around?"

He chuckled, "lay against me."

"Oh." I situated myself between his legs and began to lean back, but hesitated. "I'm heavy. Are you sure you want me laying on you?"

He wrapped his arm around my stomach and pulled me back gently. "You're not heavy," he whispered in my ear, and finally handed me my glass.

His heart pounded against my back as we moved up and down together with his breaths. He kept his arm around me, his fingers swirling tiny circles against the gap of exposed skin under my shirt. I let my head fall lazily against his neck, unable to recall the last time I felt this relaxed, this free of anxiety, self-doubt, or driven to self-preservation. In his arms I felt safe. He and Rory made me feel so... *validated* for the first time in my life.

"Warren?" I broke the silence.

I felt his heart skip when I spoke his name. "Mmm?"

"Can you sense Rory's greatest fear?"

"Of course."

"What is it?"

He shifted slightly under me. "You should ask her yourself. I'm not sure she'd appreciate me sharing."

His discretion surprised me and overwhelmed me with a sense of respect and trust. *Trust?* Oh god, please no. I couldn't afford that. "What's yours?" I forced my train of thought onward.

"I don't have one," he replied simply.

"Come on, everyone has something…"

"Babygirl, I have literally become *the* most terrifying things. The creatures and beings people have nightmares about. The ideas and scenarios that cause them to panic." His voice vibrated against my back. "I'm forced to confront them every day, be them, understand them. I comprehend fear the way no one else can, fear is me, and I *am* fear itself."

I let the words sink in, trying to understand what it would feel like to not be afraid of *anything*. To never have anxiety, never have nightmares. To have a relationship with it as one would with breathing. Fear is a primal survival instinct, it protects us, reminds us of what is important. We only fear to lose the things that matter the most. Without all that, how would we know to cherish something or someone? How would we know we were in danger? I thought about those stunt people I saw in documentaries, the ones who tightrope walk across the grand canyon, or attempt insane motorcycle jumps… People always described them as fearless. I just thought they were  stupid. Stupid to endanger themselves for a rush of adrenaline, or a moment of fame. But then again, Warren did say the feeling he got when he sensed other people's fears was akin to that rush of adrenaline… Maybe that's why he takes thugs, and hostile clients head on. Not because he's courageous. Because he's fearless.

"Does that bother you?" He noticed my sudden silence.

"No," I leaned my head back against his shoulder. "But it does make me worry."

"About?"

"About your safety. About your regard for your own well being. What's stopping you from doing something really dangerous if you're not afraid of getting hurt?"

"Common sense," he chuckled. "Just because I'm not afraid to die doesn't mean I want to. I still feel pain, and aside from your teeth against my skin…" he leaned down and bit my neck, making me squirm against him. He hummed in satisfaction, "I don't enjoy it." He tilted my chin upward with his finger, "but I adore that you care about my safety."

His eyes swam with the twinkling lights, and maybe it was the wine, but I swear I saw more than just lust behind them.

Taking them in fully for the first time, I noticed flecks of fire and gold scattered across those suns. Those bright, beautiful, expressive amber orbs that made me feel weak. Something inside me broke open.

He leaned down and kissed me, and I melted into him. His hand caressing my jaw as his tongue danced with mine. A swarm of butterflies exploded in my stomach as he held me tighter against his chest. His kiss was all passion, a desire to express something he didn't have words for. This was far more than just our bodies craving each other, this felt like… a connection. I panicked and pulled away at the realization, though even separated from him I still felt his cold tingle on my lips.

"Sorry, I didn't mean to make you uncomfortable."

"It wasn't you." I sat up, hugging my knees to my chest. "I think I've just had a few glasses too many."

"Maybe we should get you to bed then." He responded softly from behind me, pulled his legs under him, and stood. He offered me his hand, and smiled.

I took it, and let him pull me up. He rolled up the blanket as I peered through the window, realizing there was only one bed. "Where are you going to sleep?"

"I'll just roll my sleeping bag out on the floor," he shrugged.

"I feel bad, it's your place and we're forcing you to sleep on the floor—"

"Don't. I've slept in way less comfortable places. After you." He gestured back inside with a small smile.

I changed in the bathroom, and when I came back, he had laid his sleeping bag out next to my side of the bed.

"If I have to get up and pee in the middle of the night, I'm going to step on you," I whispered with a smile.

"Good. I don't want you going anywhere without my knowing about it."

I slid in next to Rory, and he pulled the covers over me as he leaned down, "sweet dreams, Babygirl." He kissed me, letting his lips linger for a few extra seconds before getting into his sleeping bag. I rolled onto my side and let my hand hang down by him as I closed my eyes. His fingers brushed against mine and interlocked with them.

# Twelve

"Wake up you drunk," Rory slammed a pillow against my back. "We gotta get going."

I groaned and buried my face in the mattress. She was always an early riser but she's so much worse when there's actually a reason to get up. Her sense of responsibility was exasperating.

"Come on. We still have to take everything back to your place," she shook me.

I didn't like the idea of her staying at my apartment on her own while we were gone. After what happened with Mrs. T, and learning that The Carver could track me, I was concerned that he would try and break in again. But both Warren and Rory managed to convince me that he already saw I wasn't there and would be more likely to follow us leaving town. So I was outvoted.

My eyelids felt like iron as I struggled to open them. We agreed on getting up early in the midst of our impromptu party, not taking into consideration how late it already was. Ideas always sound better when you're drunk.

"What time is it?" I mumbled.

"It's already 10, which is *way* later than we talked about."

For someone who was used to being comfortably asleep at 10 a.m., this was torture.

"If you two hadn't stayed up all night whispering sweet nothings into each other's ears..."

I was up.

Three people trying to shower, get ready, and get out of a tiny studio was a test to our patience. I could tell Warren was at his wits end with Rory's bossiness after the first hour, but he miraculously held his tongue. I expressed my apologies and gratitude by gently touching his arm, or giving him small smiles, which he responded to with deep sighs and eye rolls until we were finally out the door, in the truck, and on our way to my apartment.

As we arrived at the complex, I anticipated seeing the police tape and barricades still up, but of course it was as unassuming a street as ever. As we made our way up the elevator, I was psyching myself into pretending I would be fine. Pretending I wouldn't react to my belongings magically in their right places, pretending I wouldn't be on the lookout for any signs of blood. Any signs there was a murder. But I was failing.

Warren reached down and took my hand, giving it a squeeze. "You're okay," he whispered.

The doors opened and Rory confidently walked out ahead of us, as if she knew where she was going. Warren had to drop my hand to carry Dinah's cat tree, and I needed both hands to hold her carrier and my bag. I began the walk at a casual pace, but found myself slowing down as I neared my door, which was no longer off its hinges. Warren came up behind me, whispered "come on, brave girl," and somehow his words gave me enough to push through the anxiety. I unlocked my door, and let everyone in.

The apartment was spotless. Cleaner than it looked on the day I moved in. My belongings were back in their relatively correct locations, although my books were completely out of order on the shelves, making me cringe and fight the compulsive urge to throw them all off and reorganize them. Rory immediately went down the hall to my room. I couldn't bear to look yet, so I turned toward Warren who was setting up Dinah's tree in its corner.

"Huh. They did a pretty good job," Rory reappeared from down the hall with her hands on her hips. "I was sure they'd half ass it."

"Yeah. It's really clean." I agreed as I set my bag down next to the sofa.

"Alright. Well, let's get you *re*packed." She picked my bag up and took it back to the bedroom.

I hesitated to follow.

"Do you want me to go in first?" Warren came up next to me and put his hand on my lower back.

"No," I took a deep breath, "I'm okay," and headed down the hall.

Rory was already dumping out my bag on the made bed, a sight I definitely wasn't used to. It didn't even feel like my room anymore. It was *too* clean, too organized… Not to mention my gaze kept falling to the floor where Mrs. Tibbet once lay, contorted, lifeless. I suddenly felt violated. He violated my private space and took it away from me. My muscles tensed as a surge of anger swept over me. How dare he? How dare he take what I worked so hard to earn for myself. How dare he steal my peace of mind.

"You good?" Rory was staring at me.

"No," I admitted. "I'm pissed."

"At me? Sorry, I was just trying to sort your dirty clothes—"

"No. At him. At that monster. He fucked up my life, fucked with my mind… and now I'll never be the same again."

She put down the clothes she was holding and came around to the foot of the bed. "Addy. Your life has been fucked up before by a different guy, but you fought through that. And you'll fight through this."

She said it so surely. "This is different though. As much of an asshole as Scott was, he never killed anyone."

"That we know of," she smirked.

I smiled, "no, he's too much of a coward for that."

"Well that's one thing then you know you have over him, and over this evil fucker. You are one of the most courageous people I know. I always looked up to you for that. You were never afraid to stand up for others, for me. You spoke your mind, even to Mom. And although I was annoyed with you back then, I'm proud of you for telling them what I did for a living. I didn't have the courage to do it myself. Hell, I don't even have the balls to tell them I'm gay."

"It's none of their business anyway, who you love."

"See? I know that, logically. But... I can't even bring myself to cut ties with them like you did. I'm afraid to. You weren't."

"I was," I admitted. "But I needed to—"

"Even better then. Just like now. I know you're scared of this guy, who wouldn't be? But you're still trying to help Warren track him down. Addy the dude is *hunting* you and you're still after him. Fuck, if that's not brave, I don't know what is." She took my hands. "Stay pissed Addy, stay pissed and find that asshole."

I smiled at her, "alright."

The skyscrapers, concrete structures and crowded, dirty streets were far behind as I sat in the passenger seat, staring out at the flat, dry, yellowing fields. The bright blue summer sky contrasted magnificently against the golden fields, and though there was nothing much to see, it was beautiful. The sight of raptors circling overhead in search of their next meal enthralled me, and once or twice I gasped in excitement as they dove into the tall grass, startling Warren, who would grunt disapprovingly at my over-enthusiastic reactions. I began wondering why I subjected myself to the stressors of city life, when all this lay just an hour beyond my tiny little world. As farmland and orchards zoomed by, I took note of the giant tractors, trucks and odd looking machinery the workers used and remembered. I need a job, and have no idea how to farm.

"Would you ever leave the city?" I turned and asked Warren.

"Mmm. Maybe, one day. It would be hard to find work out here though."

"What if you found a different kind of work?"

"What, like a scarecrow?" He chuckled.

"No," I smiled. "Like… a farmer, or rancher."

"I have no clue how to farm. I'll cook the food all day long but don't ask me how to grow it."

"Where did you learn to cook?"

"I taught myself. At one point my foster parents had… oh… seven kids? Meals consisted of whatever they could make in bulk, and after five years of tasteless slop I was over it. One of the first things I bought when I moved out was a cookbook."

I laughed, "you're this great chef, but you were so afraid to try fries with a chocolate shake."

"I wasn't *afraid*, I just barely trust fast food as it is," he chuckled, then thought for a second. "What's your favorite food?"

"Spaghetti," I responded immediately. "But it has to be good spaghetti, like, not that canned crap. Oh and garlic bread."

He laughed, "I know a pretty good sauce recipe, I'll make it for you sometime."

"I'd like that."

He smiled, reached his hand over and put it on my knee, running his thumb back and forth across my skin.

"Your love language is touch, huh," I smiled.

He quickly pulled his hand back. "My *what?*"

"Love language," I laughed at his reaction. "It's the way you show affection."

"I didn't know that was a thing," he flushed.

"It's kind of like… the reaction you instinctively have when you want to show someone you care. Mine is 'acts of service'."

"What does that even mean?"

"That I tend to go out of my way to do stuff for you if I want to do something nice for you. Rather than hugging, or giving gifts, or saying it. Those are their own languages."

"How many are there?"

"Five? I think… let me see." I counted on my fingers. "Touch, acts of service, words of affirmation, gift giving, and quality time."

He thought to himself. "But I don't go around randomly touching people…"

I laughed, "no, but like… okay. Let me phrase it differently. If you were upset about something, do you think you would feel better if I gave you a gift? Or cooked you dinner?"

"Uh. Probably cooked me dinner, but I'm not sure I'd actually feel any better… I'd appreciate the gesture though."

"Okay, how about; said something reassuring, or we went out to see a movie together?"

"Mmm… I guess I'd be more receptive to going out to the movies, but I'd still probably be mad."

"Okay then, what if I sat next to you on the sofa and hugged you? Or… how about some angry sex?" I smirked.

He smiled mischievously. "I like that last one…"

I laughed, "I thought you might."

He placed his hand back on my leg. "How do you know all that?"

"Oh, lots of self help books and articles," I sighed. "After my ex, I had a lot of healing to do."

"If I ever meet that fucker…" His fingers curled on my knee.

"You don't even know who he is," I laughed, secretly enjoying the anger rising in him.

"You don't think I do?"

"How… How could you?" I slowly turned to him.

"I have my ways of getting information. I just need to know certain details."

"Warren… you didn't search him out did you?"

"Mmm."

"Why?!"

"I just wanted to know what he looked like… and the area he lives in. For your protection. It's my job isn't it?" His grin was almost sinister, and I felt a shocking sense of satisfaction at his statement.

I looked towards the window as I hid a smile. It would be quite empowering to watch that asshole cowering from whatever he was afraid of, and at the hands of my new guard dog… I dropped the subject lest I give Warren any ideas.

The golden fields gave way to evergreens and thick forest as we crossed through the mountain range dividing the states. The canopy shielded us from the sun as we wove through the trees.

"I've never been out this far." I marveled at the towering woods.

"Have you never been camping?"

I shook my head. "We weren't really a 'camping' type family. We were a 'force the kids into their Sunday best and drag them to church at 5 a.m.' kind of family."

He burst out in laughter. "Here." He rolled the windows down and a blast of sharp air hit my face.

I gasped, "it's so cold up here!"

"Yeah," he chuckled.

I rested my arms on the window, and leaned my head out. The air was so… *clean*. So pure. Like I could wash away my insides by just inhaling. There were no sounds of cars, no honking, or people shouting. So silent, and peaceful. I closed my eyes.

He reached forward and blasted the heat on his side.

"Oh, I'm sorry. We can roll them back up if you're cold."

"No. I'm fine, go ahead." He smiled at me, "enjoy it."


The steep incline forced him to slow as we wove up it, but I didn't mind. It meant more forest for me to immerse myself in. We took a hard turn and a flash of white sped past me.

I did a double take. "Did you see that?"

"What?"

"I don't know, it was bright."

I watched more intently and noticed several more patches of white on the forest floor. Some small, others mounds. At first I thought they were rocks, but it suddenly hit me. "Oh my god! It's snow! Warren! Snow!" I turned and tapped him, pointing out my window.

He laughed. "I see it, Babygirl. But I have to keep my eyes on the road."

"It's so white!"

"Yeah, that's how it comes down. It's the yellow stuff you want to avoid," he chuckled.

I was enraptured. It looked soft and sparkly. Like tiny little clouds had fallen from the sky. We drove a bit further, and he turned off the highway.

"Are we stopping?" I asked as he pulled up a side road.

"For a minute, let's stretch our legs."

We drove into a large, empty parking lot with a public bathroom and some picnic benches. He parked, and pulled on his jacket, zipping it up as I hopped out. My stiff muscles were immediately thankful for the break after three hours of sitting. I groaned as I stretched, relieving the tightness.

When I stepped up over the fallen log that acted as a parking bumper, I was met with a scene from one of my fantasy books. A large pond with ducks and egrets lay below my line of sight, surrounded by boulders large enough to sit on. A tiny stream ran down the hill beyond into the larger body, causing miniature waterfalls as the water fell off the edges of the boulders in its path. All around the perimeter of the stream were small mounds of snow, hidden where the sun couldn't quite reach them.

I didn't realize my hands covered my mouth until Warren came up behind me and slid his arms around my waist. I lowered them onto his arms and let myself sink into him.

"It's beautiful," I whispered.

"I thought you might like it," he grinned into my ear. "Come on." He pulled away and took my hand, leading me down a path towards the stream.

We climbed over a few of the smaller boulders to get as high up as we dared, and right in front of me, at the base of a tree was a decently sized pile of snow.

"Can I touch it?" I looked back at him.

"Yeah," he laughed. "It won't bite."

I smiled and pressed my hand directly into it. The hard and icy mound didn't sink in like I expected it to. I picked up a handful and let it melt between my fingers, leaving behind small twigs, leaves and dirt. I wiped my hands on my jean shorts, sending a shockwave of stinging down my leg at their coldness.

"It's hard!"

"Yeah. This slush is what's left over after the rest starts to melt away. Come winter when the snow is fresh, that's when it's soft and pliable, like you see in the movies."

"Are you a snow connoisseur too?" I laughed.

"I've made this trip a lot," he smiled, "in many seasons. I used to camp pretty often when I was younger too."

"Will you take me camping?"

"Sure," he chuckled. "Though I've gotta warn you, most city girls don't like it."

"Only one way to find out," I beamed.

Warren let me explore the area as long as I wanted. He laughed when I attempted to jump from one side of the stream to the other, and fell in, soaking my shoes and socks all the way through in the icy water. But I didn't care, I was having too much fun. He sat on a log and watched me with a gentle smile on his face as I found various pinecones, acorns, and pretty rocks that I thought were interesting and held them up proudly to show him.

He humored me when I wanted to build a stack of rocks on the side of the stream, like others had done. He helped me collect various size stones and crouched next to me as I balanced them on each other. I could have spent hours there with him, but it began to get cold, and he started to shiver. We bought some snacks and drinks at the little truck stop in the parking lot and continued on our journey.

As if a curtain lifted, we began our descent and the landscape changed yet again. The trees became sparse, the rocky terrain turned from grey to red, and the dirt turned to sand. I rolled the window up at the first blast of dry desert air and sat back in my seat. Warren turned his heat off as the temperature rose yet again.

"You would be happy living out here." I made a face as I checked the temperature on my phone. 110°. Yuck.

"What makes you think that?"

"It's hot as balls. You'd never be cold again."

"It gets pretty cold at night out here too. The desert weather is bipolar."

"You told me once it was your dad's fault you run cold, is it because he's a demon?"

"Yeah. His plane of existence is really dark, all the creatures from there have similar body temperatures to mine, otherwise they'd freeze to death."

"Have you ever met him?"

"No. And I don't plan on it," his voice darkened.

"How do you know about his… what did you call it? Plane of existence?"

"My mom had a bunch of books about other worlds, dimensions, creatures… I was curious as a kid. I think part of me hoped that if I learned enough I could figure out how to become… normal."

"There really isn't such a thing anymore, not with mutations."

His lips tightened and pulled downward. "Name another person, mutant or not, who is part demon."

"Well, I don't know enough people to have that privilege, but if demons exist, then other people like you must exist too," I insisted.

"Mmm."

He didn't sound convinced. "Demon or not, for what it's worth, I'm glad you are the way you are. I wouldn't be here if it wasn't for you, and," I put my hand on his lap, "I like you this way."

His eyes flashed down at my hand quickly. He cracked a small smile. "Do you now?"

"I do, actually."

"So we've evolved from me being a dick to you actually liking me?" He smirked.

I scrunched my nose at the trap I fell into, "fuck you." I pulled my hand away, dramatically rolling my eyes.

"Name the time and place, Babygirl," he purred.

Damn, he's good.


The sky painted itself in a watercolor of light when I first spotted the large, bright, colorful city amidst the desert. Pink, orange, blue, purple… all blended together behind the neon lights as the stars sparkled above it all. It was an odd sight, this colorful oasis in the sand. Nothing else for miles and miles, yet this city was alive and thriving. Warren explained to me that our contact, Paul, or Paulie as he was known to his "friends", was the coordinator of a series of illegal fighting rings. Fights that pitted mutant against mutant for profit. This massive underground business that everyone knew of, but no one talked about. Celebrities, businessmen, and high end government officials, all were known in the ring as having their fingers in this person's pocket, or that person's inner circle.

"The first fight isn't until tomorrow, but Paulie is in a better mood the day before. He tends to get pissy as his fighters get injured, or lose."

"But doesn't he control the outcomes?"

"To an extent, but you have to realize these people, these mutants who sign up for this are in it for the money, and if someone pays them more to take a dive, or play dirty, you bet your ass they're gonna take it."

We drove down the main street and I couldn't even tell it was night anymore. The lights were so bright, the sky looked blue again. Signs everywhere pointed us towards this club, or that bar, or this casino. Each one promising the best night of our life. He pulled down a side street, and in through the back of a parking garage of one of the massive hotels. The stagnant heat smacked me in the face as I stepped out of the truck, and immediately I began to sweat.

"Oh, one more thing, don't say anything. Don't talk to him, don't ask him anything. If he talks to you, respond in as short and simple sentences as possible." Warren walked around to my side of the truck.

"Why? Is he so dangerous?"

"Yes. But that's besides the point. In this industry it's about respect. And he doesn't know you, therefore you haven't earned the right to talk to him."

"Wow. That's not condescending at all."

"I know, but if we're going to get what we need here, we have to play the game."

"Fine. I'll be good."

"Thank you," he smiled, then took a deep breath. "Stay close to me."

There were two big-ass men standing at the doorway to the hotel entrance dressed in men-in-black style suits and shades. At night... they were wearing their sunglasses in a parking garage at night... like a couple of douchebags.

Warren approached them confidently. "Paulie's expecting me."
The men looked at each other, nodded in unison, and they each pushed open a door to allow us to walk past.

Apparently the bottom floor of this hotel also doubled as a casino. There were slot machines and groups of people everywhere. It was difficult not to get distracted, but it would have been more difficult to find Warren again if I lost him in the crowd, so I followed closely behind as he maneuvered among the rows of games, some of them taller than me. The flashing neon lights of the digital machines grabbed my attention this way and that way, and a few times groups of drunken gamblers stepped in front of me. I grabbed the back of his jacket, afraid to get separated from him, and in response he reached his hand down for mine. I took it, and he laced his fingers in mine. He seemed to know exactly where he was going.

As we emerged from the last row of machines, he gave my hand a squeeze and dropped it before approaching an elevator where another large man, in an identical get-up as the first two, stood, Warren and the man nodded to each other, and the man pushed the button to ascend. He then followed us in, and pushed the button to the very top floor. We rose, slowly, in dead silence. I stood slightly behind Warren and looked between him and the man, hoping someone would say *something*. Some fake pleasantries, directions, but nothing, all the way to the 65th floor.

We exited without a word into a lobby of some kind, where expensively dressed women were seated at a bar to our left, and a gaggle more of them sprawled over several laughing men with cigars in a lounge area to our right.

189

Warren continued straight towards a set of huge, white double doors, with yet another set of large men standing guard. *Fuck, did they make these guys in a factory?* Warren knocked loudly on the doors without hesitation, the booming sound they made caused me to jump. "Come in." A voice from inside commanded, and he opened the doors.

A palatial room with white marble floors and walls made my jaw drop. Floor to ceiling windows towered above us on three sides, framed in gold curtains. A ridiculously long red and gold runner led our path directly towards a large sunken seating area with a granite fire pit in the middle. A plump man in a navy blue suit sat a glass down on the edge of the fire pit, and stood to greet us.

"Nyte! My boy! How wonderful to see you!" The man boomed a little too happily as we walked towards him. "When I heard you were going to be in town I made sure I had an opening in my schedule to see you."

"How you been, Paulie?" Warren responded with a forced smile.

"Oh my word, kid, you have no idea what getting old does to you. My knees ain't what they used to be, I'm telling you." Paulie took Warren by the face as he descended the few steps towards him, and pulled him down to kiss him on each cheek.

"Sorry to hear that Paulie," Warren feigned sympathy.

"Ah, don't worry about it, pretty soon they'll come up with some crazy treatment to have me regrow them. I hear they're onto this new *'medication'* that makes you feel great, named after some mythical creature or some shit... Who's this pretty little thing?" Paulie looked down at me.

"This is Adelaide. Adelaide, Paulie," he introduced us.

Paulie held his hand out to me, and I reluctantly placed my hand in his. "Enchanté," he lifted my hand and pressed his wet lips to the back of it.

I cringed.

"Come sit, make yourselves at home," Paulie gestured to the leather sofa that circled around us. "Can I get you anything?"

"We're alright Paulie, thanks," Warren replied as he took a seat next to me.

"Don't insult my hospitality kid. Adelaide, darling, what's your poison?" Paulie turned to me.

I held my breath and looked at Warren, who gave me a little nod of approval. "Whatever you're having, you clearly have great taste."

"Ha! I like this one," Paulie grinned at me hungrily. "If she leaves you too I might just keep her for myself."

I looked sideways at Warren, who remained stoic.

Paulie snapped his fingers and one of his suited men poured a brown liquid from a crystal decanter into three glasses with ice, and brought the tray to each of us.

I took the glass politely and held it on my lap, while Warren leaned back in his seat and crossed his leg, as if he couldn't be more comfortable. He brought the glass to his lips and sipped. "This is a good blend, Paulie."

"Isn't it though? It was a gift from… oh... shit I don't remember. One of those CEO's... He makes computers or something. Now. What do I owe the pleasure? There's a fight this weekend if you're looking to take some cash home with ya, we both know you'll pick out the winners in a heartbeat—"

"I'm looking for someone," Warren interrupted, "and I thought you might be able to point me in the right direction. Since you know everyone and everything."

"You're right. I do know everyone and everything," Paulie laughed. "Who is it?"

"I don't know his name, but I know his abilities, and I have a description." He pulled a folded paper out of his pocket and handed it to Paulie.

"Hmm. See kid, that's a bit tougher, 'cause that's gonna require me using some manpower to figure it out." Paulie leaned back, opened the paper, scanned the information, then looked up with a smirk. "Manpower ain't free, you know that."

"I know."

"So, I suppose you came with something in mind to pay me for my trouble?" Paulie looked at me, and I began to panic.

Warren's sight glanced between us quickly and he sat upright. "How much do you need?"

"Well see, it's not about money really…" Paulie held the tips of his fingers together and grinned. "I've got plenty of that."

"Alright, what then?" Warren began to lose the touch of civility in his voice.

"Well let's think now…" Paulie stood and began to pace with his hands clasped at his back. "Ah, here's an idea. See, the chamber match is tomorrow night. It's the main event, you remember?" He paused for Warren to respond.

"Yeah, I remember."

"Seems as if I'm down a fighter, came down with something this morning. Something he ate didn't agree with him, poor guy," Paulie smirked.

"Oh yeah, I'm sure," Warren agreed dryly.

"So, you'd be doing me a great favor by standing in for him. Taking up your old mantle, so to speak. The seats would sell out in a flash with your name back in the headlines. A favor like that would more than cover the cost of manpower I'd need to get the name of this friend of yours." He held up the paper between two fingers.

I gasped and looked at Warren. He never mentioned he used to be a part of these fights, I just assumed he knew about them from his cases.

He didn't look away from Paulie, however. "I'm out of the game, you know that."

"Oh I know, I know, but with your skills kid, getting back in is as simple as," Paulie snapped his fingers.

The look Warren gave him could have turned Medusa to stone.

Paulie shrugged. "It's a fair trade kid, and you know it. I can give you 'til tomorrow morning to decide. Just remember, if you're lookin' for who I think you're lookin' for, no one else is gonna have the information you need. That, and if word gets out you're back, even if you don't fight—"

"Fine," Warren muttered.

"What's that now? Sorry kid, ya gotta speak up."

"FINE." Warren raised his voice, but not his eyes. "I'll do it."

Paulie grinned triumphantly, "see, that wasn't so hard, was it? I'll even sweeten the deal, just 'cause I like you. You can keep your cut of the earnings."

"Alright Paulie, the info?"

"Now, now, kid, fight first. Info later. What kind of businessman do you take me for?"

Warren glared at him.

"Oh, and sweetie," Paulie turned to me, "if you wanna make a few bucks we have a spot open for a ring girl too—"

Warren shot up and threw his glass down violently, shattering it on the stone floor. "Keep her out of this." There was murder in his eyes.

"Fine. Fine," Paulie raised his hands, still smiling. "Just wanted to be an equal opportunist. Ya know, feminism and all."

193

"You're as much a feminist as I am a fucking fairy princess. Come on, Adelaide." Warren huffed and stormed towards the door. I had to take two steps to his one to keep up with him.

"I'll have one of my guys send the fight info to you tonight." Paulie called out as Warren slammed the door behind us.


He still seethed when we checked in at the front desk, when we went up to our room on the opposite side of the hotel, and even still when he insisted on going in to check if the room was clear before I stepped foot in it. Although my curiosity bore holes through my skull, I was too afraid to ask him about anything that just happened. The anger shooting off him in waves made me timid.

Small flashes of memories came to mind of the simmer before the fights between Scott and me. How I could tell when something was wrong, but if I asked about it, it would set him off. Never really knowing what I did. I was so focused on Warren, making sure I didn't do anything to cause the explosion, that I didn't even notice he had booked a room with a single bed, which in any other circumstance would have left me in a tizzy.

It wasn't until I began to get hungry that I dared speak. "Warren?"

He grunted from the bed.

"Uhm. I know you're probably not... but, do you think we could order some room service or something? I'm getting kind of hungry..." I held my breath, waiting for the beratement for asking for something as trivial as food, but instead he sighed and closed his eyes.

"Yeah. Go ahead." He responded softer than the energy he gave off.

"Do... you want anything?"

"I'm not really that hungry. Thanks."

I pulled the room service menu from the desk against the wall and scanned it. Not even realizing I was shaking until I had to put the menu back on the desk to read it clearly. *I know he said he wasn't hungry, and I'm sure he doesn't feel like it now, but he hasn't eaten since that truck stop and those were just snacks. He's going to be hungry later once he calms down...* I dialed the front desk and ordered two plates of food, then sat on my side of the bed and clicked on the TV.

When someone knocked on the door, and I stood to open it, Warren hurried out of the bed to get there before me. He took in the food, and set it on the desk. "You ordered two dinners?"

"Only one is for me. I'm sorry. I thought maybe... you'd be hungry later..." I responded quietly.

He stared at me and his expression softened immediately. "Acts of service..." He mumbled. He crossed to my bedside and knelt, placing his chin on my lap. "Thank you, Babygirl."

"You're welcome." I gave him a small smile and brushed my fingers through his hair.

"I'm sorry I've been such a prick tonight. It didn't go how I wanted it to."

"I figured. That Paulie is... kind of an asshole."

He chuckled, "yes. He is. And you took him like a champ." He stood and kissed my forehead, flooding me with relief. He grabbed our plates and brought them to the bed, handing me mine before he sat down.

I felt brave enough to ask now. "So, you were a fighter once?"

"A lifetime ago," he shook his head. "Kind of hard to get a job as a mutant kid straight out of the foster system. I fell in with a bad crowd, who introduced me to Paulie... Long story short, I was his prize show dog for like, seven years."

"Wow. And you got out?"

"It's not hard once you have the money. I saved and saved… Most of us either didn't make enough or spent it all on booze and drugs, but I wanted out more than anything. Especially after Chelsea—" He suddenly stopped.

"Chelsea?"

He bit his bottom lip and closed his eyes, as if regretting mentioning her name. "Remember that girl I told you about? The only relationship type thing I was ever a part of? That was her," he sighed.

"What happened?"

"I found out she was sleeping with a bunch of other fighters. Just for shits and giggles. I might have been able to let it go if it was for money, or if Paulie put her up to it… but no. I was loyal, and she wasn't. I never let myself get trapped in a situation like that again. It's impossible to get cheated on if you're not mutually exclusive."

My muscles tensed. *That bitch*. How dare she cheat on this sweet, protective man? No wonder. "I'm sorry. You didn't deserve that, and she didn't deserve you."

He gave me a half smile. "Anyway, after I found out about her, I wanted to get as far away from this fucking industry as possible. I moved to the city, got my license… and the rest is history. But now… Now I'm back in," he groaned and threw himself back on the bed.

"Do you have to be? I mean, isn't there anything else you can offer him?"

"If there was, he would have asked. Say what you want about Paulie, but he's smart. There's a reason he's been able to keep this going for as long as he has. I bet you anything the moment he heard I was looking for him he planned all of this."

"But, why does he want you so bad?"

"Money. It's always about money. I hate it, but I was good. I drew a crowd. I'm like having a million fighters in one body."

"Is it dangerous? This cage match he wants you in?"

"I mean, yeah. They all are. But this one, it's a big deal, it's the biggest match of the summer." He rolled on his side to face me, propping his head up on his elbow. His hair fell over his eyes.

I gathered the now empty plates, stacked them on the nightstand, and lay down sideways to face him. "Do you think you can win?"

"I have no idea. I doubt I'd even recognize the names of the other competitors now. Not to mention I'm probably twice their age. But that's not the deal, the deal is I fight. He neglected to insist I win, at least…"

"How do you know he'll keep his word? I mean, how do you know he even has the information we need? What if you do this all and we don't learn anything?"

"Oh, he knows something. Probably even more than he'll tell me. He wouldn't dare make this deal without actually having something to give me. He knows my connections with the police now."

I had no idea what a cage match entailed, but I didn't like the thought of him purposely going into a dangerous fight. "I don't want you to get hurt…" I looked down at the bed spread and played with a loose thread.

"Adelaide?"

"Yeah?" I met his gaze.

"Can I ask you a favor?"

I pushed myself up on my arm. "Of course."

"Will you lay with me?"

I smiled, "yeah."

I shifted closer and let him pull my body into his. He ran his fingers through my hair, as he rested his head on top of mine. His cold fingers slid up and down my back as I pressed my face into his chest and took in his scent.

"You were right," he sighed into my hair.

"Hmm?"

"I do feel better."

I must have fallen asleep, because I woke up from him pulling himself away from me. His footsteps padded softly across the carpet, the chain fell from the door and it unlatched, then he mumbled something before closing it again. I rolled over to see the TV still on but playing a different show than before dinner.

"Who was that?" I yawned.

"My information for the fight." He responded as he opened a manila folder and flipped through some pages, "huh." He crossed the room back to me and sat on the bed again. "I was right, I don't recognize any of these people."

"What does it say?" I sat up next to him.

He placed the folder open on the bed in front of him and spread three pages out. Each respective page had a photo and a typed out profile for a fighter..

"This one's a hydrokinetic," he pointed to a picture of a man with short brown hair. "He's a five time champ, six-foot-four, two hundred and six pounds…" He picked up another page. "Oh this is interesting, they don't normally do mixed matches. She's a flier. Huh. Tiny thing."

I took that page from him. "One hundred thirty pounds, blonde; holy crap Warren, she has talons and can use something called a 'sonic screech'?"

"This last one, oh he's just your typical strong guy. Lame. Four hundred and five pounds, six-foot-ten, super strength."

"I'm sorry, what about a four hundred pound, seven foot tall, super strong man is lame?!"

"They're a dime a dozen. They have their following but personally I always found their matches boring."

"You have to fight all three of these guys at the same time?"

"No, one at a time, but at random. We'll each be in a small, enclosed cage outside of the ring. At random two of the cages will open, and those two will fight until the timer runs out, or someone wins. If there's a winner, they return to the cage and the loser gets ejected. If there isn't we both return to our cages. Then they pick the next two. It goes on until there's only one winner."

"And, how does one win?"

"Getting the other person to submit… or…"

"Or?"

"You… uh… incapacitate them."

"You mean *kill* them?!"

"No, not always… sometimes they just get knocked out."

"I don't like this…" I threw the papers down on the bed as my heart raced. "I don't want you to do this."

"Hey, hey…" he turned to me and cupped his hand over my cheek. "Please don't be scared. Please? I can't handle it right now. I can't stand to feel you like that…"

"I'm sorry, I can't help it. If you get hurt—"

"I won't. I promise. These kids won't know what hit them," he smiled.

I didn't believe him.

# Thirteen

I was shocked to see the elaborate pageantry of the arena. For an illegal underground fighting ring, they sure didn't care about drawing attention. Even entering through the back I could hear the thundering of the crowd cheering and booing at whatever match was currently underway. Warren led us through what looked like the basement of the arena to a corridor of locker rooms and dressing rooms. A few individuals stopped and spoke to him, some kindly, others insinuating he didn't belong here anymore. When we came to a door that had his name on it, he pushed it open, and we entered into a comfortable looking dressing room adorned with plush couches and a vanity. If it wasn't for the gravity of the danger he was about to face, I would be inclined to think being a fighter wasn't so bad.

"Nice." I raised my eyebrow at a crystal candy bowl on the coffee table filled with a colorful assortment of condoms.

"It's not like I asked for those," he ruffled his hair, "they put them in all the private dressing rooms."

"I assume that's just another perk of being one of Paulie's favorites?" I thought back to the elegant ladies in expensive dresses fawning over the men from yesterday.

"Pretty much. Not that I ever really took advantage of it." He inspected a series of containers on the vanity.

"You can stay here during the match if you want. I'm not sure you want to see all that…"

"No. I don't want to take my eyes off you for a second."

He smiled, "how the tables have turned."

A man in a suit knocked and opened the door without being invited in. Warren glared at him. "Boss says I'm to take you to the VIP area," he spoke to me.

"Me?"

"Yeah toots, come on."

Warren took a step in front of me. "She's staying with me."

"Boss said you'd be difficult about it. He also said to tell you he wants you to focus on the match. That she either sits in the ropes or she gets thrown in with the public," the man smirked.

I felt Warren tense in front of me, and he turned. "Go with him," he spoke down to me, "you'll be safer."

"I don't want to leave you," I protested.

"I know," he wrangled a stray curl from in front of my eyes. "It'll be okay. I'll see you after the match."

"Warren…"

He leaned down and kissed me, desperately. I wound my arms up under his jacket, feeling his muscles through his shirt. I hoped if I held him tight enough, maybe he wouldn't make me go. But to my dismay, he pulled back, gave me a few more small kisses on the nose and forehead, then nudged me towards the man in the suit.

I stopped in the doorway and looked back at him. "Kick their asses."

"Yes ma'am," he chuckled.

Holy shit, it was LOUD. The closer we got to the front of the arena the less I could hear my own heart beating. I followed the man out of a curtain on the side of a stage, down a long ramp, to a seemingly ordinary looking wrestling ring. Except for the fact that the two men in there did not resemble *anything* close to ordinary wrestlers. The crowd went nuts as a wolf man grabbed a lizard man, lifted him above his head in a semi circular spin, and threw him roughly on his back, slamming him onto the mat.

He led me through a path in the crowd towards the back right corner of the ring, where a roped off area sat several hoity-toity looking individuals. They scoffed at me as the man nodded to the security guard to allow me in. Then I was on my own.

I looked uncertainly around at the seats before me. Not a single person looked up in greeting, as if they were afraid casting their eyes on me would soil their expensive suits and dresses. I spotted an unoccupied chair on the end of the front row and claimed it. At least I'd be able to see.

"Hi." A voice next to me spoke loudly into my ear above the roar of the crowd.

I turned and looked into the face of a stunning woman with platinum blonde hair and huge diamond earrings. "Hi?"

"First match?" She smiled.

I nodded.

"Oh you're in for a treat. I heard a rumor that Nytemare is back, and in the main event no less."

"Nytemare?"

"He's a veteran, a 12 time champ. He was retired but there have been murmurs of his return for days now."

She had to be talking about Warren. He was right, Paulie had been planning this for a while.

"Oooh." She grimaced with a sadistic smile as the wolf man ripped the lizard man's tail clean off.

I gasped and covered my eyes.

"Don't worry, he'll grow it back. But that's gonna throw off his balance for sure. Which means another ten thousand in my pocket," she smiled.

As she predicted, the wolf man had the lizard man pinned under him. His huge claws dug into his chest, and without his tail, the lizard man had a hard time swiping at the wolf man's legs to get out. He thrashed and wriggled. The wolf man leaned down and said something to him, to which the lizard man seemed to give up, and tapped the mat.

"He's too soft for his own good," the woman next to me scoffed. "He's still a rookie, but he's gonna have to learn there's no place for mercy in the ring."

The wolf man let out an ear piercing howl of victory as a few others assisted the lizard man out of the ring. I noticed people were beginning to get out of their seats around the arena.

"Are you going to order anything?" The woman asked, "I'm a bit thirsty."

"Uh. No," I replied.

She snapped her fingers and a waiter materialized out of thin air to wait at her beck and call. "You sure you don't want anything? Paulie says drinks are on him tonight."

"I guess, I'll just have a soda?" I responded, more for the sake of not standing out being the only one not ordering anything.

The crewmen bustled around the ring, pulling off the mat from the previous match, and unfurling a new one.

They then began setting up four small kennel-like fixtures at each of the four ring posts. Once they were finished, a huge steel cage began to drop from the rafters. I watched in awe as it descended around the ring, encapsulating it and the four smaller cages at each of the corners. *This* was what Warren had to fight in? The set up alone was intimidating enough.

The crowd began to file back into their seats, and the lights dimmed. A tangible anticipation floated around the arena that made the hair on the back of my neck stand. Music suddenly blasted from the stage before me, a melodic sound of a heavenly choir echoed around the arena as a figure shot up into the air. The crowd erupted as she spread her golden wings and lifted her arms. Her sky blue robe flowed behind her as she flew a few circles over the crowd before landing on the floor in front of the menacing cage.

A referee opened the door for her, and she walked in, folding her wings behind her. Her robe fell to the floor and I gasped, she indeed had talons instead of hands. Razor sharp, angular, and perfect for shredding flesh. Her bright blonde hair was pulled back into a high ponytail, and she wore an exaggeratedly sparkly bra. I couldn't help but think if I wore something like that, my girls would fall right out of it.

The crowd's cheers settled to an excited murmur, and a recording of a booming roar accompanied with deep bass music caused a second eruption from the crowd. This one significantly dominated by male voices, but enthusiastic nonetheless. A hulking, monstrous figure of a man emerged from the doorway on stage. His arms were the size of my entire body, and I was not a small girl. My jaw dropped as he came down the ramp towards us, he was massive on stage but the enormity of him couldn't be grasped until he stood inside the ring across from the tiny feathered girl who stared up at him angrily. I gasped, and my neighbor smiled, "he's the odds on favorite to win tonight."

*Not if Warren has anything to say about it.*

Again, the crowd quieted as the lighting in the arena turned blue, and a torrential column of water shot out from the stage floor. A man's body appeared out from the swirling vortex, as an upbeat song heavy with cymbals began. The crowd was significantly louder for him than the other two competitors, and they stood and cheered as he allowed the water to wash him down the ramp gracefully. He took his time waving and winking to several women in the crowd, to their utter delight. When his feet finally touched the ground in front of the stairs, I noticed he wore a massive golden, metal belt around his waist, which he unfastened and held up proudly before he entered the enclosure. The cheering and entrance song for this man continued for a while longer than the others, clearly he was the fan favorite.

The lights in the entire arena went out, and I heard "here he comes" excitedly from my right. A hush fell over the crowd and the air stilled, until a beam of purple light shone center stage. The crowd lost their shit. I had to plug my ears as a slow trickle of fog crawled over the floor of the stage. I could feel the bass of what felt like a hardcore rock song playing but I couldn't even hear it over the screams and cheers of the audience. A dark figure emerged from the shadow and stepped into the light. I gasped as Warren's body stood illuminated in a purple glow.

He wore black tattered jeans, his black boots, and his leather jacket, but nothing else. His tattoos drew all the attention to his naked torso. At a drop in the bass, he looked up over his eyelashes, and his piercing yellow eyes seemed to glow in the dark. He walked slowly down the ramp, passing screaming men and women alike. His eyes focused only on the ring before him. He entered, and the other three competitors stood aside, giving him the center. At a breakdown in the song, he lifted his head back, throwing his hair off his eyes, and lifted his fists in the air. Again, another eruption from the crowd forced me to cover my ears. The whole arena buzzed with electricity. I couldn't help but feel a sense of admiration and pride at the image of him standing in the middle of the ring, arms above his head, and an entire crowd screaming for him. Lurking danger aside, it was honestly kind of hot.

An announcer with a microphone stepped between all the competitors, and they each moved towards a corner.

"Ladies, gentlemen, and beings of all natures, are you ready for our main event?!" He shouted to the cheering of the crowd. "The following cage match is for the championship. Each round the competitors will have one minute to incapacitate their opponents. If one succeeds, the loser will be ejected from the ring. The rounds will continue until there is only one competitor left.

"Now, please allow me to introduce our fighters! To my left, weighing in at a hundred thirty pounds, and joining us for her first title match, Glooory!"

The crowd cheered and applauded for her, as she fluttered her wings and waved.

"To her left, weighing in at an astonishing four hundred five pounds, the big boy himself, Buuuuddy Briiiiimstone!"

Buddy threw his arms up to loud rowdy cheers.

"To my right, returning for the first time in ten long years, a twelve time champion, weighing in at two hundred twelve pounds, Nyyyytemaaaare!"

I found myself smiling at the overwhelming reaction of the crowd.

"And last, defending his title, weighing in at two hundred six pounds, your champion, Lir Suuuurge!"

Lir held the belt up above his head, turning slowly around in the ring beaming.

The referee entered the ring and began commanding the fighters to their assigned cages. Warren took the one facing me on the far right side. My eyes were glued to him, and I wasn't the only one.

"He hasn't aged a day…" The woman on my right commented, "just as handsome as ever."

I fought the urge to snatch her drink from her hands and pour it over her head, and kept my attention on the ring. A series of spotlights shone over each of the four cages, and the crowd hushed again. My heart pounded as the spotlights began to flicker in turn, increasing in speed until they stopped. One on Buddy, the other on Glory. Their cage doors opened, and neither of them wasted a second to explode out of it towards each other.

Buddy charged forward in an attempt to tackle her, but she agilely lifted herself out of reach.

She dive bombed him, talons outstretched, and he swatted her out of the air like a fly. She tucked her wings and rolled gracefully towards the cage wall, before taking flight once more.

He was ready for her this time, as she lifted into the air, he jumped and tackled her to the ground, but not before she sunk her sharp nails into his back, drawing blood.

He let out a hoarse wail and attempted to throw her off, but she pushed off him, fluttering above his head, and throwing him a wide grin.

He swiped at her feet, and she tried to rise further, but the top of the cage was already at her head. She tucked her legs in and latched to the roof like a little golden fly.

Buddy roared, crouched, and leapt with an impressive force, managing to grab a hold of her ponytail. He pulled her down violently, slamming her onto the mat. Her wings splayed out on either side as she groaned in pain.

Buddy saw his opening, and launched himself at her, aiming to stomp her head into the ground. But she rolled aside at the last second, and he barely managed to step on the tip of her wing.

She attempted another take-off, but the damage she sustained to the tip was enough to keep her from getting more than a few feet off the ground.

Now it was Buddy's turn to smile menacingly at her, as he rushed forward, both hands outstretched.

She stood her ground, took a deep breath and released a shrill, crackling screech that caused several audience members behind Buddy to cover their ears.

Buddy screamed and fell to his knees, covering his ears with his massive hands, until she ran out of breath, and the sound stopped.

She nimbly leapt over his hunched body and sunk her talons into the muscles in his back, raking down.

Blood poured from his gaping wounds, and he roared again. He turned to face her with murderous intent, and the buzzer went off.

For a moment neither of them moved, but the referee stepped between them, ushering them back to their little kennels like the animals they were.

As soon as their doors were closed, the lights dimmed again, and the four spotlights shone on the competitors. They flashed, faster and faster… and suddenly stopped.

One on Lir, the other on Warren. My heart leapt to my throat as the cage doors opened.

Lir stepped out first, almost cautiously, while Warren didn't move. He stood in his cell with his eyes closed, then suddenly a smile crept over his lips, his jacket dropped off him, landing in a heap on the floor, and he transformed.

His body melted into what looked like a heap of brown goo, and then reformed into the shape of a person.

This person had no distinguishable characteristics, other than that he dripped with brown sticky liquid. *Oh, shit, he's made of* mud.

Lir's eyes went wide, and though I couldn't hear it, he mouthed the words "no fucking way…" and sent a forceful vortex of water straight at Warren.

Warren split his form in two, letting the water rush between him, to the shock of the crowd behind him who were immediately drenched.

He then melted into a puddle on the floor, and with surprising speed bubbled over to Lir, who panicked and jumped aside.

Lir conjured a torrent of water to rain over Warren's puddle form, beginning to thin and spread him, but Warren reformed into the shape of a person, and shot a rope of mud towards Lir, wrapping around his throat.

Lir gasped and grabbed at the mud, causing his rain to dissipate. His fingers desperately clawing, but unable to grasp anything solid.

Warren slid his form towards Lir, surrounding him in a casing of wet, thick, sludge. It began at his feet, then quickly traveled up his legs, to his torso, and began to encompass his face.

Fear grew in Lir's eyes as he was buried alive, before they flashed with an idea, and wrapped both of them in a bubble of swirling water.

Through the surface I could make out the shape of Warren's form thinning, being stripped off Lir's body, until the swirling water took him, and the bubble turned a dark, murky, brown.

Lir let the bubble drop, splashing muddy water all over the mat.

He stood, panting heavily, and waited. In a few seconds small funnels of mud began rising from all around him, shooting back towards each other as Warren reformed.

In a split second, they both shot a torrent of their respective elements towards each other, meeting in the middle. The splashing of mud and water splattered everyone in the front rows. The buzzer sounded.

Both men dropped their arms, and Warren turned back into himself. His chest rose and fell with effort, and he was dripping wet, but otherwise I exhaled heavily to see him unharmed.

They returned to their cages without the referee's intervention, and once again, the doors closed, and the lights flashed above them.

This time, they stopped on Buddy and Warren. I felt a surge of injustice that he had to fight again while the others got a moment's rest.

Again, Buddy charged out of his open cage towards Warren, who didn't move but for a roll of his shoulders.

Buddy's hands were mere inches from him when to everyone's shock, Warren transformed into a little girl.

Everyone in the audience stood at once, straining to get a look at the tiny thing that stopped that behemoth dead in his tracks.

She stepped out of the cage, and Buddy staggered backwards, absolute terror on his face.

At first glance, I couldn't comprehend how this innocent creature would be remotely dangerous or frightening. Though as she stepped into the light it became apparent that her face was pale except for red spiderwebs of veins that ran around her eyes, which were lifeless, grey, and sallow. Her neck was black and blue, and would move strangely as she walked.

The silence that fell over the crowd was deafening.

"Daddy?" The little girl spoke.

Buddy's mouth opened wide, and he screamed as he tripped over himself stepping back. "No... baby... no..."

"Daddy? Can I have a hug?" She extended her arms out in front of her, pressing the giant man further into the center of the ring.

"I'm sorry, baby... I'm so sorry." He broke down, getting on all fours and covering his head in his arms.

"Don't you love me anymore, Daddy?" She tilted her head and her bones protruded from under her skin.

"Please... Please make it stop... I tap. I tap," Buddy blubbered through his hands.

The referee signaled for the match to end, and Warren transformed back into himself. He looked down at Buddy, shaking, cowering, and began to retreat back to his cage, but he paused and turned his head. "Sorry," he whispered, so only he and Buddy could hear.

Murmuring and hushed chattering filled the area as a few officials helped the seven-foot tall man out of the ring.

The next round pitted Glory against Lir, and they were quite evenly matched, but my focus was on Warren in his cell. He watched intently as the two fought, but I thought I noted a hint of regret in his eyes since his encounter with Buddy that didn't dissipate.

I was drawn out of my thoughts by the shouting of the crowd as Glory shielded herself from a column of water falling from the sky with her wings, and in an instant dove at Lir, hands first, digging her talons into his neck.

Blood spurted from the puncture wounds as they fell to the ground together. The crowd gasped as the water that splashed around them turned pink, then red…

A referee called from the sidelines, asking Lir if he would submit. He gasped for breath as he clutched his throat, while Glory stood over him, turning deathly pale, until he finally nodded to the referee's requests, and they called for the bell.

Medical personnel rushed into the ring and immediately bandaged Lir's neck, staunching the flow of blood enough to get him onto a stretcher and out of the ring.

Glory turned her attention to Warren, who slowly moved his gaze upward from the floor to her. They locked eyes and waited.

The referee ordered Glory to step back towards her corner, and Warren's door opened.

In the blink of an eye he changed. His body elongated and pulled as his skin turned to scales. A massive cobra circled its body around the ring and raised its hooded head up as high as the cage would allow.

Glory took flight with great effort with her badly damaged wing, but she brought herself level with the snake's head. Her eyes showed fear, though her face furrowed with determination.

If she wasn't trying to kill Warren I might have admired her bravery.

She lunged for his eyes, and the snake dodged, striking from behind as fast as she did, his sword-like fangs barely missing her leg.

It tightened in its coil and repositioned itself for another strike, but she was too quick, and slashed across its body, leaving three jagged wounds in between his scales.

I screamed as he recoiled, but he used the momentum to bring his entire body back down on her, slamming her into the mat.

He took the advantage and curled around her body, squeezing tightly as he held her up in the air. But she was able to bring her wings around her body as a barrier, push them outwards, and drop down to the mat once she folded them back in.

The snake unraveled, finding her crouched under him, and she threw herself forward into another screech aimed right at his head.

The snake however did not seem bothered at the shattering sound, and brought his head down quickly in a strike, impaling her in the arm with his fang.

Her face contorted in agony, but she managed to bring her talons on her other hand up, and dug all five of them deep into the snake's neck.

He threw his head back, and she pulled down, revealing pink flesh as she tore his body open.

I shot out of my seat. "WARREN!" I lunged for the barricade and got stopped by Paulie's security.

The snake had Glory constricted in his grasp, the blood dripping down his body saturated the mat, and poised to strike again, but at my shout he looked in my direction.

He paused, let Glory go, and turned back into Warren. Then dropped to all fours as he held his shoulder, reached a shaky hand up, and tapped twice.

The crowd erupted in cheers, screaming Glory's name, the sound drowning out my cries for him.

I watched helplessly as the medical personnel crowded around him, helping him to his feet. They dragged him up the ramp as I pulled away from the guard.

I lost sight of him as I fought my way through the crowd, who were all trying to get towards the ring.

Hoards of bodies crowded around me, and I couldn't see over any of them. I pushed in the opposite direction of everyone else, hoping that eventually I'd get to the end, and I did, but by the time I could see the stage again, Warren was nowhere.

I ran to the curtain I initially came out of, only to be stopped by another guard.

"Let me through! I need to get to Warren!" I flailed as the massive man held me back with one hand. "Please… he's hurt…" I began to panic.

"It's alright. She's with me," a familiar voice called out from behind me. I turned to see the woman I sat next to walking towards us.

The guard looked down at me and dropped his arm.

"Thank you," I gasped at the woman, and ran in the direction of the dressing rooms.

I had to dodge fighters and staff as I scrambled down endless hallways, taking a few wrong turns. My panic caused my sense of direction to disappear entirely. I turned down the correct hallway completely by accident, and finally found his room with the door open.

He lay on the chaise, his naked torso messily wrapped in bandages. He looked up at me when I entered, and smiled weakly.

"Warren…" I felt tears welling up. "Oh my god…" I hurried to his side and sat next to him.

"So, how'd you like it?" He chuckled.

"That was awful," I shook my head. "What did she do to you?" I began inspecting him.

"I'm fine, Babygirl, they patched me up." He tried to reassure me, but the pain in his voice was obvious.

"They did a shit job at it." I huffed back tears as I noticed the bandage on his shoulder wasn't even wrapped around him, just laid on top. "Can you sit up a bit? I want to fix this."

"What? Are you a doctor now?" He grunted with the attempt to pull himself up.

"No. But I know I can do better than *this*," I held up a piece of gauze that wasn't even covering anything.

"You *would* think that," He rolled his eyes with a smile.

"In her defense, the medical staff aren't exactly board certified." The woman from the audience appeared in the doorway.

Warren's face paled. "Chels?"

"Hey," she smiled.

I looked back and forth between them, the situation not occurring to me immediately. But the moment I recognized her name, unadulterated rage roiled inside me towards this woman.

"What are you doing here?" Warren asked in a raspy voice.

"I'm an investor now," she entered the room uninvited. "Didn't you know?"

"No. How would I?"

"I thought maybe Paulie told you, oh well. That was a hell of a match." Her eyes fell on me, "oh, I didn't realize you were acquainted."

Warren looked between her and me. "I didn't realize *you* were acquainted."

"We weren't until tonight, we had the pleasure of sitting next to each other." I recognized her fake, and manipulative smile from Scott's face. "What did you think of his match? It being your first fight and all."

"It was horrible," I replied immediately. "No amount of money is worth watching you get hurt like that —" I turned to Warren.

"Oh well, the industry isn't for everyone." She moved towards the coffee table, and smirked as she picked up a condom from the candy bowl. "I don't mean to be rude, but, could I have a word in private with Warren?" She didn't even look at me.

"No. You cannot," he grimaced as he pulled himself into a sitting position. "If you have something to say, say it and get out."

"Ouch," she smiled. "You're really still holding a grudge? We were so young, we both made mistakes."

"The only mistake I made was trusting you. We weren't that young. You knew what you were doing."

"Well, I see your opinions on extracurricular activities have changed at least. Maybe I'll come back after you two are finished—"

"What do you want, Chelsea?" He spat.

"You did well today Ren. I was very impressed. You haven't missed a beat. I told Paulie that you still had it, and he promised me first dibs if you made it past the second elimination—"

Warren shook his head. "Stop. I'm not interested. I don't care what you and Paulie discussed."

"Come on Renny, don't you remember what a good team we made? I'm much better off now too, I can give you so much more."

"I don't want anything from you. Not anymore."

"You think that, but I know you, and I know what you crave more than anything—"

"You don't know anything about me."

"Oh but I do," she moved towards us. "People don't change *that* much Renny."

I felt him tense next to me, and I turned to him. His eyes were full of hurt and shame. She was bringing things back that he really didn't need to be dealing with. *She's hurt him enough.* "You know what?" I stood and my eyes hardened on hers. "He said no. You can go find another man to use and abuse."

"Mind your business you little groupie," she snapped at me.

"He *is* my business," I took a step towards her. "You gave up the ability to drown him in your manipulation when you broke his heart. You didn't deserve his energy then, and you sure as hell don't deserve it now. He wants you to go, and so do I."

Her eyes flashed with anger. "And who the fuck are *you* to speak for him you little whore?"

"She's my girlfriend," he growled from behind me, "and you can do what she said and walk your cheating ass out of here."

She scoffed, and turned on her heel, muttering something about "fat" and "poor" on her way out as I slammed the door behind her and locked it.

Warren collapsed back into the lounge with a grunt. "I didn't know she was still involved…"

"It doesn't matter anyway," I moved back to him. "Hold still," I continued my unwrapping of his messy bandaging.

He smiled up at me, "thanks."

"Well *someone* has to redress this atrocity—"

"No, I mean, for standing up for me. No one's ever done that before."

"Oh. Yeah. She's a bitch, and you're in no condition to be dealing with her right now, nor should you have to." I slid the first aid kit on the coffee table over to us.

He chuckled, "my hero."

"Whatever," I smiled. "This is going to sting, brace yourself."

He groaned and hissed through his teeth as I washed out his wound with antiseptic. "Mother *fucker*…"

"I warned you." I used a clean cloth to pat it dry as gently as I could, but he still hissed and swore with pain. "Grow a pair, would you?" I teased.

He glared at me. "It fucking hurts okay?

"Yeah yeah, I've had paper cuts worse than this."

He gritted his teeth, "you're asking for it little girl…"

I chuckled at his empty threat. "You're so cute when you're helpless."

He grunted and relaxed a bit as I re-bandaged his shoulder. "Is this punishment for what I said?"

"It should be. Don't think I didn't hear it."

"I was just saying it to shut her up."

"I know. There," I finished with his shoulder. "Better?"

"I mean, it still hurts like a bitch…"

"I'm sure it does. It's pretty bad, but you'll live. Big baby…" I added with a smirk under my breath.

"You know what…" He growled, "keep racking it up. See what happens…"

"Yeah. I'm so scared."

He smiled, "brat."

"Hey, you're the one who declared me your girlfriend, it's not my fault you have bad taste," I smiled back.

He rolled his eyes and lay back as I stood to get him a bottle of water off the vanity. "Here," I opened it, and held it up to his lips, supporting his head with my hand. He took a few sips, and I lay his head back down. "I'm going to go see if they have any painkillers or something for you." I moved to get up, but he took my hand.

"It's too bad we don't feel anything for each other," he looked up at me with soft eyes. "I think I could get used to the idea of calling you 'my girl'."

My heart pounded at the thought as I met his gaze. "Maybe if you weren't such a sarcastic asshole all the time."

His voice lowered as he smiled. "Maybe if you weren't so nosey."

"Maybe if you weren't so stubborn…" I leaned into his touch as he cupped my face in his hand.

He slid his hand down, trailing his fingers down my arm to my waist, and guided me on top of him. "Maybe if you could see how strong you really are…"

I let him move me to straddle his waist. "Maybe if you would acknowledge how sensitive you really are…" My hands ran gently up his cold, bare chest, as I carefully lowered myself onto him.

He slid his hands up my back, winding his fingers through my hair. "Maybe if you could learn to trust a monster like me…" His eyes begged mine.

"Maybe if you could learn to love a broken girl like me…" I whispered, inches from him.

"Maybe I already have." He pulled my head down, pressing my lips against his.

He kissed me as if I were the painkillers he so desperately needed. His tongue parted my mouth in search of mine as his hands ran down the length of my back, sliding sneakily under my top. His cold fingers shocked my skin at the contact, and I inhaled sharply, taking in the scent of sage and cedar wood mixed with his sweat.

I allowed him to explore me. Allowed him to slide his hand into the waistband of my shorts, allowed his weaker arm to grasp at the back of my neck, allowed him to hold me down. I allowed myself to give into him.

My hips gave an impulsive rock forward and he smiled against my lips, pulling back slightly. He released his grip on my neck, and I opened my eyes. He held my head in place, staring.

I blushed, "what?"

"You're so beautiful."

The heat intensified in my face. I suddenly felt very shy, and averted my eyes.

"No," he tipped my chin towards him, "look at me."

I obeyed, even though it caused me to shake slightly with nerves. His golden eyes were hypnotic, softening as the tiny wrinkles creased in the corners. My eyes scanned his perfect, artwork-covered skin, noting a few faint freckles scattered over the bridge of his nose. I put my full weight on his chest as I moved my hand up to his face, tracing its outline gently with the tip of my finger.

He closed his eyes with a pleasant sigh as I followed his angular contours. His hand on my back began tugging at my top in a gentle hint for me to remove it. I froze, and pushed myself up, pulling the edges of my shirt back down as I stared self-consciously at his chest, not daring to look him in the eye.

He lowered his hands and placed them on my legs as he studied my face. He huffed an understanding chuckle. "You never have to be afraid of that with me, Babygirl."

My sight locked into his in surprise.

"Your body is perfect. Every curve, every inch of skin… I find you absolutely irresistible." He slid his thumbs back and forth over my thighs. "But, if you don't want to share it yet. You don't have to. It's okay."

I relaxed my grip on my shirt. "You haven't even seen it, you don't know what it looks like."

"Doesn't matter. I know I'm going to love it, because it's *you*." He smiled up at me, adoration shone in his eyes.

I let go of my shirt and lowered my hands.

He took their place, pulling at the fabric. "May I?" He begged softly.

I nodded, and he slid my shirt up as I helped pull it over my head and tossed it aside. My body trembled.

He hummed as his hands brushed against my sides. "Fuck," he gasped, "your *gorgeous*."

A tear slid out of the corner of my eye.

"No, Babygirl, don't cry…" He smiled and pulled me back down onto him, kissing me softly.

"Shut up, I'm not crying," I mumbled.

He chuckled, "there she is."

I pushed myself back up, and he groaned softly as I accidentally pressed too hard on his left pec. "Oh, sorry," I lifted my hand.

"I'm not sure if you cause me more pain or pleasure," he laughed.

"Which one do you want?" I smirked.

He pushed his hips up, bucking me slightly. "Mmm. A bit of both?" He bit his lip.

My girl pulsated. "I don't want to actually hurt you. You can't even use your arm."

"I don't need it," he traced his fingers up my stomach and in between my breasts. "I just need you to take this damn thing off," he pulled at my bra.

I chuckled and unclasped it with one hand, allowing it to fall onto him.

"God… *damn*," he growled, and grabbed my breasts greedily with both hands. Wincing slightly as it stretched his wound.

I gasped sharply at the coldness of his fingers as they swirled around my nipples, causing them to stiffen. "Fuck, your hands are cold…"

"So warm me up, pretty girl."

I fell back onto him, kissing him feverishly. His muscles tensed and flexed under mine as I ground my hips into his waist. He nudged my face aside with his head, suddenly biting down on my neck. I moaned into his shoulder as the tingling spread over my body. He took the sound as an invitation, biting again, harder. My girl clenched with desire as another moan escaped my lips.

"You make the most delicious sounds…" He whispered against my skin, before nibbling on it again. He moved his lips further down my shoulder, and planted soft kisses on the top of my breasts as I held my body over his. He let himself linger just above my nipple, and I gasped as he flicked it suddenly with his tongue, as if testing my reaction.

Pleased with the results, he took it into his mouth, sucking slightly. His tongue softly grazed it, as he held me between his lips. He took my soft whimpers as a challenge, and brought his free hand up to my other, slightly pinching my nipple between his fingers. My head fell back at his touch as a sound of agonizing pleasure exploded out of me. His lips curved against my skin triumphantly, and he doubled his efforts, hoping for another.

My nails raked against his chest and down his stomach, stopping where I was positioned on him. I needed more. Adjusting my legs, I moved down his body, feeling his hard figure pressing against his jeans as I slid over it. I unfastened his pants and began to pull them down. His member pushed aggressively at his waistband, as if it were dying to escape. My breath caught as I finally allowed it to, standing at full attention between my legs. I gasped at the size.

"Are you okay?" He softly asked at my sounds.

"Yeah… you just… uh." I wasn't sure how to articulate my inexperience with such a well endowed man. "You're much… *bigger* than I'm used to."

He chuckled, "I'm going to try not to let that stroke my ego."

"Oh great," I smiled, "what have I done?"

"You can see *exactly* what you've done…"

My pulse quickened as he twitched under me, dripping with anticipation. I undid my bottoms, sliding them off less than gracefully. We laughed together as I had to assist him with his own, before I repositioned myself on top of him, kissing him passionately.

I stretched to the candy bowl beside us and pulled out a condom.

He grabbed my wrist as I unwrapped it and began sliding it onto him. "Are you sure?"

I nodded with a smile, lifted myself, and pressed his tip against my opening. I gasped as he stretched me, and pulled slightly off him. "Fuck. I don't know if I can take you…"

"Come here," he pulled me down gently, and kissed me. "I'm not in any hurry," he smiled, and nudged my nose with his.

My body relaxed as we kissed. I let myself succumb to his gentle touches of my skin, his nibbles on my lips, the sounds of his moans and gasps as I bit him back. My hips instinctively began to rock against him once more, and slowly, his tip pressed back into me.

"Don't think, Babygirl," he whispered against me, drawing my eyes. "Just focus on this… focus on us. Focus on our skin touching. On the sexy fucking sounds you make for me. On how it makes you feel when I bite you…" He led by example. "How wet you are for me… and how hard I am for you…"

I slid onto him, letting him open me completely. I opened my mouth to scream in pleasure, but the sound caught in my throat.

"*That's* my girl," he moaned. "*Fuck.* You good fucking girl…"

I couldn't get him any further in, our height difference forcing me to choose between his lips and his cock. Right now, the decision wasn't difficult. I pushed up, letting him sink deep inside me.

"*Fuck.*" We both moaned simultaneously, and quietly laughed.

He held my hips, digging his fingers into my skin as I rode him slowly, staring down at him. I let my hands trace over his tattoos, taking notice of each design, each color. His muscles rippled under my touch as I ran my fingers over his curves, goosebumps broke across his skin.

He bent his knees, bringing them up against my back, and changing the angle that he hit inside me. I immediately felt myself tighten around him as his head pressed on an extremely sensitive area.

"Look at me," he growled with the depth of his demand.

I didn't realize my eyes were closed. I had a hard time focusing, but I met his gaze nonetheless.

"Do you know how fucking good you feel? Do you know how many nights I've dreamed about being this deep inside you? How it feels to have your warm, wet pussy wrapped around me as I fill every fucking inch of you? How it feels to sense your pulse quickening, your heart pounding as you ride your orgasm out on me?"

The pressure built inside me as we hit a rhythm.

"Breathe with me, Babygirl." He kept the tempo as I followed his breaths, in... and out...

"Focus on that warmth spreading..." He grunted with the effort of forming a sentence, "on that sensation of my cock hitting that spot..."

My breath shortened.

"That's it... feel your clit rub against me..." He panted, "cum for me..."

Fuck that did it. I screamed his name as I let him pull it out of me. Waves upon waves of ecstasy crashed over me, and amidst it all, he threw his head back in an equally emphatic moan as he pulled my hips down, pushing into me as deep as he could. We rode the tide together as I rocked a few more times against him, before his facial expression betrayed how sensitive he was.


I lay on him, letting him slide out of me, and we laughed. He wrapped his arms around me, holding me tightly against his chest, and kissed the top of my head as our chests rose and fell together.

"Fuck…" He panted with a smile, "I don't think I've ever come that hard in my life…"

I sighed giddily, and lay my head down on him as I traced one of his tattoos with my fingers. "I thought we agreed 'no feelings'."

"My bad," he murmured into my hair, then chuckled.


His arms tightened around me when someone knocked. "What?" He snapped, turning his head towards the door.

"Boss wants to see you," an unfamiliar voice responded.

"In a minute."

The footsteps faded as they moved down the hall. He grunted and lay back down. "We did our part, now he owes us some answers." He gave me a smack on my bare behind, "c'mon."

"Ow," I smiled and reluctantly rolled off him, sitting on the side of the chaise.

"There's some wet wipes on the vanity," he groaned with extreme effort as he lifted his body. "I don't want you getting an infection."

I hummed a chuckle at his knowledge of female anatomy, and turned to comment on it, but my attention was diverted by a set of three long scratches down his back. I softly touched the swollen skin around them, and he tensed and hissed. "Why didn't you tell me she got in you in the back too? I would have dressed them—"

"That's why I didn't say anything."

"They're not as bad as the ones on your shoulder. Let me clean them at least." I stood and went around to the first aid kit, grabbed the antibiotic ointment, and sat behind him. "Be a brave boy for me," I cooed through a smile.

"Very funny," he chuckled.

# Fourteen

Several people congratulated Warren as we made our way out of the locker room area. Younger fighters kept stopping to ask him for advice, and several groups of women eyed me angrily as he guided me back out to the hotel floor with his hand on the small of my back. This time, he seemed to be in no rush as we made our way across the crowded lobby, letting me stop and inspect some of the more interesting looking games. He would not, however, let me play any of them. "We've gambled enough today, Babygirl."

A group of people approached us purposefully as we neared the elevators. The only people who would recognize him were from the fights, so I assumed they were fans of his.

"Hey, Nytemare." A balding, harry-armed man stepped forward, and we stopped. Warren didn't respond, but his hand hardened against my back when he met the man's eyes.

"You cheated," the man spat. "Buddy had that match. He should be our new champ, not some rookie, flighty broad."

"He didn't cheat!" I stepped in front of Warren. "If your guy has skeletons in his closet, that's on him."

The man glowered at me, and he flicked a forked tongue in my direction before turning to Warren. "You let your valet speak for you? Pathetic."

Warren moved next to me. "I don't tell her when or how to speak, she can do what she wants, and she's right, Buddy's going to have to get used to losing as much as he does winning in this industry." He turned to walk away.

"You didn't even belong in this match, your time's passed you fucking *monster!*" The man shouted.

My pupils dilated. "Fuck you, asshole!" I strode towards him. "Your fat ass can't even walk ten steps without getting winded and you have the balls to tell him he doesn't belong in a match? Go back to your trailer park and fuck the anger out on your blow up doll!"

"You better watch your mouth you little bitch! You have no idea what I'm capable of!" He raised his hand, and Warren flew to my side inhumanly fast, grabbed the man's wrist, and changed.

Shadow swirled around him as darkness encompassed everything in our vicinity. The games went dark, the lights went out, and people screamed as a black mass with red eyes stood in Warren's place.

*"And you have no idea what* I'm *capable of!"* A booming, gravely voice seemed to come from all directions at once. *"You think your man had it rough in there? That's nothing compared to what I'll do to you for raising a hand to my girl!"*

The man shook with his arm still in Warren's shadowy grasp, a wet spot formed on his torn denim pants. "I'm... I'm sorry... I didn't mean..."

*"You're not fucking sorry. You're just scared shitless."* Warren's form grew, everything around fell pitch black. *"But I'm about to make you realize what it means to be truly sorry..."*

"Oh my fucking god... No! Please! Not again!" The man crumpled in front of us, crying.

As much as I enjoyed watching this guy piss himself, he had learned his lesson, and Warren didn't need more blood on his conscience. I placed my hand on the swirling void holding the man's arm and it went numb. Touching pure shadow was like going into a sensory deprivation chamber, all feeling, all sensation had been sucked from my arm. Warren turned his dark, featureless face towards me.

I reached up, not needing to see his details to know where to put my hands, grabbed his face, and pulled it down towards me. I kissed him, and with my eyes closed the tingle of the numbness gave way to the feeling of his cool soft lips. I didn't feel the shadow creature, I just felt him. His arms wrapped around me, giving into my touch, and when I opened my eyes, he was himself again, and the darkness in the room had disappeared.

"He's not worth it," I whispered. "We have work to do."

The man sat on the floor, still cowering, but we ignored him. Warren smiled, took my hand, and let me into the elevator.

The doors shut, and his eyes glittered down at me. "You weren't afraid." It wasn't a question.

"Of course not. It was just you," I smiled up at him.

He kissed me again, uncaring of the security guard standing a foot from us.

"I heard you insulted one of our biggest benefactors." Paulie stood facing away from us, looking into the fire. "Nyte, you know better than that."

"In our defense, you neglected to mention she was a benefactor. Which I *know* you understood the significance of." Warren placed his hand on my lap in an obvious show of possession that forced me to fight the rising blush in my face.

"My divulging any information regarding relationships from your past was not part of our discussion, if I recall correctly." Paulie turned to him, smiling.

"No, it wasn't, and barring further insults I hope we can fulfill our agreement so we can get home." Warren didn't take his eyes off Paulie.

"So political. You would have been a great apprentice kid, I really hate you for not sticking around—"

"Paulie, the information we are owed, please."

Paulie fell silent, and for a moment I thought he was going to make Warren jump through more hoops. I tensed, ready to argue, but Warren squeezed my leg in a silent request for patience.

"A long time ago, before the fights were what they are now, there was a man with a reputation for his viciousness in the ring. He was not overly agile, strong, or intelligent, but his ability to disconnect from the other fighters as people, *that's* where he held the upper hand." Paulie folded his hands behind his back. "Other fighters naturally hesitate when they injure another, even for a second. It's our nature to do so when we see another of our kind in distress. We want to show sympathy. But not him, once he drew blood... well, let's say we had to keep a sedative on hand. I was only running security then, but I'll never forget those eyes."

I held my breath.

"What was his name?" Warren asked.

"Connor Borges."

A heaviness settled in the room at the name, and I began finding it difficult to take any air into my lungs. My heart began racing, and the enormous room shrunk around me.

"Thanks." Warren stood and took my hand to guide me up.

"If you need any other favors, kid, you know how to find me," Paulie winked.

Warren placed his hand on my lower back, guiding me towards the doors. "I know. It's alright," he whispered to me, "we're leaving."

If it wasn't for his hand, I wouldn't have been able to maneuver the overstimulating lights and sounds as we moved through the hotel, checked out, and exited towards the parking garage. Everything swirled around me as I fought for each breath. *Why… Why was this happening? You're safe, you're with Warren.* I repeated over and over, but it wasn't doing anything to quell the panic ripping out of my chest.

He didn't move his hand away until we were at his truck and he opened the door for me. The moment I was inside and he closed the door, I began shaking.

He got in, started the truck, and put his hand back on my leg. "Breathe, Babygirl, just breathe."

I had to make a conscious effort to obey. I closed my eyes and counted to myself. *In… one, two, three… out… one, two, three…* I felt the lighting change on my eyelids. We were out of the parking garage and moving, and I was able to take in a solid breath.

"Good," he rubbed my leg, "good girl."

"Thank you," I whispered as I opened my eyes.

"You fought that all on your own," he smiled.

"I'm not sure why that hit me so hard."

"Probably because you can finally connect the face to a name. I'd be surprised if anything related to him didn't trigger you." He glanced at the back seat quickly. "There's a water bottle in my backpack."

I looked behind me, and pulled his bag onto my lap, digging through it I found a full bottle, opened it, and handed it to him.

"Not for me, for you," he chuckled.

"I'm not thirsty?"

"You haven't had anything to drink, and we did quite a lot of exercise today. Drink some water," he softly demanded.

I was going to argue, but he had a point. I drank, and when I started, I didn't stop. I almost finished the entire thing. *I was thirsty after all.*

He patted my leg in approval.


We had only been on the road for an hour before the desert sunset began its nightly art session. We stopped by a drive through coffee shop since Warren had already begun to yawn. He wouldn't acknowledge it, but I noticed his shoulder also bothered him. He kept changing positions, stretching, attempting to roll his neck, but everything seemed to hurt. I dared to offer to drive for a while, to which he gave a firm "hell no" as if I had asked to harvest his kidney. I attempted then to keep him awake by dissecting what we knew now about Mr. Borges.

"So he's a mutant, with a heightened sense of smell, who can turn his fingernails into spears…"

"Not to mention a complete dissociation to the rest of humanity," he added. "Being in his head, god that was a trip."

"Right. He normally goes after sex workers, why?"

He shrugged, "easy targets? That's my best guess."

"Do they have the same pimps? Or work in the same circles?"

"No, that's the first avenue I went down. I asked all of Jenna's co-workers if they knew anything. Other than their line of work, and their gender, they have nothing in common."

I stared down at my lap in thought. "How the hell is he selecting his victims? Could it really just be random?"

"Sometimes it is. A lot of serial killers work off opportunity, they just lay in wait, hoping their prey falls into their lap." He yawned.

"Are you gonna make it all the way home? After the day you've had—"

"I'll be fine. " He cleared his throat and drank a long swig of coffee. "Just keep talking to me."

"Okay…" I glanced at him suspiciously. "What are the cities he's hit again?" I pulled out my phone, and as he listed off the names, I typed them into the search on the map app. "Even his travel seems to be fucking random."

"He's hit a few places twice, but never in a row," he noted. "I keep waiting for him to go back to the ones he's only been to once."

"There has to be a better way than to wait for another victim. With what we know, can't we get ahead of him? Isn't a name and a witness enough to arrest him?"

"We need evidence connecting him to the murders and the rapes. Even if you identified him in a lineup, they have nothing to hold him past questioning." He slowed as we began our ascent into the mountains.

"That's so infuriating. We know he did it," I grunted.

"Well, we still have to make sure this guy is the same one you saw. Paulie's got good intel but there's always a chance he gave us the wrong name."

I held the handle above my door as we took a sharp curve. I began to feel uneasy about being on this road in the dark. Aside from what our high beams illuminated, there was no way to see what was coming around a corner.

"Don't worry, I've taken this route hundreds of times." He responded to my fear without taking his eyes off the road.

"And how many times of those was hours after a rough fight, where you lost blood, and then fucked a groupie?"

He chuckled, "are you demoting yourself?"

"I'm just making a point. How do we make sure it's the same guy then?"

"That part's easy. Do a quick run on his name, if you can identify him by his photo under a different name, then I can at least try to get him arrested on fraud. Get him off the streets."

I tensed as he took another sharp curve.

He sighed, "Adelaide, we'll be— *Shit!*"


My stomach lurched as we swerved hard to the right. Everything in the truck tumbled and rolled as he violently found a turnoff on the side, bumping and jostling us as we went over rough terrain, narrowly missing being plowed over by a small box truck that barreled towards us. It took up the entire two lane road as it rounded the curve ahead of us with disregard, nearly running us into the mountainside.


"WHAT THE FUCK?!" He slammed on his brakes, the screeching echoed in the mountains. He whipped around to me as soon as the truck stopped. "Are you okay?"

"Yeah… Yeah." I was a ball of nerves, but alive. "What the fuck was that?"

"That asshole nearly took us out, he was all over the road! What the fuck is a delivery truck doing up here at this hour anyway?!"

I was a bit relieved to see he was as shaken as I was.

"*Shit...*" He scrunched his face in pain as his hand reached up to his shoulder.

"Are *you* okay?" I turned my body in the seat and leaned in to check his arm.

"I'm fine. I just pulled it in a weird way." His jaw clenched.

"That's it. We're done." I unbuckled my seatbelt.

"What?"

"You're done driving for tonight. We'll sleep here for a few hours, and pick up again in the daylight."

"I told you I'm fine, I can make it." He rubbed his arm.

"I don't give a shit what you told me." I reached over him and turned off the ignition, then took the keys out. "*I'm* telling you we're done."

"Give me the keys, Adelaide..." His voice deepened in an attempt to intimidate me.

I shoved them down my shirt between my breasts. "Make me."

"You just watched me kick three other mutant's asses... you sure you want to challenge me?"

"Two," I folded my arms. "If I recall, the woman kicked *your* ass."

Even in the dark I could tell his pupils contracted as he watched me. He *really* hating being told what to do, and I found it kind of fun to rile him.

He snorted angrily and flung the door open, stomping out of the truck like a toddler. He opened the back door, threw all the bags onto the ground outside, and fiddled with the seat until it unfolded, forming a small, flat bed. Everything he did, he did defiantly. He chucked the bags back under the seat, unrolled his sleeping bag over the top with angry grumbling, crawled back into the truck huffing dramatically, and kicked off his boots before slamming the door closed behind him.

"Well?" He grunted, reclining on his good arm behind me.

"Well?"

"Aren't you coming back here?"

I rolled my eyes and crawled ungracefully into the back, kicking off my shoes before sliding into the sleeping bag next to him. We barely fit. He had to prop himself up against the door to allow his legs to stretch out in front of him, and I was all but on top of him.

"Are you going to give me the keys now?"

"No. You'll get them back in the morning."

"You know I can just reach in and take them…"

"Try it."

I lay on his good arm, and he winced as he attempted to reach across and down my shirt with his bad one, but he couldn't get the angle he needed.

"You're fucked up. Taking advantage of an injured man."

"Cry me a river and drown in it."

He bursted laughter, "so mean."

I smiled triumphantly, "are you finished pouting then?"

He glared at me with a spark in his eyes. "Are you done being a pain in my ass?"

"I'll never be done with that," I returned his glare.

"Mmm…" He traced his fingers down my side. "I'll ask you again once I have you screaming my name…"

Heat rushed to my girl, "is that a threat?"

"You're damn right it is." He pulled me into him with a passionate kiss, biting my lip, and sending shockwaves down my body. I gasped as he flipped me over with his good

237

arm, tearing the sleeping bag open with a loud rip, and pressed my chest against the seat. The keys dug into my breasts. In retrospect, boobs weren't a good hiding place for sharp objects.

"You have *way* too much lip for such a tiny thing…" He growled into my ear, wrapped his arm around my hips, pulling them up as he reached around me, and pulled the keys out of my shirt, tossing them into the front seat.

"Don't think just because you got them, means we're going anywhere…" I breathed shallowly.

He chuckled, "oh no, Babygirl. You're not going *anywhere* until I fuck this attitude out of you." He leaned back on his knees and smacked my ass.

I let out a quiet whimper as he pulled down my shorts and panties.

His teeth came down on my bare cheek as he bit. "Fuck… your sexy sounds turn me on…" He kissed where his teeth marks indented into my skin, and trailed his lips down to my thigh.

I was dripping for him already, and he saw it when he pulled me apart to run his finger from my clit to my opening. "Mmm… My girl knew she needed to be punished." His warm breath puffed between my legs and I shook with anticipation. "Don't fucking move," he demanded before plunging his tongue into my folds.

I whimpered a moan, resisting the urge to push against him as he flicked and lapped at my clit. His lips curved and he sucked me into his mouth, swirling the tip of his tongue around me. My legs shook with the strain of holding still, and I made the mistake of grinding slightly into his mouth.

He pulled away. "Nu huh…" He purred.
"*Fuck.* Warren… please…" I begged.
"Are you going to listen like a good girl?"

"Yes. Fuck… *yes*." I gasped as he pressed back into me, pushing his tongue into my hole.

"Fuck… you taste so fucking good…" His voice vibrated against me, making me spasm and gasp.

He sucked my clit back between his lips, using his tongue to play with me. The pressure built behind it as my heart rate rose. I knew he felt it, because he didn't stop, didn't alter his motions, letting my orgasm bubble to the surface.

"Fuck… Warren… you're going to make me… *FUCK*!" I screamed as I came on his tongue, and he continued to play through it.

He chuckled as my legs shook, and he sat back for a moment.

I began to let them fall.

"No no, we're not finished yet," he pulled me back up by my hips. "I promised to fuck that attitude from you remember?"

"Ohmygod…" I gasped. "I don't know if I can…" I sucked a breath as I felt him plow into me. "FUCK." I turned my head as far as I could, "please, tell me you put on —"

He smiled down at me, "of course. Now you're going to take me, you bad girl."

I moaned as he slowly slid out, then back in, letting me feel every fucking inch of his magnificent self. I had never felt more full in my life…

He groaned above me, "goddammit… you're so fucking tight…" He kept his pace controlled, steady, and gentle, though I wasn't sure if it was more for his benefit, or mine. His hands gripped my hips as he guided me. "Fuck, Babygirl… you take me so well… Such a good girl…"

His head found my spot, and I tightened around him as he massaged against it with each thrust. "*Ohgod…*" I gasped as I felt him push another eruption towards the surface.

"I know, Baby. I feel you…" He purred. "Do you want to cum for me again?"

"Mmhmm," I couldn't fucking speak.

"Ask nicely."

"Fuck… please," I gasped.

"Please… what?" He grunted, as his breaths shallowed as well.

"Please… Daddy…. let me cum…"

"With me then Babygirl…" He reached around me, and swirled his finger around my clit, "cum with me… *oh fuck.*"

His fingers pulled it out of me once more, I screamed his name into the seat while he thrust hard against me in his own release.

My legs shook uncontrollably, we were both beaded in sweat and the windows were completely fogged over as he lay next to me, and pulled me on top of him.

"If you could do that the whole time why didn't you just take your keys?" I laughed as I caught my breath.

"Because I like this smart mouth of yours," he purred with a smile. "I wanted to see how much trouble you could get yourself into."

I giggled and adjusted myself on him, but fussed with my uncomfortable bra. "Hold on," I sat up, unhooked it from under my shirt, and pulled it off.

"How do you do that?" He stared at me, his eyes resembling small moons in the darkness.

"What? Take off my bra?"

"Well, yeah, but under your shirt like that. When you did it at the hotel pool that night I was really… intrigued."

"Really?" I laughed, "it's not that impressive, a lot of women can do it— wait. *You were watching?!*"

He laughed, "I couldn't resist, you sexy little thing." He bucked under me playfully, "and just because it's not unique doesn't mean it's not impressive."

Again, he drove me to shyness, and I hid my face in his neck. I wouldn't consider anything I could do 'impressive'. Rory, now she's an impressive woman. A successful attorney, a healthy love life, she owns her own home... While I rented a small apartment, in a rough neighborhood, worked a dead end job for a shitty boss... I'm not exactly a catch. A broken girl just trying to catch the pieces of her shattered life with a net shredded with holes. How anyone could learn to... I suddenly remembered his words.

"Did... you mean what you said? In the dressing room?"

"Babygirl, I said a lot of things," he chuckled.

"About... learning to... uh... about me being broken..."

He pulled back slightly to look at me, "yes."

I felt guilty. Guilty that I didn't say it back. Guilty that I wasn't sure I felt the same way. I couldn't fight that I cared about Warren anymore, obviously this asshole had a hold on me, but the "L" word? I couldn't even bring myself to think the word let alone feel it. It makes me too vulnerable, too susceptible to blindness.

"It's okay," he smiled knowingly. "I'm the one who broke our deal. Funny thing about feeling this way, it's not conditional on reciprocation."

"I do... you know... give a shit about you..." I felt the need to explain.

He chuckled again. "Good to know." He shifted down slightly so his head lay against the door, which forced me to also move down in the seat. One benefit of being short, I could lay out fully and still have room if I wanted. He held me tightly against him once more.

"Mmm. So warm…" He muttered sleepily.

How he could be so blasé about his unrequited feelings I couldn't fathom while I was conflicted with guilt, defiance, and if I was honest with myself, jealousy. I remembered what it felt like when you first fell for someone. Those butterflies when they looked at you. The warmth that spread over you at their touch. The driving desire to be with them day and night. The honeymoon phase, they call it. Because after that it all goes downhill, and I won't fall off that cliff again. But he… he was willing to. For me.

"Warren?"

His breaths were deep and slow as his exhales brushed my forehead, and his body lay completely relaxed under mine. A butterfly escaped its enclosure and fluttered into my chest. I lay my head on him, and closed my eyes.

A damp cold bit my nose and cheeks as I pried my eyes open, we were surrounded by grey. The windows were coated in condensation, and seemed to melt against the fog pressing in from the outside. Warren had me pulled tightly against his chest, his legs bent and intertwined with mine. It was like spooning with a goddamn snowman. Poor guy, if I was cold I could only imagine how he felt.

I rolled over to face him, his nose and cheeks were pink with chill. I scooted up slightly, and pulled his face down into my chest, trying to give it some warmth. He sighed softly and nuzzled in between my breasts, his icy skin stinging mine through my shirt. I cradled his head in my arms while my fingers played with his hair, making sure to keep his ears covered. It was my idea to sleep here, and it never occurred to me how cold it would be this high up. His breaths puffed into my chest, and his face slowly began to thaw. These big girls were good for something after all.

He wormed his hands around my waist, his fingers just as cold as the rest of him. I suppressed a yelp as he slid them up my back under my shirt. I tried to fall back asleep, but it was too cold and too bright, plus I became aware of his lips planting soft kisses between my breasts.

"You're supposed to be asleep," I muttered with a smile.

"Not with these in my face." His voice muffled from inside the sleeping bag. He bit at my top and pulled the fabric with his teeth.

"Hey," I giggled. "You're going to rip it."

"Good." He bit again.

"Oh my god, I like this shirt. Here…" I shimmied out of it, and pulled it over my head. "Fuck, you're insatiable…"

An evil chuckle came from below me. "My plan worked." He continued kissing them softly, covering me in goosebumps.

"You know this was just me feeling sorry for you." I fought a gasp as his teeth brushed my nipple. "You were cold…"

"I'm still cold," his breath tickled my sensitive skin and his fingers grasped my back.

I yelped. "No kidding, your hands are ice."

"I can remedy that…" He slid them down, grabbing my ass before I had a chance to protest.

"Fuck! Warren!" I gasped. "That isn't your personal hot water bottle."

"No? How about this?" His fingers slid around between my legs.

I convulsed at the strange pleasure of his freezing touch against my clit.

"Mmm. Much better." He used a single finger to gently rub back and forth.

"*Fuck...*" I exhaled as my legs parted for him of their own accord.

He didn't say a word, keeping his mouth busy with my breasts as he alternated his fingers when one would thaw. Each time his biting touch caused me to spasm and gasp, though none more so than when he slid his fingers inside me without warning.

"Oh god... Warren..." I moaned as he curled his finger.

"So fucking *hot*..." He mumbled, taking one of my nipples between his teeth.

His thumb slid up to my clit, while he drove his fingers inside me. Cold... so fucking cold... but it felt so good...

"Mmm... the more I play with you, the warmer you get for me... my little heater...."

"I'm so fucking close already..." I panted, "fuck..."

He pulled out of me.

"What?! No..." I threw back the cover of the sleeping bag. "Why..."

He blinked up at me with an absolutely devilish grin. "I warned you, you were racking up the points."

"You've gotta be kidding me..." I tried to push myself against his hand, but he slid it completely out from between my legs. "I thought you punished me last night..."

He chuckled and kissed my breasts, "last night was for last night. This is for you playing mean nurse."

"Fine. I'll do it myself..." I adjusted myself and slid my hand down into the sleeping bag.

"Oh no," his eyes flashed. "No you fucking don't," he grabbed my wrist and pinned it behind my back. "For that, you're grounded, Babygirl."

"What the fuck is this? You don't get to tell me what to do—"

"No? If you want this…" He slid his fingers lightly up my clit, and my head flew back as my eyes rolled, "you behave, and wait. Do you understand me?"

I was dumbfounded. Was his touch actually worth this torture? *Yes. Oh my god, yes…* my internal voice screamed.

"Say it," he growled.

"Yes."

"Yes what?"

"Yes, Daddy?"

He grinned, "good girl."

My girl throbbed at the praise. What was happening to me?

# Fifteen

I could *not* sit still. I kept crossing and uncrossing my legs in an attempt to draw his attention to them, because he just sat there, actively *ignoring* me as we continued our drive home. I knew he was paying attention, because he drummed his fingers on the steering wheel when my knee was close enough to touch, as if fighting the urge, but then he'd just smile to himself, shift his arm onto the door, and lean his head against his hand. And then… *then* that asshole smiled while he played with his hair. He fucking knew what he was doing…

I huffed, crossed my arms, and turned my body towards the window.

He chuckled. "What's the matter, Baby?"

I ignored him. Two could play at this.

"Aww. Does my Babygirl want attention?"

I scolded my girl for pulsing at his words. *We're taking a stand lady. Have a little self-restraint.*

"Okay. Okay," he laughed. "You've been punished enough. Stop pouting. It's too fucking cute, I can't stand it."

I gave him a side eye, fighting a smile.

"Wanna pick the music?" He held his phone up.

I did. We had been driving in silence since we left our parking spot this morning, and I had nothing to distract me from the burning desire I still felt. All part of his master plan, I'm sure. I nodded.

He smiled and unlocked it, then handed it to me. I tried to get the phone to connect to his stereo but there was absolutely no service up this high. "Ugh," I groaned.

"What?"

"No signal."

"See if you can get a station on the radio then?"

I flicked the input to FM, static… static… oh. Voices.

*"Police are baffled at the lack of evidence found at the scene…"*

"News. Boring." I tapped the scan button.

"Wait." His tone hardened. "Change it back."

*"…the gruesome condition in which her body was found. This marks the thirteenth murder for The Coastal Carver, who apparently has now left the coast for our bright little city in the desert."*

I gasped and looked up at Warren. "You don't think that's…"

"I do." His face tightened. "We need to get somewhere we can get signal."


A few miles out we saw a sign for a small town, and he took the exit. This place looked like something out of a travel ad for gold mining country. One main street with a few open businesses, no cars, few people, and one stoplight right in the middle, serving a seemingly useless purpose. We parked in front of the general store, and both pulled out our phones.

"I have a few bars," he noted. "I'm going to step out and make a call."

I nodded, and glanced back down at my screen once the door closed behind him. I, too, had service, and I opened my browser, searching for any articles relating to the most recent killing. As we suspected, another sex worker had been killed mere blocks from the hotel we were staying in the night before last. The same manner of torture and mutilation was used on her as the other 12. Fuck, I led him right to her…

Warren opened the door, and saw my face. "What's wrong?"

"He was hunting *me*… He followed me and this girl was killed because of me… *again*."

"You don't know that—"

"Seriously? Warren. What are the odds he was down the street from where we just were? For the first time in 13, no, 14, murders he left the state. *We* know he killed Mrs. T. And why? Because I did. I brought him there." I covered my face with my hands and broke down.

He slid across the seat to me and took me in his arms. "You're not doing this, he is. Babygirl, you can't blame yourself for the actions of other people."

"I… can't…" I sniffed.

"You can't what?"

"I can't do this to anyone else." Determination swole within me and I sat up straight as a horrible idea crossed my mind. "If he wants me, he can come get me."

"What?!"

"He's proven that he's going to keep tracking me, follow me wherever I go. And where are we going now? Home? No. I'm not bringing him anywhere near Rory," I choked. "The best thing I can do is lure him away from the public."

"What are you even talking about? The plan is to identify him and get him in police custody—"

"That's not going to work, not fast enough," I shook my head. "By the time we can prove anything he'll have claimed another victim, probably someone near me, because we're not tracking *him* anymore, he's tracking *me*. So use me! Your original plan, use me as bait to lure him to us, then… then you can do what you need to to stop him."

He sat back and stared at me, mouth agape. "You are out of your goddamn mind. I'm taking you home, *and* putting you under fucking house arrest after this."

"Why?! Why is it such a crazy idea when I agree to it, but it was completely solid when it was all yours?"

"It *was* a terrible idea when I came up with it!" He raised his voice. "I never said it wasn't! I was a piece of shit for even thinking it, and I'll never forgive myself! I will *never* do anything to put you in harm's way ever again, do you hear me? We're going back, we'll go to the cops with the information we have, we'll get you extra security—"

I pulled away from him and flung myself out the door, storming to the sidewalk, and folded my arms. "I'm not going."

He slid across the seat and stood in front of the open door, his gilded eyes piercing mine. "Adelaide, get in the truck."

"No! I'm not going anywhere near Rory, or any other cities where he can find a potential victim. I'll hike into the fucking woods if I have to. As a matter of fact…" I glanced over my shoulder at the general store and burst into it, the bell ringing angrily as I swung the door open. I took a moment to look around. It was small but the aisles were packed full of random assortments. I caught eyes with the cashier. "Camping supplies," I demanded, and he pointed fearfully towards an aisle near the back of the store.

The bell rang behind me, followed by heavy boot-falls.

"Adelaide…"

I marched towards the back aisle, and began pulling whatever seemed like something I would need to survive in the woods for a few days, and a few things I thought might come in handy for potentially killing a man. The clerk behind the counter watched us wide-eyed as Warren chased me around the store, and I frantically collected what probably appeared to be a DIY kit for murder.

"Will you please stop?" Warren rounded the corner.

"If you're not going to help me, I'll do it myself. Even better, I'll get him alone… then…"

"Then what? You're going to kill him?" Warren shouted louder than he should have as he followed me up and down the store. "Do you realize how insane you sound?"

"Better insane than—" I dropped a flashlight from my pile and it rolled towards him.

He bent down, picked it up, then walked over to me, holding it out for me to take. "Scared?"

I froze. He was right, I was scared. Fucking terrified. Terrified he'd find me, terrified he'd find Rory, terrified to venture into the woods alone to lure a rapist serial killer away from other women. But I had to do *something*. "I'm not going back." I looked him dead in the eyes, "not until he's behind bars or… or…"

"Alright. Alright…" He sighed and shook his head. "Let me think." He looked over towards the clerk, who had backed away from the register nervously. "I'll go find out where we can stay up here. I'm not letting you venture into the woods alone. In the meantime, will you please put that stuff back? I don't even know why you'd need a… what is this anyway?" He picked up what looked like a folded chain mail handkerchief.

"I don't know," I admitted. "It looked rugged."

"Huh," he read the tag. "It's a cast iron scrubber. I might actually need this," he smiled.

"See, I know what I'm doing," I held my head up.

He chuckled, "I'll be right back," and went to the register.

"I really would have ended up dying in the wild. I have no idea what the fuck I was grabbing." I muttered to myself as I put back a collapsible salt and pepper shaker set. Warren returned from talking to the poor cashier, who definitely was still expecting to be killed by one of us.

"There's a cabin up the way that's vacant. He's calling the owners to see if they'd rent to us for the week." He grabbed a few things I had dropped and put them back on the shelves. "I still don't like this 'isolation in the woods' idea."

"It's the safest thing for everyone else."

"I'm only concerned with *your* safety."

"Well it's a good thing you're coming with me then."

He sighed.

"Sir?" The clerk called to Warren.

"We're not finished discussing this." He went back to the counter, and returned a few minutes later with a set of keys.

The entire road up to this cabin wound incessantly, until we thankfully rounded the last curve to the sight of a small log house amidst the trees. I wanted isolation, I got isolation. There were no neighbors, no cross-roads, and we didn't pass a single other vehicle on the way in. We parked, and I hopped out. Out here, Borges would have to choose between me or continuing his usual killings. Either I was safe, or the other women were, there was no way to have both.

I carried the bags of clothes and groceries into the cabin, while Warren went around the back to flip on the breaker. After setting everything down I went about opening the windows to clear the mustiness. It was sparsely furnished with a table, refrigerator, and oven in the kitchen. The living room had one sofa facing a wood burning stove, and a coffee table. The bathroom had a toilet, sink and standing shower, and the bedroom was small with a queen size bed, a dresser, and nightstand, though the mattress had no sheets.

"We should be good," Warren entered. "Try turning something on?"

I flicked the bathroom light on, and thank god it worked.

"Thank you for doing this," I walked towards him.

"You didn't give me much of a choice. Short of kidnapping you and dragging you home."

"I know. I'm sorry. But you know I'm right. If I went back home, I'd be putting every woman in the city in danger."

"Not every woman, he has a specific target." He shut the door behind him.

"Well, there aren't any sex workers up here."

"But *you're* up here. You literally put yourself in the perfect situation to be murdered. No one would know," he crossed his arms.

"You would."

"You were about to come out here on your own."

"You wouldn't have followed?"

"Of course I would, you know I wouldn't let you —" He dropped his arms. "Wait. Were you counting on that?"

"I mean yeah…" I responded without thinking.

He spoke quietly. "Did it ever occur to you that his fear may be something I *can't* turn into? That we'd be facing him just as we are?"

*No, it hadn't*, I realized with a sinking feeling, the answer to his question apparent on my face.

"I get it." His face fell, "it's easy to make dangerous decisions when you can put the big bad guard dog between you and the serial killer, right?"

"I didn't mean it like that, the fact that I knew you wouldn't leave me and that I needed to come up here are two separate things…" I began to second guess myself.

"It's fine. You're right. My job is to find and protect you from The Carver." His lips thinned and his voice shortened. "That's what you *hired* me to do. No feelings, right?"

"Warren…" I reached out to touch him, and he moved his arm away abruptly.

"If you need me, I'll be in my truck." He stormed out, slamming the door behind him.

What the fuck just happened? I sat on the kitchen chair as the tears pressed against my eyes. I came out here to lure Borges away from everyone else, away from civilization, but to what end? What was I really going to do when he found me? *Rely on Warren to fight for you.* My inner voice replied. Oh my god… I *did* use him. I didn't mean to, but I saw him as a shield, a weapon to be used at my behest. Would I really have marched up here *not* expecting him to follow me like an obedient puppy? No. I just assumed he would.

In my panic, I didn't consider the possibility of him getting hurt trying to protect me. I was only thinking about the other women, about Rory. What's worse is even though he didn't agree with me, he still went along with it, why? *Because you have him wrapped around your little finger.* Fuck me…

When did I turn into this person? The person who sacrifices others for a means to an end? The tears rolled down my face, and I stood to run after him, to tell him I was sorry, and I was a selfish bitch. But… what then? We hug, kiss, makeup, and we go back so *he's* out of immediate danger, but then Rory's right back in it…

I couldn't win. There was no solution where both of the people I loved would be safe… *Fuck* I said it, didn't I? I threw the chair over with every ounce of energy I had, and the clattering of wood echoed through the empty house. I never felt more alone, but… maybe that was for the best, I had become a danger to be around. *I should just leave.* Stick to my plan and go off alone, lure Borges away from everyone, including Warren, and try to take care of him myself. If I survived, well, problem solved. If I didn't, then Warren could focus on tracking him down without having to worry about me. Either way, everyone would be better off.

I peered out the window. Warren sat in the driver seat, looking down at his phone, his face tense.

I decided to pack some stuff, but wait until it gets dark, that way he wouldn't notice me leave. I began to search the cabin for anything I could use as a weapon. There was a hatchet leaning against the wall behind the stove, but I could barely lift it. We did buy a small set of kitchen knives to bring up here, so I grabbed the sharpest one of those. My handy dandy mace still hung from my keys, and I found a pretty-damn-sharp iron log poker that I could swing with ease. Okay, now onto supplies.

I emptied out Warren's backpack, stacking his papers and laptop neatly on the kitchen table. There was a cute little coffee table book on survival in the wild that I snagged. I threw in some bottles of water, a roll of toilet paper, and whatever non-perishable foods we bought. A first-aid kit would have been handy, but I left it in the truck. I opened every cabinet, every drawer in search of one they might have, and managed to scrounge up some bandaids but not much else. Okay, fire, right? Being able to start a fire was important in the wilderness. We bought a lighter, but there was also a pack of matches on top of the stove. I threw them both in.

I definitely had not packed clothes for camping, so I had to borrow one of Warren's hoodies from his duffel. I picked the grey one he wore when we first met, it smelled the most like him. I threw a few extra socks, underwear, and shirts into the backpack. I wished I had packed a pair of pants, but in my defense it was the middle of summer and we were traveling to the desert. Satisfied with what I was able to put together, I sat on the sofa in the living room, and waited for the sun to go down.

I flipped through the survival book, which was in fact pretty educational, until my eyes were straining to make out the words, which I took as my sign it was about time. I checked out the front window again, and Warren still sat in his truck. Though his seat now reclined back and his arms were folded over his chest as he stared at the ceiling.

I went to the bedroom, and snuck out the window as if I were a teenager again. Sticks and leaves crunched under me as I landed, and I swallowed back the panic of self-preservation. For once, I wasn't going to worry about my own selfish needs.

I looked skyward. According to the book, I should always note the location of the sun. It set behind me, which was also the direction we drove in from, so I walked away from it with the intention of leading Borges away from people. Though I couldn't have been walking for more than a half hour before the forest thickened, and got significantly darker. I couldn't make out exactly where the sun was, and I hesitated. What if I ended up walking around in circles?

*Don't panic*, the sky looked lighter where the sun set, right? *Move towards the darkness.*

Funnily enough, I thought I might really enjoy this nature stuff in a situation where I wasn't using myself as bait. If I survived, I'd make an effort to come out here more. *Warren did promise to take me camping.* My heart dropped. I felt like an absolute piece of shit for taking advantage of him.

I walked for maybe an hour before it got cold enough for me to pull out his hoodie. His scent cocooned me as I wrapped myself in it, and I had to fight back tears. I didn't even apologize to him for what I did. What if I never saw him again? I should have told him how I felt, but I was too much of a coward to even realize it before it was too late. "I'm sorry Warren." I whispered out loud, hoping the trees would carry my message back to him.

I finally had to tap the flashlight on my phone. It was too dark to see anything, and a creepy prickle on the back of my neck let me know that I was surrounded by creatures who could see *me* just fine. I also kept tripping on roots and rocks, and was going to twist an ankle if I kept on. I definitely couldn't fight a serial killer with a twisted ankle, so I found a spot beneath a tree and set the backpack down.

Okay, to keep warm and have some light, I needed fire. *How does one start a fire?* I pulled out my new bible and of course, it had an entire section dedicated to it. Though even following its instructions I struggled, and went through half the pack of matches before I got a flame to survive long enough to catch anything. But when it did, I swear it was the most gratifying sensation. This how cavemen felt when they discovered fire. I was sure of it.

I sat on the forest floor, in front of my magnificent burning miracle, and stared into the darkness. What does one do in the woods, alone? I wasn't tired, not quite hungry yet... I pulled out my phone and tried to open social media.

*Duh,* no signal. The sounds of rustling leaves, hooting, chirping, and I swear I heard footsteps, kept me on edge. It was amazing to think how alive the forest was, though I couldn't see a foot past my fire. There's no way I'd see an animal, or worse, sneak up on me before it was too late. How much longer would I have to endure this stress? *There's no way I'm falling asleep out here...* "Maybe I'll get lucky and Borges will just kill me quickly."

"You would wish that, you twisted woman."

I almost fell face-first into my little fire stumbling to run, before I recognized Warren stepping out from the trees. "You almost gave me a heart attack!" I shouted. "What the fuck are you doing out here?"

"Me? What the fuck are *you* doing out here?!"

"My plan." I straightened up, trying to hide the fact that my heart still raced, forgetting once again that he could sense it.

"And that is what? To get eaten by a mountain lion?"

"No," I folded my arms. "To kill Borges before he can kill anyone else... including you."

"Oh, suddenly you care if I get killed protecting your dumb-ass?"

"I've always cared..." I lowered my arms.

"You're making it really difficult to keep you alive," he scoffed. "Get your shit and let's go back to the cabin."

"You go back. I'm staying out here. You're not safe with me."

"Fucking hell, Adelaide. Make up your mind. Do you want me to follow you into danger or not?"

"N— No."

"Yeah. Real convincing. I'm freezing my ass off out here... Is that my hoodie?"

"I had to borrow it—"

"Dammit! That's my favorite one, and I would have probably never seen it again if I hadn't found you. I will throw your ass over my shoulder and carry you back to the cabin if I have to, *let's go*."

"Will you just stop and listen to me?!"

"No. Look where we are now from listening to you —"

"YOU WERE RIGHT OKAY?" I barely noticed the tears had already begun.

He closed his mouth, and watched me.

"Fuck! You were right. I used you. I'm sorry. I didn't mean to, I didn't realize I was doing it, but I did," I threw my hands up. "I was so worried about Rory, and about all the other women I was endangering, I didn't think about how I was endangering you. All I cared about was keeping him away from them, and I was willing to use you to do so."

He looked down.

I cried as I paced. "You've been protecting me and watching out for me for weeks, and I began to take you for granted. I knew you cared about me, and you wouldn't let me go alone, and I used that to my advantage. You don't deserve to be treated like that, so please, leave me out here. I have weapons, provisions… Let me deal with him. And whichever one of us comes out alive… that's one less person for you to have to worry about." I collapsed, sobbing into my knees. "I'm so sorry. I'm a horrible fucking person."

His crunching steps echoed in the stillness as he approached me and knelt down. "This all sounds very familiar."

The sleeves of his hoodie were soaked. "I just… don't know what to do… I can't protect you both…"

"It's not your job to protect me, or anyone else."

"It is… It's the only thing I know how to do… Protect the people I love… and I can't even do it right…"

I jumped when he wrapped me in his arms and pulled me into his crossed legs. I couldn't fight it, I wouldn't. I fell against his chest, heaving tears into him.

"You do realize, if anyone understands using someone as a means to an end, it's me right?"

I sniffed and looked up at him. He had tears in his eyes too. "What?"

"Babygirl, I did the same thing to you. But *I* knew what I was doing, and I was doing it for revenge. You didn't, *and* were doing it to try to save others."

"That doesn't make it okay."

"Maybe not, but I get it. You're *not* a horrible person. You're an amazingly *selfless* person who throws herself into the line of fire to protect those who can't protect themselves." He hesitated. "Do you want to know the truth? The real reason I was upset?"

I nodded.

He took a deep breath. "Because I realized that I was willing to sacrifice myself for you if it came down to it. Because the thought of you getting hurt, *terrified* me. Can you understand what that was like for me? To realize I could still feel fear? Adelaide, you made me experience something I never thought I'd be able to again, and I *hated* it.

"I hated that you drew that intense, primal sensation out of me. How everyone else deals with this feeling every day of their lives, I can't fucking imagine. I understand how you feel about Rory, because I feel the same way about you. To realize you love someone *so* much that your greatest fear becomes losing them… It's agonizing."

I had no idea that even through my breakdown I was holding back until a dam burst inside me. Everything rushed out of me at once. Fear of my love for him. Fear of the situation I was in. Fear for him. Fear for Rory. But such an overwhelming relief that I was in his arms, that he tracked me down, that he understood me. That he loved me…

"I… love you too." I blubbered unromantically.

The sparks of my small fire danced in his eyes as they illuminated the darkness that surrounded us. He pulled my face up and kissed me. It was wet, messy, and perfect. Our tears blended together on our faces as I attempted to express the most intense and incomparable love I had ever experienced. I had no resistance left, but I didn't need it. I was his, fully and completely.

He smiled and wiped my tears. "Whatever we do, Babygirl, we do it together. I'm never leaving your side, and if that fucker even *tries* to lay a hand on you, I'll rip it off, and feed it to him."

"On a hotdog bun?" I sniffed.

He choked a laugh through his tears, "on a hotdog bun."

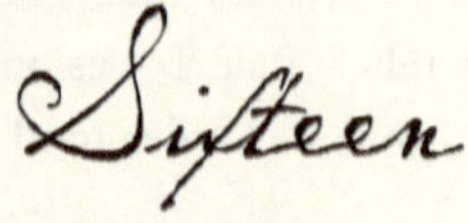

We maneuvered carefully over roots and fallen branches as we made our way back to the cabin. He held my hand tightly with one hand, and in the other he held a flashlight.

"How did you even find me?" I used his hand to balance as I stepped over a rotting log.

"You've been a nervous wreck since our fight," he chuckled. "An air horn would have been easier to ignore."

"And I thought I was being so sneaky," I grumbled.

He smiled, "I was also just waiting for you to try something stupid like this after your crazy-ass bait plan."

I stopped and put my hands on my hips. "Excuse me. I was *very* well prepared."

He turned. "Really? You didn't even bring a flashlight."

"I have my phone."

"And what happens when the battery dies?"

"I'll just charge… oh." Damn. I forgot phones need electricity.

"*Exactly*," he laughed. "I will give you this though: I was very impressed with your fire."

"Yeah? It was a perfect campfire, wasn't it?"

"It was." I could hear the smile in his voice as he took back my hand. "I guess you won't be so helpless on a camping trip after all."

Pride swelled in my chest. *I fucking knew it.*

We finally broke the tree line, and the silhouette of the cabin with its glowing windows greeted us warmly.

Once safely inside, we went around securing the windows and door. I knew *I* was securing them against Borges, but I got the sense that Warren was securing them against me trying to sneak out again.

"We have a full day ahead of him, if he does decide to follow you here," he commented as he latched the last window. "At least if he's driving."

"What if he has super speed or something?"

He shook his head, "no, not one of his abilities. He's an animal yes, but not an abnormally fast one. He has to walk or drive like everyone else. He's been smart enough to not get caught on camera, and they haven't been able to identify any of the same cars in the vicinity of each of the crime scenes. Which means he's probably stealing a new car in each city."

I stared at the floor in hard thought.

"These are all things I, and the police, have been racking our brains over for months," he came up to me and took my waist. "For the time being, I want you to go take a hot shower, while I make us dinner, and try not to worry about it."

"Easy for you to say," I looked up at him.

"There's nothing we can do up here but follow your insane plan. If you're going to stress me out with it, I ask that you at least let me take care of you while we wait."

It wasn't an unfair request. "Fine," I submitted.

"Go shower, you're covered in dirt," he smiled.


I emerged a while later in a cloud of steam with a towel wrapped around my body to the smell of something delicious wafting from the kitchen. I stopped in the doorway to watch him cook. He had his hand on his hip as he stirred something in a saucepan, brought a wooden spoon up to his lips, paused, then reached for something off the counter and added it. He turned the heat up, and leaned against the counter, picking up a glass of red wine and taking a sip. He noticed me over the rim of the glass, and smiled.

"It smells amazing." I walked towards him, and looked into the pan. Red sauce simmered lightly, and a larger pot of spaghetti noodles boiled behind it. I beamed. "Spaghetti!"

He chuckled and set his glass down, picked up the wooden spoon and dipped it in the sauce. "Taste," he offered it to me, "careful, it's hot."

I brought the edge of the spoon to my mouth and took a bit off. My eyes widened. Oh. My. God. I would never be able to eat any other spaghetti sauce ever again. "How… How are you so good…" I licked my lips.

He laughed. "Now this," he held out his wine glass.

I didn't even know what he gave me, but the combined tastes made my knees weak. I closed my eyes and released a contented sigh.

"Good?" He smiled.

I opened my eyes and took him in. *This sexy motherfucker*… "Did I tell you I love you?"

He threw his head back in laughter, "Is this all it took?" He pulled me in and kissed me. I could still taste the wine on his lips.

"Don't go taking advantage of it," I purred.

"No promises," he smiled. "Now, as much as I could stare at *this* all night," he looked me up and down, "you're dripping all over my kitchen. Go dry off. But, feel absolutely free to come back wearing nothing."

"I'll think about it," I smirked.


His hoodie was thrown on the bed in the room. I picked it up, and inhaled. *God, I fucking love his scent…* I knew he'd be annoyed if I took it again but I didn't care, it looked

263

way too comfortable. I threw it on, along with a pair of panties, tossed my curls back into a messy bun, put on my lotions and deodorant, and hurried back out. I wanted more of that wine.

A wicked smile broke across his lips when he saw me. "You stole it again."

"I did."

He clicked his tongue at me, "bad girl."

"What are you going to do about it?"

"Maybe I'll just rip it off you."

"No you won't. It's your favorite, and now it's mine too." I avoided his grasp as I passed through the kitchen, stole his wine glass off the counter, and took it into the living room.

He raised his eyebrow with a huff, "excuse me?"

"You're excused," I smirked as I lay across the sofa.

"You're lucky I have to keep an eye on the sauce, little girl." He growled as he leaned against the fridge with his arms folded. "I would have poured you your own, you just had to ask."

"But I didn't want my own, I wanted yours."

"Oh I'll give you something of mine alright…"

"Hmm?" I pretended not to hear him.

"Go on, keep fucking around," he taunted with a smirk.

I smiled to myself as I drank and looked around the living room. A pile of cut wood stood next to the stove, and since I was a professional fire starter now, I took it upon myself to get one going while he finished cooking.


He served me, *he served me*, and we sat on the floor in front of the stove, using the coffee table as a dining table. This man definitely missed his calling, he was a natural born chef. His pairings were perfect, from the pasta to the wine, even the lettuce and dressing for the salad was picked specifically. I prayed that Borges didn't find us tonight, for the mere fact that we were both too full and happy to fight anyone. We moved to the sofa, and I stretched out on it, laying my feet on his lap.

"I was thinking," he took one of my feet in his hands, and began massaging it, "that fire poker you grabbed made a decent weapon for you, but you have no idea how to defend yourself."

I exhaled a quiet moan as he pressed his thumbs into my sole. How he expected me to hold a conversation while he did this to me I had no idea… "I mean, swinging the pointy end at him was the plan."

"That's a start," he chuckled, "but I'd feel better if you let me teach you some basic defense moves."

"Fuck…" He had begun kneading into my arch. "Sure… whatever you want…"

"Will you actually let me, or are you just agreeing with whatever I say?" He smiled.

"Yes," I exhaled softly.

He laughed and placed my foot down. "Alright then, get up."

I groaned. "No… Not right now…"

"When then? Baby, if he shows up tonight…" The concern in his voice was enough to remind me why we were actually here. This wasn't a romantic getaway, I was about to face a murderer.

"Okay, you're right." I stood up, "what's first?"

We pushed the furniture aside, clearing a space in the middle of the room. "The good news is, he isn't as tall as me, so you should be able to reach his more vulnerable areas easier. Eyes, throat, groin. If all else fails, target those areas." He moved my hand along as he explained, then made as if to grab me by the throat, "if I came at you like this…." He

265

moved me back, and gently pinned me against the wall, "what would be your first instinct?"

I bit my lip as heat rushed to my face, afraid to respond.

He rolled his eyes, and sighed a smile. "Get your mind out of the gutter."

"I can't help it with you…"

He leaned down and kissed me. "You have to focus, Babygirl. Work now, play later okay?" He released me.

"Okay, okay. I'm focused." I took a deep breath. "Come at me again."

He placed his hand back around my neck. "He's going to try to subdue you, take away your ability to breathe. What do you notice that can save your life right now?"

"Uhm," I feigned a kick between his legs.

"Good. What's more, from this distance you can reach my eyes right? Use your thumbs and press into them, hard. You want to hurt him, so the harder the better…"

I smirked.

"Don't…" He chuckled, "I walked into that one."

Our impromptu lesson continued for a while. He taught me how to use my low center of gravity to keep myself steady. How to hit with the side of my hands and how to make a proper fist. I even learned how to break someone's nose. Each time I got something down, I wanted to learn more. He made me feel so powerful, so enabled, and for the first time in my life, proud of myself. I didn't have to rely entirely on him to protect me anymore, and I slowly realized I felt a little less afraid of the man hunting me.

He was explaining to me for the hundredth time how I would have to aim lower for Borges when I went for a throat punch, that I realized all the practice, everything I learned wouldn't mean anything if I froze when I stood face to face with him. If I couldn't even hear his name without falling into a panic attack, how was I supposed to defend myself against him? I stopped.

"What's the matter? Did I hurt you?"

"No, I was just thinking, I think we have to practice with you as *him*."

"What?"

"None of this is going to help me if I can't face him. I need to get past my fear."

He studied me. I expected him to argue, to try to convince me it wasn't necessary, but instead he simply asked, "are you sure?"

"No. But..." I took a deep breath and looked him in the eye "Do it."

He kissed me on the forehead. "It's just me, okay?"

I nodded and he changed.

My breath caught in my throat as he rose to full height. Those dead, evil eyes blinked absently, and his mouth was shut in a frown. He looked like Borges, but not the one I remembered from my nightmares. This one was passive, like a portrait of him coming to life. He didn't move, and watched me cautiously, almost like *he* was afraid of *me*.

"Are you okay?" His wheezing voice ground my nerves. I shuddered and closed my eyes.

"Mhm. Just... One step at a time..."

He grunted in acknowledgment.

Another deep breath, and I opened my eyes. "Can I see his nails?"

Without a word or expression, his nails grew into cone-like spears at his sides. I inhaled sharply. He opened his mouth as if to say something, but quickly closed it.

"I'm okay..." My heart raced. "You need to look more menacing... like you want to hurt me, but also find joy in it."

He frowned at first, then opened his mouth in a wide smile.

I shut my eyes quickly as my entire body tensed. *Breathe… one, two, three…* I opened my eyes at the exhale and nodded. "Just get it over with."

"I'm not going to hurt you." The horrifying pitch of his tone echoed in my head, and before I was able to process the fear, his clawed hands came at me, pausing just above my neck. He took a step back.

"Again," I instructed.

And he did. Again, and again Warren came at me from different angles, letting me practice what it would feel like to try to avoid Borges' grasp. My body shook, my nerves were on high alert, and every time he spoke I wanted to run, or throw up, or both, but I focused on defending myself. Until finally, I was able to look him in the eyes while I threw a punch at his nose, which I would have actually landed if I wasn't shaking so badly.

He stepped away, and changed back, panting. "That's enough for tonight."

My adrenaline dropped at the sight of Warren's face and I felt faint. I stumbled to the sofa, and sat heavily.

"I'm *so* fucking proud of you." He rushed to me and grabbed my face in his hands, kissing me on the head. "Baby, that was amazing."

"I feel dizzy…"

"Just relax." He hurried into the kitchen and brought back a glass of water. "Small sips, keep breathing." He knelt at my feet, watching my face closely.

I had to close my eyes to keep the room from spinning.

"You did it Babygirl, you looked him right in the eyes." He spoke softly and with such admiration. "Pure evil, and you took him head on."

"But you weren't really trying to hurt me, if it were actually him I don't think I could—"

"You can, because if it was actually him, I know you wouldn't hold back. God, you're fucking amazing."

I opened my eyes and tried to focus on him. "I was still terrified. It didn't work. I'm still scared of him."

"So fucking what? Now you know you can do it even in spite of that."

I wanted to feel relief, pride, even satisfaction at my accomplishment, but instead I just felt drained. The ordeal had sucked the very life from my veins. "I'm tired," I whispered.

"I'll lay the sleeping bag out on the bed." He smiled and kissed my hand before going into the bedroom.

I looked around me. We were going to have to put this living room back for the owners before we left, we had made a mess of it. Though we could tell them to add "combat training studio" to the available activities on the rental listing. I yawned. I really was tired, but the thought of trying to sleep in that dark, tiny bedroom made me nervous. The warm glow from the wood stove expanding over the open floor suddenly felt much more inviting, where I could see and hear everything happening around me, where I didn't feel cornered…

"Warren?"

"Yes, Babygirl," he responded from the room.

"Can we sleep out here tonight?"

A pause then, "sure."

To my surprise and amusement, he dragged the entire mattress into the living room. "I'm too fucking old to sleep on a hard floor," he complained as he set it in front of the fire and opened the sleeping bag over it. Then piled a few blankets he had grabbed from his truck on top.

"Get some sleep, Baby, I'm going to take a quick shower. I feel gross after being him." He draped a blanket over my shoulders as I lay down.

I felt silly asking, but the idea that something could happen while he was in the shower crossed my mind. "Will you leave the door open? So I can hear you?"

"Yes," he kissed me softly. "I won't be long."

I lay facing the stove. The bright flickering behind the iron bars cast odd shadows across the blankets, and the warmth on my face was enough to start lulling me to sleep. The shower turned on, and I heard the glass door open, and shut. The splash pattern changed as the water hit his body, and the cabin slowly filled with steam that spilled out from the bathroom. I blinked, and the next thing I felt was pressure at the foot of the mattress as he crawled towards me. I drowsily turned my head to him.

"Go back to sleep, Babygirl," he whispered. So I did.

I became mildly aware of warm breath tickling my inner thigh, but I wasn't sure if I was asleep or awake. Then lips, pressing softly against my skin as they inched further upward. *Fuck, if this was a dream, please let it keep going…* I had a flash of awareness the moment his tongue slid up my opening, the sensation rocking my entire body. I wasn't dreaming. I blinked dazedly at the shape of his head under the blanket between my legs.

"I'm so sleepy…" I mumbled. "I don't know if I can stay awake…"

"Then don't," he purred. "I want you completely relaxed. Sleep, and let me taste you…"

Somewhere between a dream and consciousness I felt his lips press against me. I thought I moaned but it could have been in my head. I had no energy to contribute, but he didn't seem to care. I drifted in and out of sleep as he sucked, and licked methodically, only truly waking at the sensation of pressure building between my legs.

I was barely able to form a sound before my eruption of ecstasy, to which he responded by smiling against me. As my body relaxed, and he moved his head away, I felt his fingers slowly slide out of me.

My body radiated with heat from him and the stove, and I squirmed out of his hoodie half-asleep, tossed it aside, and noticed that he had already managed to get my panties off at some point during his expedition under the blankets. My heart still pounded as he came to lay behind me and pulled me into him. His hard cock pressed against my back as he wrapped an arm around my chest, and planted soft kisses along my shoulder and neck.

I turned my head to face him, and he smiled down at me, the firelight glowing in his eyes. I pulled him down to me, and our lips connected. I didn't care that he tasted like me, his stubble still soaked in my desires, kissing him was sheer bliss.

His hand moved up and down my body, trying to feel all of me at once. He grabbed my breasts, ran his fingertips over my nipples, and dug his fingers into my skin as he bit my neck, shooting alternating waves of goosebumps, electricity, and primal desire up and down my skin. I pressed myself against him.

He hummed quietly in my ear, "my Baby wants more?"

I nodded, wanting to, so badly, but I was so freaking exhausted. "I'm just not sure how much I have left in me… Not after what you just did…"

"If you want it, I don't need you to move a muscle, Babygirl. Stay relaxed for me."

He rolled over for a moment, fished something out of a bag and tore open a wrapper. Then returned to me, lifted my leg slightly with his arm, and pressed his tip against my opening.

I gasped at the pressure.

"Deep breath, Baby," he whispered, before filling me completely.

My back arched as he pulled my hips towards him, releasing a soft moan into my ear. He slowly thrust himself in and out of me as he released my upper leg, letting it come to rest. "Is that comfortable?" He panted.

"Uh huh," I wasn't capable of words. The way he fit inside me, how every inch of him hit something perfectly, left my mind completely blank.

I could feel every flex of his muscles, every breath he took as he was pressed against my back. His heart pounded aggressively in time with mine, and he lifted my chin to him again, and kissed me. As quiet little whimpers escaped both of our lips, they found homes on each other's tongues. He looked into my eyes as another orgasm began to build in me.

"I love you," he breathed the promise into me with another kiss.

I gripped the back of his hair in response, as we moaned into each other. A sound of desperation vibrated from my lips into his as I came for him, while his grasp on my side tightened as his breathing shallowed, then caught. His thrusts slowed and he buried his face in my hair, breathing heavily.

I rolled over to face him, the dying fire at my back, and looked into his smiling eyes. I couldn't believe how hard I fought not to be in love with this man. No one has ever made me feel so protected, so wanted. Even in the midst of the greatest danger of my life, I felt safe in his arms. I was gathering the breath to return his promise, when he pressed his forehead against mine as if in response to my thoughts.

"You're *mine*," he whispered.

# Seventeen

Sometime in the early hours, I woke and felt around for his hoodie. The fire must have gone out, because it was fucking cold. I sat up slightly to slip it back on. Warren must have also been cold, and gotten up to grab one of his other sweaters, because in the dim lighting I could make out his silhouette in the doorway of the hall. I lay back down and pulled the blankets over me, and felt his arm wrap around me.

My heart stopped, and as I began to gasp Warren's eyes shot open.

"Wha—" He never got to finish.

I didn't even have time to scream before a clawed hand launched itself at me from across the room.

Warren tackled the body out of midair, and they landed on the coffee table as its legs gave out with a loud shatter.

"RUN!" He shouted at me while he attempted to pin two lethal hands above a manic Borges.

I flew off the mattress and found the fire poker on the floor as Borges managed to kick Warren off him and went for his throat.

"NO!" I ran at him swinging as hard as I could, and heard a crack as I made contact with his jaw. The unearthly sound he made as he reeled made skin crawl.

We had a millisecond to get to our feet and escape out the front door. Warren shoved me in front of him as we made it outside.

It was still dark, damp, and cold. The mist from the early morning clouds had not yet dissipated. The only light source was the sprinkling of moonlight that broke through the canopy. My mind raced, I didn't think I was breathing. Everything in me told me to run, but as we made for the truck, I turned around.

Borges flew out the door, his jaw hanging at a disturbing angle. He smiled when he saw me and drool dripped from his broken mouth.

"What are you doing? Get in the truck!" Warren screamed at me from somewhere farther ahead.

"I can't... We have to stop him..."

"Knew I'd find you," Borges wheezed. "So delicious..." He scrambled at me like a feral animal on all fours.

I stood my ground, the iron rod over my shoulder in preparation. Warren frantically ran to intercept him, coming to a stop just ahead of me.

Borges closed in, but Warren was still Warren. "If you're going to change, now's the time..."

"I... can't..." He gasped, and Borges swatted Warren away with his massive daggered hand, knocking him to the ground, leaving five bloody gashes across his chest.

I screamed as I swung the rod at Borges again as he reached me, but he caught it, and held it above my head as he reached for my neck with his other.

Instinct took over, and I kicked as hard as I could at his crotch, but it only seemed to anger him more. I dropped the rod and ducked as he swung at me, narrowly missing my face with the tips of his nails.

"He isn't afraid of anything!" Warren shouted agonizingly as he forced himself up. His bare chest was black with blood. "Adelaide, *run!*"

Borges' eyes shifted slightly at Warren's screams, and I took the opportunity to bolt into the forest. *Lead him away from Warren, lead him away from people… He's not afraid of anything, he's going to kill you…* my thoughts shot through me faster than I could process them. The rocks, sticks, and debris scraped and cut at my bare feet as I sprinted blindly into the darkness.

The sounds of haphazard running, wheezing, slurping, and desperate grunting followed close behind me.

My lungs burned, my feet screamed at their injuries, but I couldn't stop. Stopping meant death.

I narrowly missed tripping on a fallen branch and stumbled as I caught myself, my ankle twisting unnaturally. I screamed in pain as I forced weight on it, my vision blurred with tears, but Warren's voice echoed in my mind. *"Run."* I fought the pain, fought the fear, dragging myself through the trees.

I couldn't hear Borges anymore, which was more frightening than knowing he was at my heels.

*Where did he go?*

I hid behind a large tree, planting my back firmly against it. I panted and sobbed.

*I left Warren…* I just fucking left him. Without being able to transform, he was just a man against a monster. What if Borges went back for him? I wanted to run back to the cabin, to run back to Warren, but I was frozen with fear.

A twig cracked behind me, and I covered my mouth to suppress a scream.

My hearing sharpened. Sniffing… Something was sniffing… No, *someone*. If I ran, he'd see me, and there was no way I could outpace him now. I held my breath, hoping, *praying*, that he somehow wouldn't find me.

It felt like hours passed as he padded around the area, a wolf tracking a wounded deer. I wanted to close my eyes, curl up into a ball, but I didn't dare move a muscle.

Suddenly he stopped moving, and fell silent. There was no way to tell how close he was.

A frantic scramble, the whistle of something swinging, a horrible pain in my head, and darkness.

Warren scrambled to his feet as she ran into the forest. He could see the dark, warm liquid pouring from him change from black to red as the first blue light of the morning broke overhead, but he felt no pain, just terror.

Borges wasted no time in taking off after her, and Warren tackled his legs in an attempt to take him down. They crashed to the ground, knocking the wind from him.

Borges kicked hard at his face as they wrestled. He wasn't even trying to slash at Warren anymore, his only goal was to get after her.

*He has to fear something...* Warren tried to concentrate as he received another blow to the face with a steel toe boot, causing his vision to flash. It was enough for Borges to get away.

Warren forced himself up, and watched the world spin around him before he collapsed to the ground.

He blinked into the bright sunlight, and the pain that shot through his head made him sick. He rolled over, and expelled the contents of his stomach onto the dirt, then gasped at the pain that alternated between his head and torso. His hand came up and felt the sticky, dried, dirt and leaf caked blood that covered him. "Adelaide..." He croaked and attempted to rise to his feet, only to feel sick again.

He supported himself on all fours, attempting to steady his breathing. "Have to get to her..." he reinforced his will, and stood unsteadily, before padding into the woods in the direction she ran.

He searched for hours on his own, but found no traces of her or Borges. Shivering violently, sick to his stomach, and naked except for his sweatpants, he miraculously found his way back to the cabin.

He dug around the debris of the struggle from the previous night to find his phone, and called the sheriff to report the abduction. Then he dragged the blanket off their makeshift bed, wrapped himself in it, and began to cry.

In less than an hour, the local sheriff, rangers, and the FBI had the cabin surrounded. Warren had to be forced into the back of the ambulance to get his wounds treated, which to everyone's shock were long and gruesome, but not deep. They attached an IV to him, and the FBI questioned him.

"Why did you wait so long to call it in?"

"I went to look for her after I came to." He knew how it would look from their perspective. "It didn't occur to me how long I had been unconscious."

"Can you guess as to what time you lost sight of them?"

"It was around sunrise, I… don't really know the exact time."

"Is there any possibility that she knew him?"

Warren glared at the agent. "She knew him from when she witnessed the murder before last. He has been hunting her ever since, which is why she hired me in the first place," he partially lied.

"And as part of your agreement, you brought her out here? To an isolated cabin in the woods?"

"*I* didn't bring her here. She *chose* to come here, and I followed, as she asked. Her crazy plan to lure him away from civilization actually worked, which means she got further in this case than any of your agents." His jaw clenched.

"I'm not understanding what her intention was with that, did she think she could subdue him herself?" The agent raised his eyebrow.

"Yes," Warren lied again. "She felt a sense of responsibility for the deaths that followed wherever she went. She wanted to keep him from hurting anyone else."

"Well, stand-up job you did protecting her." The agent scoffed.

Warren's eyes flashed first with murderous intent, but then quickly turned to shame.

"If you don't mind, agent, I need to take his vitals again before I release him." The EMT chimed in, then she waited until the agent walked away before saying; "You did everything you could. No one would have been able to take on that monster."

But it didn't do a thing to quell the guilt overtaking him.

My consciousness returned to me in the form of a massive throbbing at the back of my head, followed by a dull pain in my shoulders. I tried to open my eyes, and was met with resistance from a large strip of duct tape. I panicked, and opened my mouth to scream, but it too, was sealed shut. I shifted my body and pains shot through it from several areas. My arms were numb, and I realized I was being suspended by them. Tight bindings around my wrists held my entire body weight as I knelt on the floor. I tried to stand, but my feet were bound, constricting the swelling occurring in my right ankle, making it that much more unbearable.

Fearful tears pooled in my eyes and at the corners of the tape. *Don't panic.* I told myself as I began to hyperventilate, noticing my nose was not covered. *You can still smell, hear, and feel Addy. Use your senses.* I didn't recognize the voice in my head, but I obeyed nevertheless. I stopped struggling.

All I could hear was a low rumbling of an engine as I became aware that I was rocking slightly. *We're moving.* The voice confirmed. It was cold. Very cold, like a walk-in freezer. A wet chill hit my bare face and legs. *Get up.* The voice demanded. I brought my legs under me and with an extreme effort and muffled scream I balanced on my bound feet, scraping against what felt like a metal floor.

As my body rose, the bounds tightened, pulling my back against something solid. *Rocks?* The voice reasoned. The various sized lumps pushed into me uncomfortably. They felt frozen. *Who would freeze rocks?*

I listened harder, but from what I could make out I was alone, in a freezer full of rocks. That didn't make any sense.

"The dogs found something!" One of the rangers shouted from the tree line.

Warren pulled his head up from his hands as he sat on the front steps of the porch. He and numerous other law enforcement officials hurried to follow the ranger into the woods. He recognized the path he had taken that morning, but as they continued on, he reprimanded himself for giving up. She ran farther than he would have guessed.

A pack of bloodhounds and search and rescue teams were gathered around a tree. For someone who didn't know what was going on this would have appeared to be some strange cult ritual. As he approached, he noticed one ranger kneeling, marking the ground around a lone iron fire poker. His eyes widened and his heart leapt at the recognition of her weapon.

"There's blood spatter on the tree as well." He overheard a forensic specialist telling the FBI Agent.

"Who's blood?" He asked out loud and approached the scene.

"Seems to be from whoever was hit with this, from the pattern." The analyst who took a sample off the bark responded. "But we'll know for sure when the tests come back."

Warren looked around him. *He caught up with her here.* He thought to himself. *She dropped the poker when she took off... He must have picked it up...*

"I don't suppose you have a light to shed on this?" The Agent approached him.

"Not past what I told you. I gave you the identity of the killer, and now he's kidnapped my— assignment," he stopped himself. "Probably after beating her with this. And knowing his M.O. she's probably dead now."

"We have no proof what you say happened is what actually happened. For all we know, you did this, using The Carver as a convenient scapegoat." The agent replied nonchalantly.

"So arrest me then!" Warren's hands flew up and his wounds stung angrily. "Arrest me and keep me in custody if it makes you feel better, just go after him!"

A Ranger interjected. "Calm down son, we're trying to find out how to track him. We just don't have enough information yet."

"Seems to be the one factor this guy has been riding on this entire time." Warren muttered and stormed further off into the woods.

I twisted my hands in every direction they could possibly go, trying to feel for a weak point in my bindings, but was only succeeding in chafing my wrists. I lowered myself back to the ground, trying to find an angle where I could press my swollen ankle against the cold floor. It was the only relief I could find from the constant throbbing, and standing on it only made it worse. I decided I would rather feel my arms numb and sore from being stretched unnaturally above my head.

A loud screeching preceded my body lurching to the side, as whatever I was in stopped moving, causing my head to bump against one of the several frozen rocks that surrounded me. I listened. The sound of a roll up door... Footsteps on metal, keys, a lock... Then the footsteps approached me.

I held my breath.


My arms were almost ripped from their sockets as I was pulled to my feet forcibly. I screamed through the pain, which fell short on the tape that covered my mouth.

"No... No screams," a whiny voice grated from somewhere in front of me. "This is why I use the tape."

I closed my eyes, suppressing tears as I recognized Borges' voice.

The footsteps moved slightly away from me. "I hate when they scream... It makes it so... *unpleasant.*"

"I don't know what to do with you." He walked back towards me. "I thought I did, but now that I have you… I can't do it. You're… different."

I felt his presence inches from my face.

"It was fun, though, wasn't it? Our game of hide and seek? I knew I would win, but I thought, 'why not?' Change things up… See if I like something different. Oh, that's right. You can't speak. This is a problem…"

His steps padded back and forth across the metal.

"I need you to stay quiet. We're about to come to a weigh-in, and I'm really not supposed to have friends here."

*Weigh in?*

"Usually my friends are… less awake by the time I let them into my clubhouse. So… Do I wait to decide what I want to do with you and risk you making noise… Or, do I solve the problem right now?"

A sharp point pressed against my neck. I didn't need to see to recognize one of his nails. I squeezed my eyes shut under the tape to keep the tears in.

"Hmm. That's better." He moved his nail away, and huffed. "I might just keep you through to the next county." He walked back towards where I assumed the door was, and opened it.

"Or… Maybe once I find my next friend, I'll get over you." He closed the door and locked it again.

"Don't leave town. We might have more questions for you." The agent commanded gruffly before stepping into his luxury rental car that looked completely out of place in the wilderness.

Warren watched, disheartened as the Rangers and Sheriff packed up the search. "It's not even that dark yet." He said when they told him it was getting too late to continue.

"We'll pick it up tomorrow," they assured him.

But Warren knew how quickly evidence deteriorated in these conditions, not to mention every second not searching for her brought a higher chance of not finding her alive. *If she even still was.* He trudged back inside the cabin, scanning the damage. He felt defeated, guilty, angry, and scared. How did normal people deal with this? How does someone go about their day feeling the weight of dread dragging them down with every step? This was nothing like the thrill of feeling fear from others, where he looked forward to the climactic release. Right now, he would do whatever he could to avoid facing that terror at the end of the road. He tried to focus on cleaning up, maybe they missed something.

He started in the kitchen, picking up the dirty plates and pots that were strewn about the floor. The sight of the pasta sauce splattered on the counter made him think of the way her eyes lit up when she realized he had made her favorite dish for dinner. His heart ached. How could he just let Borges take her? He should have run after her, should have done more to subdue him...

The sofa in the living room lay on its back, and he stood it up. The pride on her face when she learned how to break a nose with her palm; She looked so confident, she finally began to see herself as strongly as he did... But a lot of good that did her. In the end, the only thing he didn't anticipate was his undoing. Real monsters weren't afraid of anything.

He picked the blankets off the floor, and her underwear fell out. He folded them neatly and tucked them in the duffle bag, but not before thinking how desperate he was to taste her. How he watched her sleep, and couldn't resist his cravings. How she squirmed and moaned for him, and how he wanted nothing more than to make her feel that pleasure again, and again… It was only last night, but it felt like an eternity had passed since then. He should have stayed awake, he should have kept watch all night. But the lure of her scent, the softness of her skin, way she fit against him… It was too tempting not to be next to her, and now she paid for his weakness.

"There's got to be more I can do," he muttered to himself. Had he not been tracking Borges the entire time? Did he not have the most complete profile on the man? Fuck the FBI, *he* was going to pull all his resources to get whatever was on record under the name "Connor Borges".

He threw open his laptop and realized, "fuck, I need      Wi-Fi…" The cafe in town had a sticker on the window offering free internet. *Gotta hurry before they close.* He grabbed his keys and both their phones, and headed out.

The sound of hissing hydraulics peaked my senses as I lurched to the side once more, but it wasn't just coming from beneath me, it surrounded me. Rumbling, squeaking, people's muffled voices, metal doors opening and closing came from every direction. *It's a truck stop…* the voice recognized,   *we're in a truck.*   A memory of headlights beaming through the front windows of the hotel lobby flashed in my head. *It was him that night.* The sickening realization that the truck that almost ran us into the mountains was also him hit with aggressive force. He had been right there the whole time…

He mentioned something about a weigh-in, maybe they check the back of the trucks? It was my only hope. The truck moved forward slightly, then the engine turned off. For a few minutes, nothing happened, but then two men's voices came from my left, and the door rolled up. I thought about screaming, kicking, making whatever noise I could… but then I remembered Borges' threat. He would get to me before anyone else… I turned my head in their direction, hoping someone would catch a glimpse of me. The shuffling of boxes, a ramp lowering, then rising, wheels on metal, and still nothing.

*No one has any idea you're here. There's another door.* The voice reminded me of the sound of the lock. Panic and tears rose in me once more as the door closed and the voices faded into the distance. The engine rumbled, and the floor moved for a moment before stopping again. Then silence for a long while.

The winding road that led back to the main highway forced Warren to ponder how in the hell Borges could have gotten up here, and out, without anyone seeing a vehicle. If he was on foot, there's no way he wouldn't have been discovered dragging along a kidnapping victim… He rounded a bend and glanced out to his right, then slammed on his brakes.

A semi-flat patch of rocky terrain stretched off to the side of the road, where a few saplings looked like they had been broken in half. He considered moving along, it was probably just a bear tromping through… but… something in his gut told him to get out and check.

The waning blue light of the setting sun offered just enough assistance for him to tread carefully. He stepped only on solid rock, not disturbing any broken twigs or dirt, as he crouched down to get a closer look at the snapped trees. "They're all bent the same way…" he thought aloud, "and like they were pushed at the same time… Bears don't do that." He scanned the ground for animal tracks, finding nothing. "Ugh. I can't see shit." He pulled his phone out and turned the flashlight on, moving it back and forth. His eyes caught on an unnatural looking impression as the bright light cast a shadow over mounding ripples in the shallow dirt. He quickly snapped a photo with the flash, and stared at the screen. *Those were fucking tire treads.*

It could easily have been a passing camper, pulling off for the night, but what were the chances of fresh tire treads in the loose dirt, off an isolated road, down the way from the cabin where they both just happened to be? If it was just a camper, maybe they heard or saw something? If it wasn't… He glanced at the time. The forensics lab would be closed by now, he'd have to wait until morning to talk to his guy, but he could at least send the photos. He continued into town, in the meanwhile he could still do a search on Borges' name.


He pulled up in front of the cafe to dark windows and a locked door. They had closed 20 minutes before. "Dammit, this little fucking town…" He was used to city business hours. He leaned on the hood of his truck and looked up to the sky with a forceful exhale. The sounds from the bar down the way caught his attention.

The chatter halted as he pushed the door open, and everyone turned to watch him. The dimly lit room was darker than the moonlit night he just emerged from. His eyes adjusted to the rustic red woods, worn out pool table, and, was that an actual jukebox? Ignoring their gazes, he found a booth in a corner, and slid into the red vinyl seat. The chatter slowly returned to normal as a woman with a tiny apron and rather disheveled ponytail approached him.

"You're the guy who rented that cabin where that girl went missing, right?"

He nodded. Word does get around.

"I hope they find her," she smiled uncertainly. "What can I get you?"

"Wild Turkey on the rocks." He didn't even look up at her.

She nodded and left. He pulled out his laptop, set it on the tiny table, and began a broad search on Borges. Either he was the most upstanding citizen on the planet, or he used an alias, because the only record he was able to find was a birth certificate, which aged Borges at 53.

"Dude's fucking spry for a man his age..." Warren scoffed as the waitress put his drink down in front of him.

"Thanks," he acknowledged, handing her his card. "Open a tab for me."

He brought the glass to his lips and drank deeper than he probably should have. The burn was the first warmth he felt since he held her in his arms last night. The anger and fear swirled in the pit of his stomach once more, threatening him with a lump in his throat as he swallowed. He immersed himself in scanning through genealogy reports with anyone of the same last name, searching "Borges" and "truck" in the same line, anything that might randomly throw a clue in his face.

He was a third glass in when he felt a phone vibrate in his jacket pocket. He pulled it out. It was hers, and Rory's face was on the caller ID. His heart dropped, but he swiped the green button.

"Hey…"

"Oh, hey. Can I talk to Addy?"

"Uhm." How was he going to explain that he failed at the one thing he was meant to do? How was he going to tell her sister that he let her get kidnapped by a serial killer? That he let her down.

"Hellooo?"

"Uh. I'm not sure how else to say this… but, Adelaide was taken last night… by The Carver."

Static from the other end.

"I'm so sorry," his voice cracked and he cleared it, suppressing tears. "I fucked up. I couldn't protect her… He's not afraid of anything… I was useless…"

"Please. Tell me you're fucking with me…" Rory's voice was small.

"I really, really, wish I could." He broke, and told her *everything*. From the fights, to Paulie, to admitting their love for one another. His hand grabbed his hair forcefully and pulled it back as he rested his head in his hand, spilling the contents of his heart over his keyboard. The words on the screen blurred behind his tears as he covered his eyes with his hand, trying to push them back in. "I don't know what else to do," he choked.

Rory fell silent again, though he heard sniffling. "I believe you," she said quietly. "That insane plan sounds exactly like something she'd come up with. She was always willing to throw herself in front of the train for someone, even if she had no business doing so."

"I shouldn't have let her… and now she might—"

"Don't. She's alive. If I know my sister, she's alive and fighting, and you're going to fucking fix this. You're going to get my sister back, do you hear me? He normally kills them on site right? Dismembers them and takes off with their breasts?"

Warren cleared his throat and took another drink. "Yeah," he responded shakily.

"Well, he took her. Her whole body. Why? He wants something with her, alive. Otherwise what would be the point of lugging her all the way down the hill?"

She had a point.

"We'll find her. You'll find her, I'm not giving you a choice. And you can consider yourself lawyered up. Don't worry about the FBI. Just do what you need to do find my sister. I'm officially hiring you."

Warren nodded against his hand. "I will. Whatever it takes."

They exchanged personal numbers and hung up. He rubbed his face in his hands and exhaled, then swallowed the rest of his drink. "I've found people with less." He muttered determinedly and returned to work.

The door came up again, footsteps, the lock, and the other door, then more footsteps.

"You did well." Borges' voice churned my stomach. "Though part of me kind of hoped you would give me a reason to add you to my collection. Still..."

A burning shock shot across my face as the tape, skin, and hairs were ripped from my eyes. I blinked, blinded by the excessively white light, as my sight came to focus on the face of The Carver.

"See? I treat my friends nicely." He smiled grotesquely, but was not looking at my face, he was staring at my chest.

As my vision cleared, I began to make out the textured lumps of the rocks covering the walls. But these were strangely colored, tans, pinks, browns… My eyes finally focused. They weren't rocks. I let out a muffled wail as I recognized breasts plastered all around me. Frozen, hanging, like cuts of meat, of all shapes and sizes. I gagged when it dawned on me that when my head slammed against the wall, it came to rest on another woman's stolen body parts.

He didn't react to my realization at all, his eyes not moving from my chest. "It's torture not to look at them when I'm speaking to you… but I know once I see them I won't be able to resist. And they keep so much better fresh." He reached for my neck, and pulled down on the zipper just enough to expose the top of my collarbone. Even without his nails grown out, his fingers were disgustingly long and bony, reminding me of spider's legs.

"I really should get through my frozen supplies first," he continued, completely ignoring the tears streaming down my face. "Oh well." He moved away from me, and stared at his prize wall for a moment, before yanking a breast off a hook with force, tearing the skin.

I wished he would put the tape back on, I didn't want to watch him turn the severed breast over in his hands, inspecting it like it was a prime cut of beef, but I couldn't look away.

"Yeah. She's good." He weighed the breast in his hands. "I don't suppose you'd care to join me for dinner?" He grinned sadistically at me before chuckling darkly, and walking out the door, locking it behind him.

I released a sob, letting the tears finally fall freely as they melted little spots of frost off the metal floor. Why didn't he just kill me? Why torture me? What did he want? *You have to survive. You have to find a way to escape.* The voice insisted. I dared to look around again. All these women… There were clearly more than the 14 victims we knew about. I noticed some breasts were hanging in pairs, while others were single. No doubt ones he'd already consumed. *He won't touch me.* I wouldn't let him break me. I had to believe that Warren was alive and out there, looking for me…

The night wore on, and the bar began emptying, but Warren still sat at his booth. Though the only progress he made was on his level of inebriation. At some point he requested the rest of the bottle be brought to him, to save the waitress the trips back and forth. He decided to fill out an official case file for her, which brought him back to tears. The server startled him when she approached the table.

"Last call hun, I'm about to close up."

He looked up at her blearily, and grunted.

"Was she someone special to you?"

"Yeah…" He forced himself upright.

"I know everyone's sayin' you did it… but, I've been watching you all night, and… any man who's this broken-hearted about his girl bein' lost definitely didn't have a part in it."

"I didthough…" he slurred, "I letit happ'n… couldn' saveher…" He slammed his laptop shut and shoved it in his bag, crushing other papers in the process.

She backed away as he clumsily slid out of the booth. "You gonna be alright? You got a place to stay?"

"Yeah." He slung the strap of his bag over his shoulder, and stumbled out the doors.

The cold bit his face and he wrinkled his nose at it as he glanced up and down the street. "Shit." He almost tripped on the curb. *That's what an entire bottle of whiskey does.* Where the fuck was he parked again? The only vehicle left on the street was a truck down the block, so he assumed that was him, and forced his legs to move in that direction.

"Thankgod..." he whispered as he reached the back door and unlocked it. He didn't even bother unfolding the seat before he collapsed onto it, sighing. The entire truck spun, and he held his eyes closed, picturing the night they spent together in it. A sad smile crept over his lips. *She can be so bossy*, but he loved that about her. When she finally put her foot down on something, that determined little glare, the way her fists clench... He would never admit to her that she was right about that night, he was exhausted, and after that truck almost—

His eyes shot open. In his many travels through the mountains, how many times had he seen any semi's or box trucks making deliveries after dark? None. That road was a difficult drive for them during the day, and extremely dangerous at night. To try to make it overnight, one of them would have to be desperate... *or insane.* He racked his memories, trying to remember any details of the truck, but all that flashed in his mind was the brightness of the headlights, and the panic he felt at the thought of her getting hurt.

He fished his phone from his pocket, and winced at the bright screen as it awakened, '2 a.m.'. Still too early to call him, *normal people are sleeping at this hour,* he reminded himself. He searched for delivery companies that traveled between the two cities, moving companies, anything that might give him an indication of the identity of the truck that almost ran them over. He scrolled through hundreds of pages of results, before finally losing the battle to his drooping eyelids, and the phone fell from his hand.

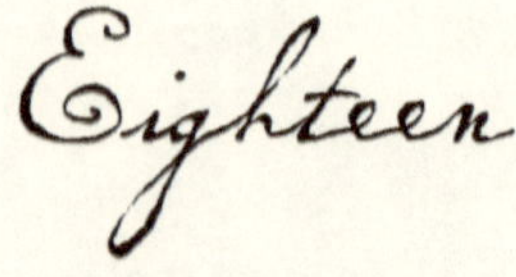

# Eighteen

Warren gasped in surprise at his ringtone and sat up forcefully, blinking into the bright sun. "Fuck…" he muttered as his hand blindly felt for his phone on the floor, finally finding it.

"Nyte." He cleared the rasp from his voice

"Based on the width alone, I'd say it was some kind of large truck. but that's just on initial glance." The voice on the other end of the phone confirmed Warren's suspicions without a greeting.

Warren rubbed his eyes. "Do you think it's enough to find a make or model?"

"I mean, we've gotten matches off less, but it's still going to take some time. It's only a partial tread."

"I get it, but a life is at stake here, whatever you have to do…"

"Why is it you never have a quick job for me man? Gimme a blood sample or something sometime."

"Thanks Ax." Warren acknowledged and hung up.

His head lay back against the seat with a sigh. *This has to lead somewhere… it* has *to*. He thought as he rubbed his eyes with his thumb and index finger, the pressure relieving a bit of the dull thud that pounded against them. What the hell does he do in the meanwhile? He felt a twinge of loneliness as he lay in the back of his truck without her, then shook his head. He couldn't afford to dwell on feelings right now. He had a job to do.

*Dig I dig.* Find out what businesses on the block where the last victim was found had deliveries that day, for a start. He sat up, forgetting for a moment he was parked in front of the cafe. "That's convenient," he muttered as he stepped out of the truck and stretched, mentally preparing himself for the homework.

The cafe was quiet, small, but fairly well lit. The square counter sat in the middle of the room, trapping the barista inside. He ordered his latte with a double shot of espresso and a breakfast sandwich, and turned to sit. His options were to sit at the counter, or at a small bar table against the window, so he chose the latter not needing more attention on him than he already drew in his disheveled state from the three hours of sleeping in his truck. He opened his laptop, and began.

Talking to some of these low level employees reminded him how much he hated kids these days. Lazy, unwilling to do the bare minimum. He had to ask very specifically for them to go ask a manager about the delivery schedules or to tell them to check when they responded with "uhh. I dunno. I didn't work that day." Like the extra effort to problem solve was too much for their little brains to process. He grunted loudly as he hung up for the fifth time with no useful information. He heard her voice in the back of his head, *grumpy old man.* He smiled sadly, he missed her teasing.

He had been at this for hours, and was running on a few hours of sleep, caffeine, and anger. He felt like shit and he knew he wasn't going to do his best work in this state. He needed a shower, and a nap.

He hesitated to get out of the truck when he pulled back up in front of the cabin, *now I know what she felt like at the hotel.* He forced himself out and through the front door. She wasn't there waiting for him, and it pulled at his heart. He dropped his bag on the table, went straight into the bathroom and stripped down. "Geez." He looked at himself in the mirror.

He was more bandage than man, and he had a pretty impressive black eye where that steel toe connected. "I look like hell," he chuckled. No wonder everyone had been staring at him. He peeled his dressings off, revealing some partially healed wounds across his chest, and mostly healed ones on his shoulder. A few areas were still raw and stung with the hot water, but the external pain was a welcome distraction for the emptiness he felt internally.

He dressed in a maroon v-neck and a different pair of black jeans, started a fire, and lay down on the sofa, staring at the mattress on the floor. "I'm sorry," he whispered. "Fight Babygirl, for as long as you can. I promise I'll find you." Though he couldn't fight his body anymore, and drifted into a deep sleep.

I had no idea what time it was, but I knew we had stayed in the same spot for long enough for him to sleep, and then began driving again for hours. Yesterday, he only stopped for the weigh in. Today, he seemed to stop more frequently, doing drop offs of whatever cargo he carried beyond my cell. Each time I heard the roll up door, I dared to hope that this time, maybe, whoever was back there might notice the lock. Might think "that's strange, maybe I should ask about that." But each time they didn't I fell deeper and deeper into despair.

I held myself as far forward on my bindings as I could, trying desperately not to touch his morbid collection. He kept the lights on. These horrible, blinding, LED lights that kept me from sleeping. Though without the tape over my eyes I finally got a good look at my ankle, which was much worse than I thought. It may have been because it had been constricted but the swelling bubbled around the zip ties and tape, and I had all but lost feeling in that foot.

For a while I tried to use my saliva to weaken the adhesive on the tape covering my mouth, but I was too dehydrated to make any real progress and I only succeeded in chapping my lips. So on top of the pain from my arms, legs, and now my stomach cramping, my lips burned as well. To tie the whole package together, my bladder was full to bursting, and thinking through an exhaustive list of possible options, the only actual doable one was to go where I lay. So I continued to hold it as best I could.

The truck stopped again, but this time, I didn't hear any other voices come to the back with him. In fact, he didn't come to the back right away, it was only after what I assumed were a few minutes that I finally heard the door open and the lock click. I didn't even bother looking up.

His feet stopped under me. "Scream and die." The sentence was short, but clear. He ripped the tape from my mouth, forcing me to suppress a cry. A cardboard to-go cup with a straw was held down to me, and though my thirst urged me to drink whatever he offered, my survival instinct fought back.

"What is it?" I could barely form words after not speaking for god knows how long.

"Drink."

"Why?"

"You can't die… No… Need you fresh." His voice was emotionless, uncaring. This wasn't about pity, it was simply necessary.

I stared down at the cup. If I took anything in, I would only need to use the bathroom more, and I was barely holding it as it was. "I need to pee."

"And?"

"If I piss myself, it's going to stink up your whole meat locker."

He huffed, placed the cup down on the floor, exited, then came back with an old 5-gallon bucket and placed it behind me. "Pee."

I waited, but he didn't leave, didn't turn around, or avert his eyes. I fought tears as I balanced as best I could on the rim, and relieved myself. He didn't offer anything to wipe with, nor was I about to ask for anything else from this monster, so I let myself drop to the floor once more, letting my knees fold under me. He moved the bucket back against the wall, and held the straw up to my mouth, this time forcing my head down.

"Drink, or die."

I obeyed, and some form of fruit smoothie fell into my mouth. Poisoned or not, the sensation of liquid on my tongue was enough to force my reflexes to greedily take the rest as fast as I could. Once I couldn't force any more through the straw, he tossed the cup aside.

"Why are you doing this?" I begged.

"You broke all the rules."

"I don't know what you're talking about."

"You saw me. Weren't on the list…" He grasped my face roughly and dug his unevenly sharp nails into my cheeks, breaking skin, and forcing me to my feet. "Your smell… I *knew* I needed your cuts. Not like the others… I need yours *fresh*. Breaking the rules." He sneered and dropped me, reached into his back pocket, and pulled out a roll of tape.

"No—" I began before he shut my mouth with another piece, picked up the bucket, and left me alone again.

We didn't move again for several hours, and though I tried, I still couldn't sleep with the constant stream of light. The cramping in my legs dissipated a bit after my liquid meal, but though I had relieved myself, the cramping in my lower abdomen did not. A fresh surge of panic flooded me when I realized it was close to that time of the month. *Please for the love of anything holy, wait… Wait until I either get rescued, or die…* I begged my uterus, as if it had ever listened to my pleas before.

A few hours after we begun moving again, I felt the first trickle drip down my legs, and I cried.

Warren's phone rang from the kitchen table, and his eyes fluttered open. He drug himself across the room, half awake.

"Yeah?" He yawned.

"It's a pair of back tires on a box truck." Ax responded. "Specifically a reefer, you know, the refrigerated ones?"

His heart rate picked up. "Can you tell a brand?"

"I'll do you one better, I can tell you what companies use these tires."

"Shit," he smiled. "You didn't have to do all that."

"My brother in Christ, you needed all the help you could get with this one. Just say you owe me."

"You're a fucking genius, and I definitely owe you."

"I know, it's a curse," he could hear a smile in Ax's voice. "I'll send you the results, good luck man."

Finally, a lead. *It only took losing her to get it.* He frowned. *Not worth it.* He shuffled back to the sofa and sat while he waited for the email, noticing daylight streaming through the windows. "Shit, how long did I sleep?" He checked the time, "fuck, 12 hours?"

He got the notification, and squinted against the bright screen as he read the report. At least 15 different trucking companies used these tires. He grunted at the thought of the groundwork that lay ahead of him. This had always been his least favorite part. Following people, snapping photos, even the angry confrontations were preferable to, *ugh*, phone calls. *It's for her.* He reminded himself, and he would literally do any number of unpleasant tasks to get her back.

Each company he called received the same interrogation. 'Did they have any trucks in the area? When were they scheduled to arrive or depart? What stops were they scheduled to make?' The answer to each question either prompted the next, or ended the conversation. He spent the better part of the morning on hold or being transferred. Was it too much to ask that a single person could answer all his questions? He only had five more on his list when to his utter shock, this dispatcher answered each question to his liking.

"Who's the driver?" He tried to hide the excitement in his voice.

"I'm pretty sure that's Pete's route." She typed something in the background. "Yep, he likes taking the long ones."

"Do you know what the rest of his route schedule is like, and his last name? I want to try to get a message to him at his next stop," he lied.

"Uhh. Well it's Brown, Pete Brown… but I'm not sure I should be giving out our route information—"

He put on an air of informality. "Oh I get it, it's a weird request, but he and I got to talking about barbecue and I promised I'd send him a recipe. And darn it if I lost his number…"

"Well… I guess there's no harm in it. It's not like he's making secret deliveries or anything like that," she laughed.

"You're an angel," Warren gushed. "I'll let him know to thank you."

"Oh stop it," she sounded flustered. "Looks like he's got a few more stops on his route, did you want to write them down or should I email them to you?"

"Email would be great. We know how I am with losing information," Warren forced a flirtatious laugh.

"No problem," she giggled.

He recited his email, and thanked her with a few extra compliments, only feeling mildly guilty about lying. He then did a search on "Pete Brown" and was less than surprised when the face of Connor Borges stared back at him on the screen.

"Got you, fucker."

The notation dropped down that the email from the dispatcher came in, and he opened it. She had not only sent the next few stops, but his entire route schedule, and he quickly noticed that each stop was within a five-mile radius to a location of a murder. "Oh come on. This is too easy."

The next scheduled stop was a six-hour drive, and Borges was due at 5 p.m.. He did some quick math. "Fuck, I won't make it." But the following day's delivery was only four hours away. He could cut Borges off, get there before him. His adrenaline surged as he sat up and began packing everything messily into the bags, except her things, he took his time to fold her clothes and put them nicely away.

Then he drove, like a madman.

My cramps had always been unbearable, debilitating, ever since I was a teenager, and of course this time was no different. Even with my arms bound above my head, my extremities beginning to sting from the freezing air, and my ankle combined, I couldn't focus on any of it above the sharp, stabbing shredding that occurred in my abdomen. With my legs bound, there was no way for me to avoid coating my legs in my own mess, and I really had no strength to try to hold myself up, so I non-consensually surrendered to the humiliation.

We only stopped once today, and I seriously considered screaming this time. This torture wasn't worth it, death sounded like sweet relief… But the thought of Warren finding my mutilated body, imagining him going through what I did when I found that girl… I couldn't do that to him. I closed my eyes and forced myself to think of him. I teared up again as I thought of that stupid, attractive, way he runs his fingers through his hair when he's thinking. That dimple that betrays his smiles when he tries to pretend I'm annoying him. How he comes off as so dangerous, sees himself as a monster, but was really one of the sweetest, most sensitive people I knew…

I was startled out of my daydreams by the sound of the lock. I hadn't realized we stopped again. How long had it been this time? Borges entered and immediately honed in on the smell of my blood. His expression turned feral.

"What's this?" He licked his lips and walked eerily slowly towards me before ripping the tape of my mouth.

"It's called a period," I answered dryly.

"You… You weren't supposed to bleed yet…" He sniffed the air around me, his voice becoming more like a whine.

"I don't really have control of it, genius. It comes when it comes."

"Still… breaking… rules…" He ran his finger up the dried blood on my leg, and licked it.

I suppressed a gag.

"Mmm… Different seasoning than the rest… I wonder how it compares…" He ripped my hoodie open, revealing my chest to the icy cold as he grew one of his claws out to a piercing point.

"No… nonono…" I begged pointlessly as he sliced down the side of my breast.

His bony hand covered my agonizing screams as he lapped the fresh blood off my skin and smacked his lips like a dog after a meal.

"Hmm. No. Definitely better…" Then he suddenly pushed me over, snarling. "NO. No… You were supposed to be fresh. Can't wait…" He shook his head violently. "Not time… Not time for harvest… Need new friend…" He backed away as if my presence was killing him and slammed the door.

"Oh god… He's going to kill again," I whispered, realizing the tape missing from my mouth.

Warren double checked the address of the restaurant he had stopped in front of. "Yep, this is it." Borges was due to make his delivery here in a few hours. He pulled back out into traffic, and around the corner to the back of the building, and parked across the street to begin his vigil. He downed the rest of his energy drink and cracked open another. There was no way he would risk nodding off.

These poor employees had no idea that their delivery driver was a serial killer. He observed a few of them come out back for a smoke break, or to take out the trash. How many people does this asshole interact with in a day? How many times does he have an opportunity to take another victim?

He considered for a moment about contacting the local police, but decided against it. What good have any cops done for this case so far? Besides, they'd need to do things by the book, follow the law... He wasn't bound by such inconveniences, and he wasn't planning on handling Borges in a legally-upstanding manner.

He reclined his seat, opened a chess game on his phone, and waited.

A small reefer truck rumbled through the alley towards the restaurant, and Warren slouched further down in his seat. The company name on the side of the truck matched his notes. His heart pounded as it backed against the loading dock, turned off, and Borges exited from the drivers side. Warren had to use all his self-restraint not to leap out and attack him in broad daylight. He had to follow

305

Borges, find out where he was hiding her, or her body. As much as he wanted Borges dead, his priority had changed. Recovering her became so much more important.

He watched in disgust as Borges exchanged pleasantries with the restaurant workers, cracking jokes and helping them unload. How could someone fake being so normal, and be such a fucking psycho? "C'mon..." Warren drummed his fingers impatiently on the steering wheel, "take me to her." Finally Borges got back in, started the truck, and took back off down the alley.

Warren followed as Borges made an unnecessary amount of turns and changes of direction, even getting back on the freeway for a moment, before turning around and heading towards the seedier part of the city. The sun set as they passed by several strip clubs and bars, their lights turning on for the night. Borges slowed his truck at each one as if he was shopping.

"Fucking creep," Warren muttered.

Borges made a sharp turn into an alley two blocks from the main businesses, between a warehouse and office building. Warren passed slowly, and saw that Borges had parked the truck. He made a U-turn, and parked across the street on the same block. Borges exited, with a blue cooler in hand, and looked both ways before casually beginning his walk in the direction of the bars.

Warren hesitated. *Do I follow him? He's obviously about to claim another victim. I can stop him... But... his truck is unguarded.* His brow furrowed. If he goes after Borges, he could potentially save another woman. But he could also miss his opportunity to find clues on her whereabouts. He would have to sacrifice the woman to give himself time to search the truck. It wasn't even a difficult decision. *She matters more.* He stepped out of his truck, watched the top of Borges head move down the block, and ran into the alley.

He didn't return to me, but we also didn't move for a while. Either he had fallen asleep, or he was out searching for a victim. Maybe… Maybe he just left? Abandoned the truck somewhere? I heard the engine start up.

So much for hope.

Another journey of immense pain, and though it could have been my imagination, today's drive felt much longer. Although he left my mouth uncovered, he left my chest in the same condition, and I would have gladly traded the tape for him to have zipped me back up. I shivered violently, and could no longer tell cold pain, from period pain, from strain pain. I tried my best to curl up as tight as I could, but the smell of blood sickened me, and the closer I brought my legs to my face, the more nauseous I got.

I was tired… So tired… and so cold… I just wanted to sleep… Please, just sleep through the rest of this nightmare… I think I may have even begun to drift in and out, or at least I was delirious enough to daydream vividly, because at one point Warren lay behind me, his arm around me, his warm breath on my neck… and then he was gone.

I adjusted my position, finding that using my suspended arm as a pillow was not comfortable, and kneeled. Dinah jumped up onto my lap, purring. Her warm little body thawed my legs as I stroked her soft fur. "I'll be home soon." I said to her. "Warren and I will be home soon." I blinked, and found my fingers twitching in the air.

I jolted to the side as the squeal of the breaks echoed around me. But then, that could have been my imagination too, because no one came to the back of the truck, and I was too numb to feel if we were actually moving or not. I let myself fall into another fantasy, where I was warm and comfortable. If I was lucky, maybe I'd be in one when Borges came to kill me, and I wouldn't even notice.

Warren held me tightly and kissed my forehead. *"Brave girl,"* He whispered. *"I'm so proud of you."*

"I miss you," I whispered back.

*"I know, but here we can be together. No one can hurt you here."*

"Can we stay forever?"

*"Yes, Babygirl."*

I was finally warm, and my body no longer ached. I sighed happily as I drifted to sleep.

It was easy enough to break into the passenger side of the truck. Warren rifled through Borges' papers in this glove box, finding his registration, order forms, his company badge... all with the name "Pete Brown".

"You couldn't have even picked a more original name dude?" Warren huffed as he continued to the center console, but was coming up empty. How does he have nothing incriminating? This guy was a fucking monster and he comes across as the most basic-ass bitch. He grunted, slammed the compartments shut, and stepped out.

He moved to the back, skillfully picked the lock, and flung the roll up door open to a blast of refrigerated air. Pallets of fresh produce were piled around him. He stepped inside and moved a few boxes around, digging through them for any indication of foul play. Not finding anything, he screamed, "WHERE *ARE* YOU?!" And slammed his fist against the back wall, causing an echo behind it. "What the fuck?"

He ran his hands along the wall, tapping. *It was hollow.* His eyes widened. There had to be a door. He threw boxes of food carelessly away from it, scattering fruits and vegetables everywhere until the top corner of a frame came into view. His heart leapt, and he dragged the last pallet away from the wall to see a metal door with a padlock on it. He picked it, threw the door open, and his jaw dropped.

A macabre mural of female anatomy littered the walls. He had seen some sick shit, but this was fucking— His eyes fell to the back corner of the room, where she lay unconscious, suspended in an unnatural angle, in a pool of her own blood. He gasped and ran to her, quickly cutting her down.

"Oh… No…" He held her body as she limply fell into his arms. "No... God, *no*." He picked her up and carried her outside as the tears began to fall.

# Nineteen

"Adelaide!" I heard my name from somewhere… but I was warm, and comfortable. I didn't want to leave. "Please, Adelaide… wake up. Oh god… *please*." It was Warren, but that couldn't be, he was here with me.

No, he wasn't. I found myself alone, in the dark.

"Fuck… please, Babygirl, come back to me… Don't do this…" He sounded scared.

I had to help him. I opened my eyes.

"*Ohmygod*," Warren gasped. "Adelaide, I'm here. You're okay. You'll be okay," he pulled me against him.

Everything looked blurry, and I was still unsure whether I was dreaming or not, but his tearful eyes pleaded for me to stay wherever we were, so I tried. "Warren?"

"I'm here, Baby. I'm so sorry," he cried. "Fuck. I'm sorry. This is all my fault." He pressed my head to his chest as he rocked me.

I could smell him. I couldn't smell him before.

My vision focused, and it was no longer bright. We were outside, at night, on the floor… "Am I… dreaming?"

"No, Baby, this is real." He kissed the top of my head, and his lips were *warm* against me... I began to shiver again.

"I'm... c-cold..."

He ripped off his jacket and threw it over me. "I know, I'll fix it." His tears dripped onto my chest.

Reality slowly set in. I was in the back of Borges' truck, surrounded by his trophies... my legs covered in... "Oh... no... your jacket..." I tried to push it off me. "I'm bleeding. You don't want to touch me—"

"I don't give a fuck if you're covered in radioactive waste, I'm not letting you go." He cupped his hand on my cheek.

"Always breaking rules." A snarl came from behind us.

Warren quickly set me down. Cracked asphalt scratched against my bare legs as he leaned my back against the tire. He turned to face the voice, and stood over me.

"Stay the fuck away from her you, fucking bastard," he warned darkly.

"You... are trying to take my friend?!" Borges wheezed angrily.

"I'm going to fucking kill you, you sick fuck."

I looked between Warren's legs, finally able to lift my head. Borges stood at the entrance of an alley, clawed nails fully extended and bloody. A blue cooler in his hand dripped scarlet from the opening. He clearly succeeded in finding another "friend". Panic and guilt overtook me as I looked up at Warren's body standing protectively over mine.

311

"No…" I tried to yell, but it came out in barely a whisper. I couldn't let him get hurt again…

Borges grimaced a smile at Warren's battered face. "I won our last game… Does he want to play again?"

"Oh yes, he fucking does," Warren growled.

"For keepsies…" Borges slobbered as he looked at me on the ground.

It was enough to send Warren into a frenzy. He ran at Borges, who dropped the cooler and dove claws first.

I screamed hoarsely as I lunged forward, the effort of which sent black spots flashing in my eyes.

Warren dodged, and side kicked Borges into the brick wall, his head colliding with a loud crack.

I rolled onto all fours, straining to get my breath. Why was it so hard to gain my bearings?

Warren strode towards Borges, who lay on the ground, but as soon as he was in reach Borges slashed at Warren's leg. Fountains of red shot from his calf.

Warren fought Borges hand to hand, with no abilities, and no weapon. I panicked.

Borges was going to kill him.

Warren went down on one knee. Borges jumped up and lunged at him with a single nail aimed at his throat, but Warren miraculously grabbed his claw as it landed inches from his skin, and broke it off with a loud snap.

Borges wailed in agony as Warren chucked the broken nail behind him.

Borges' expression turned from manic, to raging. He screamed and tackled Warren, pinning him underneath him, his remaining four spears directed right at his heart.

I gasped a realization, and mustered all the energy I had. "Warren!" I screamed. "*MY* FEAR!"

My distraction caused Borges to look up just long enough for Warren to understand, and change into his mirror.

Borges looked down at him in shock, as Warren kicked out with regained strength, turning on his hand and grew out his own nails.

Both men only wasted a millisecond staring at each other, before being back at each other's throats.

I didn't take my eyes off them as one Borges slashed at the other, turning and kicking in a lethal dance. I slowly gathered enough strength to stand, but my ankle protested and failed me as I stumbled, leaning against the hood of the truck.

In the split second I looked away, I lost track of who was who. My eyes darted between them as a nail went through another's side, and the other raked the first ones' arm.

One Borges suddenly had the other pinned against the wall by his throat, and lifted its body off the ground with an impressive show of strength. Though the pinned Borges managed to get his nails into the other's arm and was slowly pulling it off his neck.

I glanced at the hand of the Borges' who had the other pinned, and saw the missing index nail. My breath caught as I realized the one hanging up at his mercy was Warren.

Time slowed as my blood pounded in my ears.

I watched in horror as his face slowly began to turn back into his own, losing the fight against The Carver. I glanced down, and the detached claw lay between us. My adrenaline surged, all pain forgotten as I ran and swiped up the discarded body part, coming to stand behind the true monster.

"Hey, stalker!" I shouted.

Borges turned, and the moment I caught sight of his soulless eye I plunged the tip of his nail through it with all my might. A crunching, squishing, sucking sound accompanied his howl as my fist made contact with his face, the end of his own weapon pushed clear through the other side of his skull.

His body wavered slightly as he dropped Warren, before collapsing in a pool of his own blood onto the alley floor.

I dropped to my knees and crawled to Warren's body, as he slowly lifted himself on all fours, spitting blood.

"Are you okay?" We both choked out at the same time, and laughed painfully.
"I will be, now that I know you're safe." He smiled weakly up at me, his lip and forehead cut open. He fell onto his hip, and raised his hand towards my face. "Baby… " his eyes fluttered, and he collapsed.

"Warren?!" I bent over him, and put my fingers to his neck. His pulse felt weak. I tried to stand, but my ankle wasn't having it. I crawled to his jacket which I left on the ground by the truck, frantically searched the pockets, and was surprised to find my phone. My hands shook as I dialed 911, and crawled back to him.

"911, what's the address of the emergency?"

"I… don't know." I began to hyperventilate. "I was kidnapped. My boyfriend is hurt…" I looked down at him, he was so pale.

I dropped the phone and it clattered onto the pavement. "Warren, please stay with me…" I scooped up his head, placed it in my lap, and brushed his hair back. "Baby, please…  don't leave me …" I felt faint.

*Have to stay awake… have to save him…*

"Mr. Nyte, if you don't go back to your bed this instant, I swear I'll sedate you again." I heard a scolding voice from somewhere in the distance. "I've told you a hundred times, Ms. Quinn is in good hands."

I forced my eyes open, and was met with a bright white light. I panicked at the thought of the inside of Borges' truck, but as I came to, I realized I was in a bed. My vision cleared to the sight of a hospital room.

"Jackie, if you don't get out of my way, I'll turn into a clown." Warren's voice sounded from outside my door.

"Don't you threaten me, you big, handsome bully!" A woman, who I assumed was Jackie, exclaimed. My door opened, and Warren stood there in a hospital gown, dragging an IV behind him.

His eyes lit up when he saw me. "You're awake."

I tried to sit up, but found I, too, was connected to a series of tubes. "And you're alive," I smiled.

He limped as he dragged himself to my bedside, which brought to my attention the numerous bandages and wrappings he was plastered in.

"Oh, Warren…" I sighed.

He looked down at himself, then back at me and chuckled. "You should see the other guy." He sat in a chair at my side.

"I never want to see that guy again," I shook my head.

"And thanks to you, no one will." He brushed my hair out of my face. "You fucking badass," he smiled.

I vaguely remembered the events of that night, but the feeling of stabbing someone through the eye would never leave me. Though I had no remorse, no guilt, and it frightened me a bit. "I… killed him…" the words sounded foreign on my tongue.

"You did," he nodded softly. "In self-defense. You saved my life, Babygirl."

"You saved mine first," I looked up at him.

"I didn't realize it was a contest." His eyes glinted as his dimple peeked out from under a bandage, and he leaned forward and kissed me softly, his lips rough from his healing cuts.

"I don't remember what happened after I called the police…" I admitted. "The last thing I knew, you were in my lap… so pale…"

"I woke up in the ambulance, but you were still out," he explained. "The medics said they found us both in the alley, passed out in front of Borges body. You had pretty severe hypothermia, they were shocked you were even able to wake up after I got you out of his truck. Your ankle is pretty badly sprained too, you're going to have to stay off it for a few weeks."

"And you?"

"A few cuts, got a few stitches, nothing I haven't dealt with before."

I looked up to the ceiling in thought, recalling the bloody cooler Borges carried. "Did… he claim another?"

Warren nodded, "yeah." He looked away. "I knew he was going to… but, I chose to search for you instead."

I found his hand on the bedside, and squeezed it. "Thank you."

His eyes met mine. "Always."

"Alright Romeo, I gave you plenty of time, now you need to get back in bed—" Jackie burst in then looked down at me. "Well now, welcome back. Not sure how you deal with this one, he's a menace." She smiled and shook her head.

Warren gave me a guilty smile and I laughed softly. "Yeah, but he's *my* menace."

The reporters were on us faster than flies on a pile of shit in summer. Jackie became my personal hero, fighting off journalists, tv crew, and FBI agents for us while we lay in recovery. They had moved him in with me after I woke up. Apparently he refused treatment until they did so, and

317

though it only took a few days for me to feel back to my normal self, Warren was worse off than he let on.

He sustained multiple deep lacerations, a few of them narrowly missing vital organs, as well as a broken nose, fractured ribs, and a concussion. I was allowed up and about on crutches while he was confined to the bed for another week, which was hell for both of us. How someone could be so stubborn, yet such a big-ass baby at the same time was a wonder.


"Oh my *god*. Please *no*! I would rather get stabbed in the liver again…"

"Seriously? Warren, it's not that bad."

"It is. I'm fighting for my life here, suffering in bed as it is, and they keep subjecting me to *that*?" He pointed at his plate of bland chicken and mac and cheese that they brought him for dinner.

I laughed, "okay, it really is that bad, but you need to eat something other than jello."

"You think they'd let me into the kitchen?"

"Not even if you were at 100%," I smiled. "For me? Please?"

He glared at me. "Fuck you and your angel eyes. You are taking advantage of a helpless man."

"Absolutely," I chuckled. "I promise you can cook for me every day for the rest of our lives, just eat this slop so you can get better and get out of here."

He smiled, and stared at me.

"What?"

"The rest of our lives?"

"Shut up. You know what I meant," I blushed.

He gave me a little growl. "Control that heart of yours Baby, I can't do anything about it while I'm stuck here —"

*"You* can't..." I smirked and trailed my fingers down his thigh over the blanket.

His eyebrows raised. "Naughty girl, do you know how *wrong* that would be?" He chuckled, but shifted his legs.

"I think we've crossed the line of right and wrong enough for *this* not to matter in the grand scheme."

His lips parted as desire glossed over his eyes. "Fuck, you're so bad..."

I smiled slyly, "don't pretend you don't love that about me." I looked over my shoulder at the closed door. During dinner they usually give him at least half an hour before checking on him. I looked back at him.

"God, I fucking do..." He bit his lip and reached for my face, brushing his thumb over my bottom lip.

I grabbed it between my lips and sucked it into my mouth, releasing it with a kiss.

He exhaled slowly, and the blanket rose between his legs.

I slid my fingers under the blanket, and trailed them across his hip, tracing his v-line down to where he was already hard for me. "Watch the door," I commanded quietly, as my fingers wrapped around the base of his cock, the tips unable to reach each other.

He gasped, and twitched at my touch.

I gave a gentle squeeze, before releasing my grasp and trailing my fingers up his length, softly tracing his seam. My girl throbbed at the feel of his silken skin under my hand.

"*Fuck,* Babygirl... your hands are agony..." He moaned quietly.

I circled his head, coaxing a drop of lust from it, before encircling him in my grasp and pushing him through it slowly.

His hips thrust under the blanket as his fingers grasped the bedsheets. I pumped my hand up and down his length, alternating pressure as I increased speed. His breaths shortened, and his muscles tensed. He winced in pain at the pressure it put on his ribs, but grasped my free hand with his in a silent beg for me to continue.

*"Mmm... fuck... that's my good girl... I'm so fucking close..."* He whispered as he panted, right before his grip constricted around my hand, and his eyes shut against his release. His body convulsed under my touch as his cum coated my hand in three long, separate streams. He fought a moan by biting his fist, as his body stilled under the blanket.

I bit my lip, fighting my own desires at the sight of him, before I stood and grabbed a towel to clean us.

"You... are going... to be... the death of me..." He panted as I sat back down at his side, letting him cup my face in his hand. "And I fucking love you for it."

I smiled at his aggressive adoration. "I love you too."

# Twenty

It was *so* good to be home. I stood in my doorway and just stared ahead at my tiny living room, basking in the silence, which only lasted a moment before Dinah bounded up to me meowing dramatically. I hobbled in on my crutches and tossed them against the couch before sitting down to pick her up.

"I missed you so much!" I kissed her fuzzy little face.

"And I barely got a 'hey'," Rory laughed as she entered behind me, and turned over her shoulder. "Better hurry, your girl is giving all your love away to a cat."

"That cat and I have a written treaty on the subject." Warren limped in last, smiling.

I laughed up at them both. "I have enough love for all three of you."

"Go sit, gimpy," she commanded Warren with a smile, and fished his keys out of his pocket. "I'll get your bags out of your truck."

He flopped down beside me, and Dinah abandoned me for him. "Slut," I muttered to her and laughed.

He chuckled as he scratched her behind the ear. "She's just coming over here to say 'I told you so'."

"For what?"

"I tried to deny it, but she was the first one to know I was falling in love with you," his eyes gleamed.

I don't think I had ever used the dining room table for anything other than storage before that night, and having the only two people in the world who mattered to me sitting on either side of me, while we enjoyed an amazing meal, cooked by my *boyfriend* made me the happiest woman alive.

"I've got good news." Rory began as she poured herself a second glass of wine, "I met with the Judge and they're going to dismiss your case on self-defense."

"Meaning what?" I asked.

"Meaning you were fully within your rights to stab that fucker's eye out through his skull," Warren explained. "Though I'm assuming that means they're also closing The Carver case with no conviction," he turned to Rory.

She nodded, "can't bring a dead man to trial. At least not in this country, but I don't think anyone is going to complain about it."

"So just like that? It's over?" I put my glass down slowly. It didn't feel real, for something so heinous, something that had baffled police for months, to just be finished in the snap of a finger.

"Thanks to you two, yes," Rory sat back in her chair. "If you hadn't killed him in that alley, who knows how long the trials would have been. Do you know how much the media would have eaten it up? He would have been given fame, money, book deals, you name it. That guy deserved nothing more than what he got, and all those women got *real* justice. Though, as your lawyer, my advice is to refrain from stabbing anyone else unless your life is in danger, okay?" She smiled.

"Noted," I laughed.

"Now, changing subjects. Mrs. Tibbet's attorney has been trying to get ahold of you."

"Mrs. T has an attorney?"

Rory nodded. "They've been holding off on the reading of her will until you were available."

"Oh." I looked down. "I didn't even think she had a will, since she didn't have family."

"I can let him know you're out of the hospital, if you're up for meeting with him?"

"Sure." I looked up at them both, "will you guys come with me?"

"Of course," Warren smiled softly.

"And I have to, being your lawyer, but I'll be there as your sister as well," Rory smiled too.

Warren held the door open for me into a huge lobby with black and white marble flooring. I gawked up at the open ceiling, revealing all 30-something floors stacked above us. Glass elevators crawled up and down on both sides, while people in expensive suits walked about on the open balcony hallways. We slowly approached the black marble reception desk, them patiently waiting for my ass on crutches.

"Good morning. Aurora Quinn for Mr. Gurillo," Rory spoke confidently. "We're his 11 a.m."

I turned my head upward again as they spoke, noting a golden chandelier hanging halfway down the building.

Warren whistled beside me. "Imagine having an office in here…"

"No kidding. I bet none of these guys ever have any old men in wife-beaters breaking down their doors." I eyed the several modern sculptures stationed around the lobby floor.

He chuckled, "well, that's no fun."

I laughed, "you would enjoy that, you twisted man."


Mr. Gurillo came down to greet us and escorted us back to his office, which was even more expensively dressed than he was. Several large, leather armchairs circled the front of an even larger mahogany desk that sat in front of a bookshelf which made me gasp with envy. The books on it seemed incredibly dull, and I imagined what it would look like in my tiny apartment, filled with my fantasy, sci-fi, and romance novels…

"Thank you for joining me, Ms. Quinn. I'm sorry to hear about your injuries." He stole my attention away from it as he sat in his chair across from us.

"Oh, yeah. Of course." Rory held my crutches for me while Warren gave his hands to help lower me in the chair, before taking the one to my right.

"And thank you for your patience while she recovered," Rory sat in the one to my left, "we know it's been much longer than the standard timeframe."

Mr. Gurillo shook his head. "Not at all. You were the sole benefactor Ms. Quinn, so we could have taken all the time we needed."

"Benefactor?" I tilted my head.

"Yes," he responded. "Her only request was that this be read to you in person."

I looked at Warren, who shrugged.

"If we're ready? I'll jump right into it?"

I nodded, and Mr. Gurillo opened a yellow folder, pulled out a sealed envelope, unfolded a letter and began to read:

*"My Dearest Adelaide,*

*If you are hearing this letter, that means I have moved on from this world, and am finally at peace. I know your wonderfully big heart is probably hurting right now, but please Dearie, don't be sad for me. I'm happy to be back with my Albert, and all my kitties that passed before me. I cannot tell you how much I cherished our chats, your visits, hearing about your life, and reliving my youth through your eyes. Even if I had an infinite amount of time on this world it wouldn't be enough to teach you everything I learned on my own, and I hope that you were able to take something away from our little tea times.*

*I know you have had your heart broken my dear, by many who should have protected it with all their might, but please, don't let that keep you from giving it to others. You have so much love to give, more than anyone I have ever met. You are a sweet, selfless, caring, courageous young woman and my wish for you is to share yourself with the world. If you promise to do just that, all my earthly possessions are yours. I only ask that you pass on your ability to love to someone else before your time has come to an end, and if it is not too much to ask, could you please watch over my babies? I know you love them as much as I do, and all their needs will be paid for.*

*Oh, and don't forget to have some fun dearie,*
*Much Love, Mrs. T."*

Tears streamed down my face as he folded the letter, and I heard Warren sniffle from my right.

"With that being said," Mr. Gurillo continued, "Mrs. Tibbet has bequeathed to you her family's home north of the city, along with the property it sits on, as well as the entirety of her savings."

"Her… home?" I coughed. "She owned a house?"

"It seems so." He picked up a paper and handed it to Rory, who held her hand out for it.

She scanned the page, her eyes widening. "Addy… this property is worth *a lot*." She handed me the paper.

My jaw dropped. "Mrs. T…" I gasped. "I had no idea… She lived in that tiny apartment longer than I did…" I handed the paper to Warren.

He ran his hand through his hair as he puffed out a breath. "Shit."

"It's yours, along with all its contents, effective the moment of her passing," Mr. Gurillo stated. "I expect you and I will be discussing the details?" He looked to Rory, who nodded.

"Babygirl, I love you, but there's no way that's going to work…" Warren sighed as he changed lanes.

"Why not? We've already pretty much been living together for two weeks now." I tried to hide my disappointment.

"What happens when I have to start working on cases again? Coming and going at all hours, being gone for days… Not to mention I need an office. Your place is too small, My Love."

"You can keep your office..." I responded dejectedly.

"I can't afford to pay rent at two places," he shook his head, "and before you even say it, no. If we moved in together there's no way I'd let you pay for everything on your own. Even with your new job. That's not fair."

I looked down silently, twisting my hands.

He glanced over, took one of them off my lap, and brought it to his lips. "I'm not saying no, just not yet." His voice was gentle. "I'm just... I'm not sure I'm ready. It doesn't mean I love you any less."

"Okay," I sighed, but my heart was still sore.

He stared out the windshield, his expression unreadable.

I understood, and I would never want to push him if he wasn't ready. After all, he had been totally fine being on his own before he met me. I was the lonely one. The fact of which didn't occur to me until Rory flew back home with two of Mrs. T's cats, and he told me he would go back to his apartment after my ankle was fully healed. I was going to be alone again, and I didn't like it. We drove in silence the rest of the way.

The road wound upward as the houses began to spread apart. Tall evergreens and granite walls jutted around the road which seemed to be paved around the natural landscape, rather than through it. The driveways got longer, and the cars in them more expensive as we began to see speedboats and fishing boats among the family vehicles. The navigator took us through a series of streets off the main road, until it had us turn off, and go down a long gravel driveway, and at the end stood a massive, dove-grey, victorian-style lake house.

I stared wide eyed as we circled around the driveway and parked in front. "This can't be the right house." I gaped as I gingerly stepped out of the truck and looked up to the multi spired, black roof.

"This place is out of a goddamn movie…" Warren came around and stood at my side.

"Did you put in the address right?"

He looked at his phone, "yeah. Go check if the key works."

I stepped up the stone paved steps and put the key Rory gave me into the lock of the double doors, and turned. It clicked. I held my breath as I opened the door.

It was dark and a bit musty. The furniture was dressed for halloween in their white sheets, but the lighting that shone through the full wall of windows illuminated dark brown, hand carved moldings and details. The house echoed under my steps as I walked through the living room's hardwood floor to look out the windows. I gasped at the sight of a dock stretched over a sparkling lake.

"Holy fucking shit…" his voice echoed behind me. "Grandma was holding out on you…"

Why on earth would she have this place just sitting, collecting dust? Why would she live in the middle of a dirty apartment building, when she could have been enjoying a life of luxury? There were a series of picture frames sitting on the mantle of a stone-laid fireplace. I picked one up, and blew the dust off to see the face of a much younger Mrs. T in the arms of a kind eyed man. "Albert," I whispered. She only had one photo of him in her apartment, and that was when they were both much older. This photo was taken on the dock outside, and they were laughing. The bright sun shone off the water behind them, where a little rowboat sat docked in the background.

As we explored the house we discovered several rooms, a few furnished as bedrooms, others as office spaces, and to my utter delight, a circular room at the top of a turret that was wall to wall bookshelves. Warren leaned against the doorframe chuckling as I gushed about it.

The kitchen was too fucking huge for my taste, but he took extra time in it. I watched his mind wander as he ran his hands over the granite countertops. Something twinkled in his eyes, and he smiled.

We moved outside to find a detached shed and boathouse, where the rowboat from the photo sat atop some wooden stilts.

"So, when are you moving in?" He laughed breathily as we sat on the dock, watching the sunset.

"Funny," I smiled. "The plan is still to sell it. I don't need a house this big for just myself and three cats." I kicked the water below me with my bare feet, sending a splash of ripples rolling away from us.

"What about three cats, yourself, and… a boyfriend?"

My heart leapt. "Any particular boyfriend you have in mind?"

"Mmm… Maybe a stubborn, grumpy, mutated one who's afraid of commitment…" He bumped me with his shoulder, then smiled down at me. "But one who's absolutely crazy about you. One who couldn't stop himself imagining waking up to your beautiful smile every morning when we saw that master bedroom. One who fell in love with you all over again when he saw your face in that library. One who wants to spoil you, cook all your favorite meals for you, let you give him attitude, just so he can fuck it out of you under the stars on this dock. One who has actually been considering this for weeks."

"Yeah?" I swooned. "What happened with not being ready?"

He sighed and looked up at the purple sky. "I don't know how it's going to work with my job. I might not come home every night, and last time I lived with someone I loved, she cheated on me when I turned my back… I was afraid, I still am," he looked back at me, the starlight reflecting off the water shone in his eyes, "but some fears are worth facing." He gripped my chin in his fingers, pulled me towards him, and kissed me.

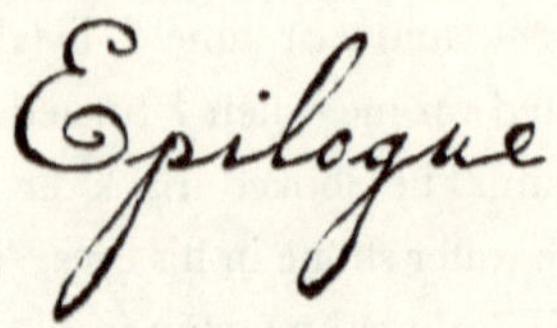



I forgot how much I fucking *LOVE* the smell of the holidays, and it was only enhanced with Warren's recipes cooking alongside Rory's. I helped Ginger set the table, as we had both been banished by our better halves from the kitchen lest we "fuck up their rhythm."

As it turned out, we had a lot in common. We were both avid readers, we both hated mushrooms, and both had plenty to complain about when it came to high schoolers.

"Oh my god, and when one of them told me that 'they didn't take fashion advice from anyone born in the 1900's' I almost fucking lost it…" She laughed. "Like why do they need to cut so deep?"

"Right?! One of them came in the other day because they were doing a report on 'ancient technology', and their teacher told them to ask the librarian if we had any VCR's!"

We both busted up.

Way too much food and alcohol later, the four of us sat cozily in front of the fireplace in Rory and Ginger's living room, watching the snowfall outside. They already had the tree up, but its twinkling lights couldn't hold a candle to Warren's eyes as he looked down at me with his arm around my shoulder. An orange tabby jumped on my lap. "Hey, Gunther," I scratched his chin, and he curled up purring.

Ginger made the mistake of asking how Warren and I met, and we recalled our summer's adventure in avid detail, to her fascination.

"…and when I saw him start to pass out in Borges' grasp, I just acted on pure instinct. I didn't think 'I'm going to stab this fucker in the eye', I just… I dunno," I shrugged.

"You went into mama-bear mode," Ginger smiled.

"Wait," Warren interrupted. "I didn't pass out until after you killed him."

"You did then too, but remember, Baby? You began to turn back into yourself."

"But that wasn't from me passing out."

We all stopped and looked at him.

"I can only take the form of physical fears." He looked at me, shocked that this was fresh information. "When that stopped being Borges, I lost the ability to hold his shape."

"What?" I tilted my head in confusion. "My fear changed?"

He smiled at my cluelessness. "Babygirl, at that moment, your greatest fear became losing me."

"You two are too fucking cute, it's disgusting," Rory groaned.

I met his shining gaze, smiling back at him. We didn't have to say a word, because I knew that we both could sense it, in a way that no one else could understand;

There was nothing better to be afraid of.

## Sinful Habit

I held my breath, waiting for someone to come back in, and when they didn't I crawled out from behind the frames, staring at the wall where the three men emerged. *If it was a drug den, and Carlos worked for the cartel, then he must have a stash of Glitter back there.* My heart sped at the prospect, and I rushed to the wood paneled wall, sliding my hands over it as I searched for the way in.

I stood back and inspected it. There was a conspicuous wood knot a few feet from where the door opened, and I ran my finger over it, feeling a slight outline. I pressed, and the wall cracked open.

I pushed my way through and closed it behind me, sealing myself in darkness. The pounding rain outside echoed around me. I pulled my phone out of my back pocket and tapped on the flashlight.

The beam shone on the corner of a steel room, where a metal table sat against the wall lined with various menacing looking tools. I recognized a few files, clamps, and handheld rotary machines, but others I could only guess at their use.

A shuffling from my right scared the shit out of me.

I turned the light quickly in that direction, and gasped.

A man was kneeling on the floor, naked, except for a pair of tattered jeans. His hands were bound individually by metal cuffs which were chained with thick steel to industrial hooks in the wall. His head hung over his torso and blood dripped from two horns on his head, staining his hair red.

As the light hit him, he slightly tilted his head upward, revealing a pair of stunning green eyes hidden behind blonde curls. He squinted against the brightness and looked down again.

Why did Carlos have a man chained in a secret room? He allowed mutants in the bar, and he's definitely not prejudiced against them. I had seen him leave for the night with one on his arm several different times, so this couldn't possibly have been a hate crime. I took a step towards the man, but hesitated. He might have been chained because he was dangerous.

"I thought we were done for the day," he muttered quietly, revealing a set of elongated canines.

"Who are you?"

He looked back up slightly, unable to look directly into the light. "Who are *you*?" Even with the bite at the end, his voice was a straight shot of spiced rum; sweet, warm, and soft.

I lowered my phone slightly. This man was chained, beaten to hell, he wasn't a threat to me. I approached him. "I'm Vix, I work here, are you okay?"

His pupils dilated in the dark. "Do I look okay?"

No, he didn't. "Why are they keeping you here?"

He eyed me suspiciously, "they need me."

"What the hell for?"

He lowered his head, and didn't respond.

I shone my light onto the bloody horns on his head. They were cracked, shaved, and broken in several areas down to a pink fleshy tissue. Then turned my light back onto the table of tools, realizing their nefarious purpose. But why? What the hell was the cartel doing with this mutants' horns?

# Acknowledgments

I am so overwhelmed with gratitude and excitement right now, I can't even express it. After a lifetime of panic attacks and trauma, to finally have someone who sees you and supports you through your healing journey is not something many people are fortunate enough to experience. So to those who are struggling: You are safe here, you are loved, and though you might be broken, you are worth the fight to keep going.

Daniel, I know I'm a handful, but really, it's your own fault for helping me heal. I never thought I would feel comfortable in my own skin ever again, especially not enough to explore all the things we've explored together. If it weren't for you, this book would have never been written. Thank you for supporting us, encouraging me to write guilt-free, and letting me use you as a guinea pig. I love you so much.

Thank you to everyone who gave their time and expertise to help me make this dream a reality. I did not expect so much kindness and selflessness from you all. Thank you to each and every indie author who came before me. Thank you to TikTok for connecting me with other writers, editors, artists, and so, SO much knowledge. Thank you to all my beta readers who gave me so much insight and constructive criticism. Alyssa, I know you know it, but you rock so hard. Jessie, you have been the absolute sweetest, and I can't wait to have you be my Adelaide. Ethan, I know you don't think so but I couldn't have made it without your push, and I feel a long work relationship ahead of us.

On to the next!

# About the Author

If you needed to describe Aura in one word it would be passionate. Passionate about what, well, that depends on her current hyper-fixation. She is a *major* nerd, a Scorpio, loves animals, hockey, anything spooky, tattoos, and the ocean.

Among her many artsy obsessions… ahem… *passions,* including (but not limited to) painting, knitting, sketching, and cosplay; writing was the one that she was most afraid to share. But with a deep breath (and a lot of caffeine), she dove in and wrote her first romansy trilogy. To her astonishment, it was a hit, and several people were reaching out to her to complete a new story. As they say: The rest is history.

She was born and raised in the South Bay, before it was known as the Silicon Valley. She currently lives in Savannah, Georgia with her fiancée, dog, cat, goats, and lizard, where they own and run a comics and collectibles store together. Yes, the animals are employees too, and yes, they get paid more than the humans.

www.ingramcontent.com/pod-product-compliance
Lightning Source LLC
Chambersburg PA
CBHW022012310726

48972CB00006B/1621